DREAM CHASERS
THE GIFT OF VISIONS

Coming soon:

DREAMCHASERS

THE DARK PLAGUE

DREAMCHASERS
THE GIFT OF VISIONS

DANIEL J ADAMS

COVER DESIGN BY CHERIE FOX

MAHOGANY
PRESS

CONTENTS

Chapter 1

Zoned Out

It was the month of April. A full moon shone brightly in the cloudless sky. Thanks to the city lights, only a few stars could be seen. The night was chilly, but it was the kind of chilly that made you want to pull on your favorite hoodie and hang out on the porch with your friends. Along with our footsteps, the only sounds I could hear were a few crickets singing in the background and an occasional car passing by. The night felt perfect.

I was nervous, my hands shaking and sweaty. I looked over at Presley as she walked next to me with her arm wrapped around mine. She looked so good, it made it hard for me to breathe. She was wearing a dark green prom dress about the same color as her brilliant eyes. Her perfectly curled brown hair bounced as she walked, and her big smile beamed at me as she caught my gaze.

We had just finished dancing the night away at our high school prom, and now I was slowly walking her up to the front door of her house. I walked slowly because I had seen this moment in all the movies and T.V. shows. It was the moment that would either make me the happiest or the most miserable guy alive. I don't know anyone who would want to rush that.

We climbed the steps to the front door and stopped. We turned to face each other, the porch light shining right above our heads.

"I honestly had the time of my life tonight, Chaz," Presley said, staring into my eyes.

"Me too," I replied, trying not to avoid her gaze too much.

She reached out and grabbed my hands. "You were such a fun date! And your dance moves are pretty cool."

"Hah, thanks." That was all I managed to get out of my mouth. The suspense of the moment was killing me.

"Today has been just about perfect. You've been such a gentleman, and so sweet to me. There's probably only one thing that could make it better."

"Yeah? What's that?" I asked as she moved a little closer. I could tell from her shaky hands that she was getting just as nervous as I was. I asked what it was, but I already knew the answer, I just couldn't believe it was really happening. I knew exactly what to do, but I couldn't bring myself to do it. My heart hammered so hard in my chest, I felt like I was going to choke. I had better make my move before things got awkward.

I closed my eyes and started to move in and–
"Chavez . . . Chavez!"

I opened my eyes and I was no longer with Presley on

her porch. I was in my high school geology class, and it wasn't even April. It was March and the prom was still a month away. Disappointed, I looked around my classroom, taking in the bland walls covered in maps and posters of foreign countries. I turned my attention to my classmates and saw the usual scene of everyone trying not to fall asleep to Mr. Durham's lecture.

Turning to my left, I found one of my best friends, Isaac, staring back at me with an annoyed look on his face. Normally, Isaac wore a small grin on his face like he knew everyone thought he was the coolest in school, and he actually kind of was. He was good-looking and tall, he had tan skin and an athletic build. And on top of it all, he knew how to make everyone laugh.

"Chaz, I thought you said you were going to quit doing that," Isaac whispered, replacing his annoyed look with a grin. "I almost had to resort to using your full name to get you back to reality."

My full name was Chavez Matthew Anderson, but only my family and close friends knew that. Everyone else knew me as Chaz. I started going by Chaz when I realized that Chavez was actually a Hispanic last name. I wasn't Hispanic and I already had a last name.

"Well . . ." I replied with a fake smile. "I'm still working on it."

"Judging from how you zoned out while talking about prom and how long you were gone, I'm pretty sure I know what you were thinking about." He started making kissy faces. "Daydreaming about it isn't going to make it come true. You do realize that, don't you?"

"Yeah, I know. It's just that, we've been good friends for so long, ya know? I'm not really sure how to go about it now."

"Uh, hello? You can ask her to prom."

"That's true. But–" I stopped short when the lights turned off. Everyone knew what that meant. Mr. Durham was done lecturing and it was time to watch a funny video that had nothing to do with the lesson just because he had run out of things to say. Everyone who had been asleep or falling asleep was now sitting up in their chairs, turning their attention towards the screen.

I turned back to Isaac and said, "We'll talk about it later."

"Okay, man," he replied.

I tried to pay attention during the rest of the class, but not even an intense video of someone almost getting eaten by a shark could keep me from thinking about Presley. I kept daydreaming about her and how I was going to ask her to prom. I couldn't completely zone out like I did earlier, thanks to Isaac who every few minutes would whisper something like, "Chaz, dude, are you watching this? This video is nuts!"

Before I knew it, class was over, and the bell started to ring. Isaac and I quickly put our things into our backpacks and joined the rush of students moving out the door.

The halls of Pleasant Valley High School were swarming with students scurrying off in all directions heading to lunch. The school's colors of green and white covered the floors and walls like ridiculous abstract art. But other than that, it looked just like any other high school. There were bulletin boards on the walls covered in flyers, pictures, and other random stuff no one paid any attention to.

"We having lunch with Presley and Jake today?" I asked as we walked through the halls, dodging students.

"You know it. Just like we always do. Why do you ask? You thinking of popping the question during lunch?"

I laughed. "No way, man! I can't just ask her the old-fashioned way. I've got to do something really unique." I stopped right next to the entrance to the men's restroom. Isaac stopped a couple of feet ahead and looked back. "I'm gonna go to the bathroom really quick."

"I'll be right here, man," he called after me.

If only he knew the real reason I was going in there. I had to make sure I was looking good for Presley.

Once I reached the mirror, I immediately began to fix my curly brown hair, making sure that every curl was in the right place, with most of it out of my face and just a couple stray curls hanging right above my brown eyes. Once I was confident my hair was just right, I began examining my face just to make sure everything looked how it was supposed to. If it wasn't for the fact that I was six foot one, then no one would've believed that I was in high school. I had always been told I had a babyface.

As I stared in the mirror, I started to wonder what I would look like years from now and what life would be like. Before I knew it, I completely zoned out.

I looked at the clock on the dashboard and read 4:36 PM. I was driving down the road in a beautiful gated neighborhood surrounded by trees and bushes. The brown brick houses were all large with long driveways, perfectly green lawns and big garages, probably hiding nice cars, boats, and other fun toys. A few of the houses had white fences surrounding the backyard with dogs barking behind them, but most of the houses had their backyards open. and every so often, a deer would wander through.

It had been a long day at work, and I was pretty tired. But at the same time, I was so excited to get home to my family and be with them. I drove the car up a driveway to a house that looked very similar to the rest and pulled into the garage. Getting out of the car, I headed inside. The first thing I noticed as I walked in was the familiar smell of my wife's homemade lasagna, which was my favorite.

I walked down the white-walled hall with mahogany wood flooring and found myself in the living room. The room was spacious with a fireplace at one end and a large television at the other. In the middle of the room were light gray couches atop a large blue and white area rug. All kinds of toys and knick-knacks were strewn over the rug and furniture, and among the clutter sat two young boys with curly brown hair.

"Daddy!" They both screamed when they finally noticed me there. They jumped up, dropped their toys, and ran over to me, giving my legs a big hug. My heart felt so happy as I took a minute to look down at both of their faces. They looked like younger versions of me.

"Dad, will you play a game with us?" the younger of the two asked as he squeezed my leg.

"Of course, I will!" I replied with a big smile. "But not until after dinner, okay?"

"Okay!" he said, letting go of my leg. The two ran back over to their toys and resumed playing.

Man was I hungry! I headed into the kitchen to take a peek at the source of the smell. Entering, I saw that the table was set with plates and utensils, as well as a large green salad. A sparkly chandelier hung above the dinner table. It was covered with candle-shaped lights. I turned to my left to find a woman pulling the lasagna out of the oven. Just from the look of her beautiful brown hair I already knew who she was. It was the same brown hair I had been staring at since 5th Grade.

"Chaz, bro. Wake up," someone said as they shook my shoulder, hard.

I opened my eyes and saw my familiar fifteen-year-old reflection in the mirror. Isaac was standing behind me with his hand on my shoulder.

"Really, Chaz?" he asked with a dumbfounded look. "You can't even take a trip to the bathroom without zoning out?"

"I'm sorry," I replied, feeling a little annoyed. "I just . . ." I didn't bother explaining myself to him. He always ruined the best daydreams.

"It seems like you're doing that more and more lately. I don't think it's healthy, man."

"Sorry. I'll try harder."

"It's all good, bro. I'm just trying to be a good friend."

"Well, you've already proven yourself after all those times you've *attempted* to be my wingman."

We both shared a laugh before leaving the restroom. We walked down the hall and headed through the glass doors into the parking lot. Right outside the door, we found Presley and Jake waiting. Jake was wearing his usual eccentric button-up with uncomfortably short shorts. Presley was looking as good as she always did, in her green shirt and denim shorts.

"Hey, you two," Presley said, smiling at me.

"There you guys are," Jake said. "Let's go to lunch."

"The Lounge?" I asked. The Lounge was our favorite fast food restaurant, and we usually went there when we went out for lunch. It wasn't as comfy as it sounded, but it was cheap and good so that's where we went.

"Yup," Jake replied as he headed towards the mass of parked cars. The three of us followed right behind him. We wove through the cars to the corner of the parking lot until we found Jake's gray Jeep.

"Shotgun!" Isaac called out as he ran to the passenger seat. He opened the door and winked at me before getting in. I had a pretty good idea of why he was winking. I was a little nervous just thinking about sitting in the back with Presley. Yeah, I did all the time, but I always thought that maybe this time would be different. Maybe this time she would whisper sweet nothings in my ear as she fell asleep on my shoulder.

Just kidding. That would be really weird.

I decided I would start trying to be a gentleman around her, so I opened the door for her.

"Thanks, Chaz," she said, stepping inside the vehicle.

I rushed around to the other side and hopped in. Jake sped out of the parking lot and off we went. I looked over at Presley and found her looking out the window. Now would be a good time to find out if she had been asked to the prom, but of course, I had to be cool about it.

"So, Presley, have you been asked to prom yet?" Isaac asked from the passenger seat. There he goes again, working the wingman like it was his full-time job. That's why we were best friends.

"Yeah, four times, I think," Presley replied. "But I turned them all down."

Isaac didn't seem to catch the sarcasm in her voice. He looked back, impressed. "For real?"

"No," she laughed. "I haven't been asked yet."

"Well, that's okay. I'm sure you will be soon."

Call me crazy, but I'm pretty sure he gave me a telepathic fist bump after that.

"Yeah," I added. "I'm sure there's lots of guys planning on asking you."

"Hopefully. Do any of you know who you're going to ask?"

"I'm planning on asking Lindsey Gerber tomorrow," Jake answered as he turned the jeep into The Lounge parking lot.

"I'm not sure yet," Isaac said. "There's too many options. I have to make a pros and cons list for each girl

I'm interested in."

The three of us laughed because we knew he was serious.

Presley looked over at me, probably because I hadn't said anything yet. What a perfect time to reveal that I wanted to ask her. She was practically begging me to do it.

"What about you, Chaz?"

"I–"

"Let's go eat!" Jake interrupted as he opened his door. "We can talk about all this stuff inside."

Darn it, Jake! Well, I probably wouldn't have done it anyway, but you never know. Crazy stuff happens every day.

Inside we were met with the smell of burgers and probably a mixture of other unhealthy things. The restaurant was spacious with bright orange walls, blue tables surrounded by comfy looking booth seats, and a few television sets hanging around the room. We approached the cashier as I stared up at the giant menu above her head.

"Hi! How can I help you?" she asked cheerfully.

One by one, we ordered, starting with Jake, Isaac, and then Presley. When Presley reached into her pocket to pull out some money to pay, I decided it was another good time to work my magic. I stepped up next to her, handed the cashier a 20-dollar bill and said, "I've got hers."

A surprised smile broke across her face. "Chaz, that's so nice of you! But it's okay, I can pay for mine. And I should be the one buying for you. After all, it's *your* birthday tomorrow.”

“Well, you can buy me lunch *then*,” I replied. I was feeling really good about myself. Man was I smooth. I was also broke; that was the last of my cash.

“That works for me. Thanks, Chaz.”

Presley started towards the table Jake and Isaac were sitting at as I accepted my change from the cashier. I used what was left to pay for my order. As the cashier sorted through the money I gave her, I start thinking about what I was going to say when Presley brought up prom again.

“So, Chaz,” Presley began. “You never told me who you plan on asking to the dance.”

She sat across the table from me, staring into my eyes. Why did she have to be so darn cute? It made it so much harder to have a normal conversation. Whatever, I gotta be smooth. Smooth Chaz is the only Chaz with a date to the prom.

“Well . . .” I said, pausing. “I was actually planning on asking you.”

“Chaz, asking a girl to prom isn't something to joke about.” She was teasing me, but I could tell by the look on her face that she was a little hopeful.

I laughed. “No, I really mean it. I just wasn't totally sure how to go about it.”

“You really wanted to ask me?”

“Hello?” A feminine voice said. “You okay?”

I came back to reality and found myself staring awkwardly at the cashier as she tried to hand me my change.

“Sorry!” I said as I grabbed the change from her. “I

was just thinking."

I pocketed the change and headed over to join my friends. As soon as I sat down, one of the employees called out Jake's order, so he jumped to grab it. Right after that, Isaac's order was ready, so he too headed over to grab his.

"So, Chaz," Presley began. "You never told me who you plan on asking to the dance."

Well, the way I pictured this moment was right on the money. Now, the question was, could I be as smooth as I was when I imagined this moment? I contemplated my response until I realized it had been an awkward thirty seconds or so that I hadn't replied.

"Oh . . . uh, I'm not sure yet."

Both of our orders were then called out.

"I got it!" I said as I rose from the table. I had blown the moment. I would just have to ask her another way.

After we all sat down, we discussed my birthday and what I had planned. When Presley found out I didn't have any plans besides eating cake with my family, she insisted that we go out and do something fun. Jake and Isaac liked the idea as well.

As weird as it sounds, I had a bad feeling inside my chest when she brought it up, but I just ignored it. What's wrong with spending my birthday with my friends?

Chapter 2

Not My Typical Daydream

The rest of the school day was a drag, as usual. I did a little daydreaming here and there, but no zoning out this time. Believe it or not, I was actually trying to work on it. After my last class, I made my way to the parking lot. The curb was lined with parents waiting in their cars to pick up their high schoolers. Stuck in between the few dozen cars, I saw my mom's familiar blue minivan with the windows rolled down. My little brother Garrett sat in the passenger seat with his foot hanging out the window.

As I walked up to the van, Garrett pulled his blue shades away from his eyes and gave me a *look* before replacing them. He was trying to be cool or something. He *was* kind of cool though. I mean, he looked and acted a lot like me so . . .

I got in the van and buckled up. My mom smiled at me through the rearview mirror. Her name was Carla and I guess she was pretty cool for a mom.

"How was your day?" she asked me.

"It was pretty good." I took in the smell of the 'New Car' air-freshener hanging on the rearview mirror. I noticed the whole vehicle looked like it had recently been vacuumed and washed. It probably had been. My mom cleaned the van and the house almost every day. I thought it was a little ridiculous.

"Anything interesting happen today?"

"Nope."

My mom didn't bother asking me anything else because I never had anything to say anyway. My parents and I didn't talk very much, and it wasn't because we had a bad relationship, I just felt kind of embarrassed about sharing anything with them. I think it's just a phase that teenagers go through.

"Are you excited for your birthday tomorrow?" Garrett asked.

"Yeah, I am."

"Good. I'm going to whoop you at all your games when you get home from school."

I laughed and gazed out the window, sinking into thoughts about Presley. If you couldn't tell yet, she was literally all I thought about. As I stared out the window the scenery slowly changed from residential to country living. We lived just a couple miles outside of town where most people had farms or large pieces of land. Mine was one of the very few families living outside of town with no farm and just a small amount of land. We lived out there because it was cheaper. I mean, who wouldn't want to wake up every morning to the aroma of manure and the sound of goats screaming?

My dad worked as a manager at the Taco Bell in town. And just like with most fast food manager positions, he didn't get paid very much. That was why we couldn't afford to live in town. Dad had really changed over the last two years. I missed the way he used to be, so driven and motivated. He used to have so many goals, so many dreams and aspirations he was working towards. One in particular was the restaurant he'd planned to open.

As far back as I could remember, he had dreamed of opening a fancy, 5-star restaurant. He was so set on making it a reality that he had even started taking business classes at our local university while he worked as a full-time manager at Chili's and saved up money. And even though he was busy with work and school, somehow, he still found time to hang out with the family and pursue his hobbies.

Then out of nowhere, Dad's dreams started going downhill fast–like, they literally snowballed.

He came home from class one day and told us over dinner that he was done going to school and didn't want to pursue a business degree anymore. Then, a couple of weeks later, I overheard him telling my mom he quit his job at Chili's because it was too much stress, but he was able to score a manager position at the local Taco Bell. Ever since then, he'd been spending less time with our family and more time watching T.V. I hadn't seen him even pick up his bass guitar or make time for any of his other hobbies since. It's like he just gave up on improving his life and doing anything that took a bit of effort.

I knew it had been especially hard on my mom. More than once, I caught her staring at Dad as he sat on the couch. "What can I do?" she would quietly murmur to herself. Last year, she decided to go back to her part-time job as a dental assistant because we were struggling financially.

I tried and tried many times to have a mature conversation with my Dad about it, but I always seemed to beat around the bush when it came to bringing the subject up. I just didn't want to make him feel even worse than he already did.

After about fifteen minutes of driving down a country road, we turned right onto a gravel driveway that crunched underneath the tires. We pulled up the long driveway and parked next to an old Chevy Malibu. If the car was there, then Dad had to be home. I slid open the mini-van door and jumped out of the vehicle. The strong smell of manure and all things country hit my nose as I gazed at our cozy, four-bedroom house with its freshly painted gray exterior and flat roof. It was always good to be home.

Garrett and I raced inside the front door and into the dim house, leaving my mom behind to shut the door. The house was always dim when Dad came home, he preferred to have all the blinds closed to prevent most of the sunlight from seeping in. He said it helped him to relax, but I was pretty sure it just helped him see the television better.

Garrett and I raced down the dark wood walls of the hall, past the doorway where I glimpsed my dad lying on the couch sleeping. I broke off to the right into my room as Garrett turned left into his. Shutting the door, I flopped chest first onto my bed with my backpack still on my back. I awkwardly shrugged off my bag as I laid on my stomach before rolling over to stare at the ceiling.

The sky-blue walls cluttered with posters of my favorite bands and video games gave me a feeling of comfort as I took a minute to relax. Though my walls were very cluttered, the rest of my room was very neat and tidy. Nothing was out of place. I probably got that from my mom. Garrett's room was the only messy place in the house.

As I lay on my bed, my mind started to wander towards Presley. How was I going to ask her to prom? If I didn't hurry up and do it, someone else would. That would be the worst. I could see it happening . . .

I was sitting at my desk in English class, which was the first class of the day and the one class I shared with Presley. Mr. Oakland, with his shaggy brown hair and round glasses, was standing at the front of the plain classroom reading from his plain power-point slides. He had a very plain personality too.

I looked to my left, past my classmate Jenna, and sitting at the desk to her left was Presley. She sat in her usual spot, pretending to be paying attention to Mr. Oakland, but I knew she was actually texting. I turned to my right and saw a kid named Danny quietly whispering in his friend Quinn's ear, who was sitting right in front of him. Danny and Quinn were honestly my least favorite people in the class. They had never actually done anything to me, but I heard from Jake and Isaac that for some unknown reason, they didn't like me. Whenever they talked to me, they acted like we were good friends, but behind my back, it was nothing but insults. Even though I didn't like them, and they didn't like me, I still tried to be nice to them.

I watched Danny and Quinn excitedly whisper to each other before Quinn handed a folded white piece of paper back to Danny. I tried not to stare too much as Danny unfolded the paper and examined it. Our desks were close enough together that I could read the large letters written on the paper. In a really cool and exquisite font, it read, Will you go to prom with me? - Quinn

Come on, Quinn. That's not a very creative way to ask someone to prom, *I thought. But at least the artwork was impressive. It looked like it took a while to do.*

Quinn turned to Danny, who nodded with a smile as he refolded the paper. Danny turned to look at me and whispered, "Hey bro, can you tell Jenna to give this to Presley?"

I took the paper from Danny. "Sure."

Because I knew what was on the paper, I was so tempted to toss the note away or rip it up. But I didn't. I slid it onto Jenna's desk. "Can you give this to Presley?"

She nodded her head in response, turned to Presley who was already looking our way and handed it to her. I watched closely as Presley opened up the paper and a small smile appeared on her face as she scanned it. She

looked up and over to Quinn who quickly caught her gaze. She smiled at him and nodded. I watched Quinn as he turned his attention back to the front of the class, a big satisfied smile on his face. Just looking at his smug smile made me want to poke him in the eye with something.

I sat up on my bed. It would be just my luck for one of my least favorite people to ask Presley out because I took too long. Alright, new goal: Ask Presley out by the end of the week. It was Wednesday, so I still had three days. It should've been my top priority to make a plan on how I was going to do that, but I had a lot of homework that was due the next day. Presley was going to have to wait.

Sitting down at my desk, I began my math homework. I worked on it for about forty-five minutes before my mom yelled that dinner was ready. When I walked into the kitchen, I found Garrett and Dad already sitting at the table. It was set with plates, cups, utensils, and a big pot of homemade mac and cheese. My mom was pulling something I couldn't see out of the oven.

"Hey, Dad," I said as I took a seat next to Garrett.

"Hey, Chaz," Dad replied as he spooned some mac and cheese onto his plate. He was still wearing his Taco Bell uniform and his dark-blond curly hair was matted against the right side of his head, the evidence of his long nap. His brown eyes looked very tired and a five-o-clock shadow covered most of his face. "How was school?"

"It was good." I took my turn scooping food onto my plate.

"Good."

We sat in silence for almost a minute before Mom finally placed some chicken nuggets on the table and sat down next to Dad.

"Let's eat," she said, shoveling some chicken nuggets onto Garrett's plate as he held it out to her. We ate in silence for a few minutes until Mom asked, "How was work, Bob?"

"It was alright," he answered tiredly. "Very stressful, as usual."

"I'm sorry, honey."

Irritation quickly grew inside me as, once again, Dad explained why he hated his job. He did this almost every time we ate dinner. Couldn't he give it a rest for once? I usually just zoned out during this part of the meal, completely ignoring his complaining, but this time, I couldn't. I listened, letting it fuel my annoyance. Why didn't he just stop whining about his hard life and do something about it? Why didn't he try to get a better job if he hated the one that he had so much? Why wouldn't he even try for my mom? She worked so hard to pick up his slack. It had been like that for almost a year and I was sick of it.

"I just wish I didn't have to deal with the things I have to deal with." Dad sighed.

"You wouldn't have to if you hadn't given up on your dream of opening a restaurant." I spoke up as I stared Dad in the eyes. He didn't respond, he just looked down and started eating again, which annoyed me even more, and I pressed harder. "Dad, you were so close! You were almost done with school. You had the money saved up. I just don't understand what happened."

He continued to stare down as he finished his food. There was an awkward silence filled with tension. After a minute, he placed his fork on his plate and looked up at me. "Life happened, Chaz. And in life, dreams most often don't come true."

With that, he got up from the table and walked out. I glanced at Mom, who stared at her plate sadly. My little brother Garrett just kept eating in silence. I quickly finished my food and headed back to my room.

The rest of the night, I worked hard on my homework, making sure I had no time to think about the conversation at dinner or how annoyed I was. By the time I got all the homework done that was due the next day, it was 8:43. I pulled out my phone and texted a group message to Jake and Isaac.

How do you think I should ask Presley to prom?

As I waited for a reply, I played around with my yo-yo until it came back up and smacked me in the face. I put it away and checked my phone. There was a message from Jake.

I have a great idea but it would be better if I told you in person.

I sent a reply.

Okay, see ya at school.

After mine sent, I got a message from Isaac.

Jake, if your idea doesn't involve flash mobs or food, then it's a bad idea.

I laughed and set my phone down. It was early, but I felt pretty tired. I slipped on my pajamas, brushed my teeth and wiggled under my warm comforter. As I lay in bed, I thought about what we could do for my birthday the next day. Slowly, my tired mind began to drift into thoughts of randomness like it usually did right before I fell asleep.

Jake, Isaac, Presley and I walked up to the counter at the noisy city fun center. The air was filled with the smell of popcorn and nachos. I gazed to my right at the twenty-four-lane bowling alley, and then to my left at the giant collection of arcade machines. Thankfully, it was a school night, so the place wasn't very packed.

"What should we do first, Chaz?" Jake asked.

"I'm thinking laser tag," I replied. As soon as I said it, I got an awful feeling inside, like maybe it wasn't a good idea. But I ignored it.

Everyone went up to pay, and they all chipped in and paid for mine. After, I led the way over to the arcade side of the fun center. We walked through the doorway into a dark room. It was lit with a black light, which made the bright colors on some of our clothing glow. There was another group of six kids waiting in the room with us, and we recognized a couple of them from school. As we waited for the game to start, we chatted with them a bit.

After a minute or two, a lady walked into the room and shut the door behind her. She started briefing us on the rules of the game and our objective. Lights on both sides of the room turned on, revealing racks of laser tag guns and vests. Even though there were six of the other kids, we were confident we could take them. Each person in our group pulled on a blue lighted vest and the other team wore the red vests. After we were all outfitted and ready to go, the woman opened a door on the other side of the dark room.

We followed the other team out the door into the game room and then split up. This room was just as dark as the previous one with multiple black lights covering the ceiling. The black walls seemed to be about six feet tall and they twisted and turned like a maze. After the game started, we ran around as a team, shooting lasers at any red glowing vests or guns we saw. After about five minutes of playing, we decided to change tactics and split into two teams, me and Presley on one team and Jake and Isaac on another.

The two of us ran around as a team for a few minutes before Presley stopped me. "Is something burning?"

I sniffed the air and noticed it reeked of burning plastic and smoke. "Yeah," I agreed. "Something is definitely burning."

"Look!" She said, pointing to a cloud of smoke rising over the top of the maze wall. Beyond the wall, I noticed dancing light reflecting off the ceiling and walls beyond as it slowly got brighter. I followed Presley as she maneuvered through the maze, away from the smoke and onto a raised platform that gave us a good view of the room. There were two kids from the other team already up on top pointing at the fiery scene and yelling for help.

I looked over to where they were pointing and saw the

source of the burning–a tiki head sitting high on the wall that shot lasers at unsuspecting players during the game. It was on fire and smoking heavily. Most of the face had melted, making it pretty much unrecognizable. The fire from the tiki head had spread to some of the wood walls of the maze and was quickly growing. As I surveyed the scene, I noticed two glowing blue vests frantically running back and forth, trying to find a way out of the fire. It looked like they were completely surrounded.

"Jake and Isaac are down there!" I yelled in shock. This couldn't be happening. Things like that never happened. And how in the world did they get stuck?

I jerked my eyes open and sat up on my bed, breathing hard, trying to calm myself down. It was all a dream, there was nothing to worry about. I couldn't believe how real it was though. I thought I was actually there. Did I even fall asleep yet? It didn't matter. My mind always came up with some weird stuff right before I fell asleep.

Resting my head on my pillow once more, I slowly relaxed.

Chapter 3

Life Gets Weird

I woke up the next morning to my obnoxious alarm going off on my phone. Quickly jumping out of bed, I turned it off, took a shower, and got ready for the day, spending extra time making sure my hair looked good. After I was all ready for school, I grabbed my backpack and headed to the kitchen.

"Happy birthday, Chaz!" Mom said as soon as I walked into the kitchen.

"Happy birthday!" Garrett said as well. "You ready to get destroyed after school?"

"I'm ready to destroy *you*!" I replied, pouring myself a bowl of cereal.

"Are you going to do anything fun with your friends tonight?" Mom asked.

"Yeah, I think so." I suddenly remembered the dream I had last night and quickly pushed it from my thoughts.

"I'm glad to hear that. You boys ready to go?"

"Yeah," Garrett and I responded in unison.

The three of us piled into the minivan, and with Mom at the wheel, we headed to school. After fifteen minutes of driving, we dropped Garrett off, and two minutes later, it was my turn.

"I love you," Mom said as I stepped out of the van. "Have a wonderful day."

"Thanks, Mom. I love you too."

I pushed through the crowds as I made my way down the hallways. On my way to class, I made my usual stop at Presley's locker. I found her there, shoving books into her backpack.

"Hey, Chaz," Presley greeted as I walked up next to her. "Happy birthday!" She pulled a little box wrapped in light blue wrapping paper out of her backpack.

"Oh! Thank you!" I said, surprised. This was the first year I had gotten a birthday present from her. Normally, it was just a card. "What's in it?"

"You'll just have to wait and see."

"You mean I can't open it now?"

"No." She playfully smacked me on the arm. "You have to wait until after you eat your birthday cake."

"Oh, fine," I huffed.

"Let's go to class."

She closed her locker and I followed closely behind her, shoving the present into my backpack as we made our way to room 104. We entered the door at the front of the class and found the teacher, Mr. Oakland, sitting at his desk typing on his laptop. There were only a few students scattered throughout the room and we still had a few minutes before class started. Most of the students usually waited until about a minute before class started to arrive anyway. Presley took her seat toward the left side of the room next to Jenna and I took mine to the right of Jenna. If we didn't have assigned seating, I would for sure be sitting next to Presley.

I waited patiently for class to start as Jenna and Presley chatted away, probably about random stuff like boys and their favorite hair conditioner. After a couple of minutes, the rest of the students quickly walked in one by one, Danny and Quinn coming in last, just before Mr. Oakland shut the door. Danny took his seat to my right and Quinn directly in front of him. Mr. Oakland immediately pulled down the screen and started his power point while most of the students pulled out their cellphones.

I gazed around the room to find Danny and Quinn excitedly whispering to one another. *What in the world are they so happy about?* I wondered. I watched in surprise as Quinn handed Danny a white piece of paper, exactly like I imagined in my daydream yesterday. Okay, this was like Deja Vu or something. As long as it wasn't a note asking Presley to prom then everything would be okay.

Sitting at my desk, I watched as closely as I could as Danny unfolded the paper. When I read what was on it, I almost choked. Written on the paper, exactly as I had imagined were the words,

Will you go to prom with me? - Quinn

The font was just as detailed and artistic as it was in my head.

What the–? Okay, either I was asleep, or the universe was playing some kind of cruel joke on me. It had to be a coincidence. Or maybe I was psychic? It was unlikely, but you never know. If anyone in this world had psychic powers, it would make sense that it was me. When I was little, I drank almost half a bottle of Windex before my mom saw and rushed me to the hospital. That had to be what caused it. But all joking aside, there had to be a logical explanation for what was happening.

Quinn turned around to look at Danny, who gave him a nod and folded back the paper back up. Danny turned to me and whispered, "Hey bro, can you tell Jenna to give this to Presley?"

No chance in this world. That was what I wanted to say. But what I actually said was, "Sure."

Okay, this was happening for real. I needed to do something quickly. I could tear it up. But then he would probably just get mad and ask her again in the same way or another. I could pretend to sneeze on it. But again, he would still probably ask her later. So, there was really only one way to solve my problem.

I handed the paper to Jenna. "Hey, this is for you."

She took the paper from me and opened it up. A smile spread across her face as she read it. "Awe, that's kind of cute!" she said.

Not really, but okay.

She looked over at Quinn, who was staring at her with an embarrassed smile.

"Should I just tell him my answer after class, or

should I do something creative like this? What do you think?"

"I'd say just tell him after class," I replied with a grin. "He's probably dying to know your answer."

"You're so right," she said before turning to whisper giddily to Presley.

I felt a tap on my shoulder. I turned to find Danny and Quinn both staring at me with dumbfounded looks.

"What did you do that for?" Danny asked.

"What do you mean?" I replied, pretending to be confused.

"I told you to give it to Presley."

"Oh. I thought you said give it to Jenna. My bad."

"Oh well," Quinn said quietly to Danny. "Jenna is cute too."

"Yeah," Danny agreed. "Maybe I'll ask Presley."

"Go for it."

Great. There's another promposal I would have to sabotage. I waited too long to ask. I was just going to have to ask her the boring, old fashioned way.

When the bell finally rang, Mr. Oakland wrapped up his lecture and told us to have a good day. I quickly packed up my things and walked out with Presley. On our way out, I watched Jenna approach Quinn and tell him she would love to go. Presley and I walked together down the hall to where we needed to split for our next class. We stopped and faced each other.

"I guess I'll see you at lunch?" Presley asked.

"Actually, I need to ask you something real quick," I

said nervously.

"Okay." She stepped closer to me. "What is it?"

Alright, Smooth Chaz, this is your time to shine.

"Well normally, I would ask you in a really cool way, but I haven't had time to come up with anything. But anyway, do you want to go to prom with me?" It felt so good to finally get that out of my mouth.

"Are you asking for real?" she joked. "Or are you just practicing to ask someone else?"

I laughed. "No, I'm really asking you. Will you go with me?"

"I would love to, Chaz."

"Sounds good. See you at lunch."

We smiled at each other for a few more seconds and then went our separate ways.

Have you ever felt so good that you thought you might be able to fly? Well, that's how I felt right then. I felt like I could run ten miles and then backwards dunk a basketball over the tallest guy in the world. I had never felt so confident before. I was going to go to prom with the cutest girl in school. Smooth Chaz did it again!

During math, I didn't pay attention in the least. I just kept replaying in my head the moment where I asked her to prom. I couldn't believe I actually did it. On my way to Geology, I met up with Isaac and told him about my accomplishment.

"There you go!" He said. "It's about time. I was ready to ask for you."

"You figured out who you're asking yet?" I asked.

"Nope. Still narrowing down the list."

After Geology, we met up with Presley and Jake on the way to the cafeteria.

"Happy birthday, Chaz." Jake said, swatting me on the back as we walked next to each other.

"Thanks," I said. "What should we do tonight?"

"Whatever you want to do," Presley answered. "It's *your* birthday."

"I'm down for anything."

"How 'bout the city fun center?" Jake suggested.

"Let's do it," I replied.

Finding the cafeteria fuller than usual, we decided to take our food outside to eat. It was chilly out, our breath fogging up the air in front of us. But it wasn't too cold for me, I was wearing my big black puffy coat. I had always been one who got cold easily, so whenever the temperature was below sixty degrees Fahrenheit, you could expect to see me in a coat.

We sat down on one of the cold metal tables on the school grounds. I took a bite of my ham and cheese sandwich and was setting it down when I noticed something going on out on the field near the school. It looked like Jace Hawkins and Trevor Green were picking on quiet little Ben again.

"Those guys just don't stop," I said, standing up.

"Chaz, what are you going to do?" Presley asked when she noticed what I was talking about.

"Maybe I'll threaten to tell the school police officer on them or something. Jake, Isaac, will you two back me up?"

"Of course," Jake said as he and Isaac got up to follow me. "They harass him way too much, and it has to stop."

Presley got up and followed close behind as we made our way over to confront the two bullies. Jace and Trevor were both taller than me and had the whole baseball team to back them up, but I wasn't very intimidated. I had dealt with them before, and I knew they wouldn't give me too much trouble.

I used to get bullied when I was younger, but once my height really sprang up and my confidence grew, I no longer tolerated anyone getting bullied. Thankfully, I had never been in a fight or had to deal with anyone too mean or stubborn. Usually, it was guys like Jace and Trevor who would harass other students until they were confronted.

As we neared the three guys, Jace squealed with laughter as Trevor pretended to cast ridiculous-sounding spells on him with one of Ben's wizard staffs. Ben always carried all kinds of fake weapons with him because he was a serious *LARPer*. LARP stands for *Live Action Roleplay*, and it's where people get together all dressed up as their favorite fictional character and pretend to battle each other. Every day without fail, you could find Ben during lunch, with or without friends, swinging his sword around. Sometimes he was in costume.

"Roses are red, violets are blue," Trevor chanted as he pointed his wand at Jace. "Pigs are fat, and so are you!"

"Not this time," Jace responded in his annoying squeaky voice. He picked up one of Ben's foam swords off of the ground and swung it in front of him. "I deflect your attack and send it towards Ben."

Ben just stood there with an unreadable look on his pale face. His long, black hair almost covered his eyes completely, helping to mask his expression. He held the wooden sparring sword he usually practiced with limply in his hand.

"Guys, leave him alone," I said firmly, staring down Trevor who was usually the one who started it.

"Hey, Chavez," Trevor said in a feminine tone. He ran his fingers through his dirty-blond hair. It flopped to the right side of his head. "Did you come to play Dungeons and Dragons with us?"

"Just leave Ben alone. If you keep harassing him like this, I'm going to get you in trouble."

"Oh, lighten up, Chavez," Jace said. He also ran his fingers through his own brown hair, which almost exactly resembled Trevor's. "We just want to roleplay with him."

"Yeah," Trevor added. "Ben was just about to get hit with my intricate fattening spell unless he figures out a way to stop it. Ben, what's your move?"

"Please, just stop." Ben pleaded quietly. His right hand clenched and unclenched as if he was struggling to control his temper.

"We'll leave you alone once someone is defeated," Trevor assured him. "If you're going to be a party pooper, I guess I'll have to defeat Jace."

Trevor yelled and ran towards Jace while swinging the staff he was holding. He looked like a crazy islander warding off visitors. Jace yelled even more obnoxiously as he charged towards Trevor with the foam sword held out in front of him. Once they neared each other, the sword and the plastic staff met as they pushed towards each other. The foam sword bent and then snapped from the pressure, leaving Jace holding only half of it as Trevor pulled away in surprise.

"Guys, stop!" Jake said, stepping forward. "You're breaking his stuff. You owe him a new sword."

"Well, if I owe him a new one, I might as well take advantage of what I have left," Jace replied. He started swinging the half sword at Trevor, who used the staff to block his attacks. Jace yelled as he started hammering the staff with the sword.

"You can't stop me!" Trevor screamed as he held the staff in front of him.

I felt anger welling up inside of me as I watched the two acting like idiots. I looked over at Ben and noticed him shaking a little.

"Stop!" Ben said a little louder. "Just stop! Please."

"Not until I finish him," Trevor said, taking his turn to hammer Jace's weapon with the staff.

"I said stop!" Ben screamed as he ran towards the two and swung his wooden sword at Trevor. There was a loud crack as Ben's wooden sword connected with Trevor's arm, making him drop the staff and cry out in pain. Trevor fell to the ground holding his arm and cursing. Ben just stared at him with a look of regret.

"I–I didn't mean to . . ." Ben stuttered quietly. "I told

you to stop."

"Are you serious?" Trevor cried. "I think you broke my arm!"

"I told you to stop . . ." Ben started backing away.

"You didn't have to go psycho and break my arm!"

"What's wrong with you?" Jace asked angrily. "You've got some issues, dude!"

I stood there in shock. I was so surprised by what had happened, I had no idea what to do. I had heard the rumors about Ben having an anger problem in the past, but I didn't know it was that bad. Even though Trevor was the one who got hurt, I felt bad for Ben. He didn't mean to do it.

"I'll make sure you regret this," Trevor warned, cradling his arm as he and Jace headed toward the school.

"Ben," I said, stepping towards him.

He wouldn't meet my eyes. He began picking up his toy weapons and shoving them into a black duffle bag.

"I know you didn't mean to. I'll make sure everyone knows what happened."

He didn't respond until he finished packing up all his stuff. He turned toward the school, but before walking away, he said, "What if . . . What if I *did* mean to."

I shared a concerned look with my friends before we headed back to school.

Chapter 4

I'm Telling You, It Was the Windex

For the remainder of my day at school, all I could think about was what happened. Poor Ben just needed some good friends. Sure, he had his LARP guys, but they barely hung out with him. I often saw him eating lunch alone.

I wasn't exactly sure how, but before school ended for the day, word got out about what happened during lunch. All of us who were involved had to take a trip to the principal's office. We all had to go in one at a time and explain what we saw happen. After everyone told their side of the story, Ben, Jace, and Trevor had to meet with the principal again with their parents. Before leaving the school, I heard through the grapevine that the three were all suspended for a few weeks. Ben was also no longer allowed to bring any kind of weapons to the school, even fake ones.

I had been told that Trevor's arm was definitely broken, and he probably wouldn't be able to play baseball anytime soon. That was very bad news. He would make sure to never let Ben live it down for the rest of his high school years. There was going to be war over this.

After my last class, I ran into Presley in the hallway on my way to the parking lot.

"You doing okay?" I asked her as we made our way outside.

"Yeah," She replied sadly. "I feel so bad, you know, about what happened at lunch. Trevor and Jace are such dirtbags. Ben just needs a friend."

"Yeah, that's exactly what I was thinking."

"Well, we can try to be his friend when he gets back from his suspension."

"Sounds good. See ya tonight."

"See ya."

Presley walked away and I began searching for my mom's minivan amidst the chaos of students trying to escape their day prison. After a minute or so, I found the van and I hopped in.

"How was school?" Mom asked as usual.

"It was weird."

"Why is that?"

"It's a long story."

I sank back in my seat and reflected on the events of the day before falling asleep.

I woke up to one of my favorite sounds of us driving up the gravel driveway to our house. When I opened my eyes, I noticed Dad's car wasn't there. Hopefully he would be home soon. I headed inside the house and went straight to my room. Setting my backpack on the floor, I sat down on the edge of the bed.

"Hey, Chaz." I looked up to see my brother Garrett standing in the doorway. "Since it's your birthday, I don't think you need to do any homework. So, we should play a game." He smiled.

I laughed. "Okay, let's play a game."

I followed Garrett into our dark family room, turned on the T.V. and opened the blinds as Garrett set up the video game he wanted to play. The light of the bright sun shone through the windows and put a glare on the television.

Garrett and I played video games for about an hour or so, getting very competitive with one another and sometimes screaming at or punching each other. While Garrett and I were in the middle of an intense round of a fighting game, I heard the front door open and someone walked into the room.

"Happy birthday, Chaz," I heard my dad say from behind me.

"Thanks," I said without looking back. I couldn't let Garrett win another round because he was already getting too cocky.

"Smells like dinner is almost ready. You boys better finish your game and come to the kitchen."

After another minute, I finally beat Garrett on our last match, so we shut off the game and headed to eat.

"You know that I let you win," Garrett teased as we walked out of the room.

"I'm sure you did," I replied sarcastically.

As I walked into the kitchen, I took a big whiff of the lasagna smell filling the air. I sat down at the table across from Dad, and Garrett took a seat next to me.

"Have you had a good birthday so far?" Dad asked.

"It was good after I left school," I answered.

"Do you have anything going on tonight with your friends?"

"Yeah, not sure what we're gonna do though. Maybe the fun center."

"Just don't stay out too late."

"You can bring your friends over," Garrett suggested. "Then they can watch me beat you again."

"I think they'd rather go out and do something fun," Dad said to Garrett.

Mom sat down and we ate dinner with little small talk. Surprisingly, Dad didn't bring up anything negative about his job. Maybe it was because it was my birthday, or maybe it was something I said last night.

After we finished dinner, Mom placed the chocolate strawberry cake on the table and stuck sixteen birthday candles on top. Dad lit the candles and all three of them sang Happy Birthday to me, and then we dug into the cake.

"Have fun tonight," Dad said, handing me a 20-dollar bill. "Let me know if you need a ride anywhere."

"Okay, I will. Thanks, Dad."

I gave Mom and Garrett a hug before slipping off to my room. As soon as I closed the bedroom door, I texted a group message to Jake, Isaac, and Presley.

I'm ready to party! You guys ready to meet up?

I sat down on my bed and grabbed my backpack. I pulled out the little present from Presley and tore the wrapping paper apart, revealing a brown cardboard box underneath. I opened the cardboard box to find a folded paper that said my name on the front. There was a black and white bracelet underneath. The bracelet looked like it was homemade, woven together out of black and white thread making zig-zagging patterns.

I wasn't much of a bracelet guy, but whatever. If it made her happy then I would wear it. I tied it around my right wrist before unfolding the paper and reading the note written in red ink.

Dear Chaz,

I'm so glad we've become such great friends. It's always fun hanging out with you. You always make me laugh. I can't wait for summer so we can spend even more time together. You better not go find cooler friends to hang out with and forget about me. Thanks for always listening even when I talk about 'girly' stuff. Thanks for always being there when I need you. You're the best. Have a happy birthday.

-Presley

PS: I know it's not much but I couldn't figure out what to get you. I made it especially for you, but I'll only be a little bit offended if you don't wear it. ;)

I couldn't help but feel a little disappointed that she hadn't confessed her love for me or jokingly called me something like "Sugar lips". Oh well. There was always next year.

It took about fifteen minutes for Jake to arrive at my

house. Once he did, I got in his Jeep and we headed to the city fun center. We arrived before anyone else and waited outside near the entrance for the other two. Presley and Isaac arrived at almost the exact same time, each of them driving themselves. I was the only one without my license yet. I was planning on getting it soon.

We walked inside and stopped at the front counter.

"What should we do first, Chaz?" Jake asked.

I glanced at the sign with the games and pricing. When I looked at laser tag, I felt that same bad feeling inside that I had felt in my dream. Even if it was a dream, there was no use risking it.

"Let's bowl?" I said, making it sound like it might have been a question instead of a statement.

"You sure?" Jake asked. "You've been wanting to go laser tagging for a while. And it looks like there's no wait."

It was true, I had been wanting to play laser tag for a while. But I decided to go with my gut.

"Yeah, I'm sure. We can laser tag after."

"Let's do it." Isaac said, leading us to the counter to pay. They all chipped in to pay for mine, then we grabbed our bowling shoes and headed to lane 11.

The four of us went to the racks of bowling balls and selected our own. I settled on an 11-pound ball that fit my fingers just right and I took it to the lane we were assigned.

Right from the start of our game, I did awful. I was never much of a bowler, so it didn't surprise me. I was just thankful I wasn't in last place–that was Presley. When we finished the first round, Jake was in first place with Isaac right behind him. Presley and I didn't even score close. For the second game, we mostly messed around and did some trick shots. I wasn't a very competitive person, so I thought it was a lot more fun that way.

During our second round of bowling, Presley noticed I was wearing the bracelet she made me.

"I like it," I said. "But I'm disappointed it doesn't give me mad bowling skills."

"It's only a prototype," she said. "I'm still working out the kinks."

"Thanks for making it for me."

"You're welcome, Chaz." She smiled.

After Isaac bowled a strike, I got up to take another turn. Just before I was about to throw the ball, a loud and obnoxious alarm started blaring overhead. Everyone in the alley paused in what they were doing and looked around, confused.

"Please evacuate the building immediately using your nearest exit," a female voice said on the intercom over-head. "I repeat, please evacuate the building immediately using your nearest exit. This is not a drill."

I stood there frozen as everyone started making their way to the exit. *This couldn't be happening! There was no way!* I thought. I mean no one said anything about a fire yet, but still. It was all too crazy. That would be twice in one day that I saw something before it happened. Again, things like that didn't just happen. Someone had to have been messing with me.

"Chaz!" Jake yelled, pulling me out of my thoughts. "Let's go!"

The four of us jogged to the exit and left the building. We found ourselves in a crazy mass of confused people. I watched as most people simply got in their cars and drove off, but a few stayed and tried to figure out what was going on.

Over the next five minutes, a small number of people continued to spill out of the building. I wasn't too surprised when most of them came out wearing laser tag gear. I was definitely a little freaked out though. Who wouldn't be when you're going through what I was experiencing?

It didn't take long for the smoke to start spilling through the front doors, windows and any other openings it could escape through. That was about the time the fire department, ambulance, and police finally arrived with their sirens wailing. The police organized the chaos as the firemen put out the fire. There were a couple of kids being treated by the paramedics because of small burns, but no one was seriously injured. After questioning anyone who might have had any info on what happened, the police dismissed most of us.

"Well, that was crazy!" Jake said as we made our way towards the parking lot.

"It's been a really weird day," I commented, mostly to myself.

"I hope your birthday wasn't too awful," Presley said.

"No, it was still pretty good thanks to you guys."

"I vote we do it again," Isaac said.

"Do what again?" Jake asked.

"Chaz's birthday. Let's redo the whole thing another day. This time without the excitement of people getting suspended and fires."

"Yeah, maybe," I replied. "But I think I can wait until next year."

"Suit yourself." Isaac opened his car door. "See you guys at school."

"I should get going too," Presley said. She gave me a quick hug. "Happy Birthday, Chaz."

"Thanks, Presley," I said, grinning from her hug.

I hopped into Jake's car and we left the parking lot of the still-smoking building. I got home and quickly got ready for bed. Unless another one of my dreams suddenly came true, I wasn't going to worry about what happened that day. It might have been nothing, just two coincidences in one day. Life could play tricks on you sometimes.

I slipped under my covers and it didn't take long for me to doze off.

Chapter 5

There Had Better Be Dragons

I awoke to a light breeze tickling my skin, making me shiver. I ignored it and tried to go back to sleep. I quickly became annoyed by all the birds chirping. They were so noisy, it made it impossible to go back to sleep. Why in the world were the birds so loud this morning, and why was it so chilly? I reached for my comforter so I could cover myself from the wind, but I didn't feel it anywhere. I didn't feel my soft bed either, instead, I felt . . . grass?

Opening my eyes, I quickly sat up and found myself in the greenest forest I had ever seen. Hundreds of white trees with bright green leaves surrounded me in every direction. The ground was covered in bright green shrubbery, and yellow and pink flowers and weeds were everywhere I looked.

What the–?

I looked around frantically, completely confused and unsure of where I was. Okay, I was obviously dreaming. I had to be. I was such a light sleeper that I knew it wasn't possible for someone to kidnap me while I slept. And this didn't look anything like Utah. How would they smuggle me out of the state without me waking up? I figured it may have been possible if they'd drugged me or something, but I hadn't eaten anything weird.

I looked around, feeling so awake, it was hard to believe I was dreaming. And usually, when I noticed I was dreaming, I would wake right up. But not this time. I stood up and looked down at my clothes. I wasn't even wearing my pajamas. Instead, I was wearing my gray t-shirt and jeans. Yup, it was definitely a dream. Who would take the time to dress their abductee for the occasion?

To my left, I noticed what looked like an animal trail about six feet in front of me. I decided to follow it. I moved through the undergrowth for a few minutes but stopped when I heard a quiet growl to my right. Startled, I jumped and searched for any kind of animal that might have made the noise, but I saw nothing, only trees and shrubbery. There was a good-sized bush that I thought would be the perfect place for a predator to hide while it waited for prey. Maybe it was a bear cub? If so, it would probably leave me alone if I kept walking.

I heard movement behind the bush and another quiet growl. I slowly started backing away, when something black and round jumped over the bush and landed in front of me. The creature didn't look like any animal I had ever seen before. It was completely covered in black fur, and its skin underneath might also have been black because it was the darkest animal I had ever seen. It was almost as round as a perfect circle, with dog-like legs protruding from the bottom and skinny arms extending from the sides.

The most terrifying part about the creature was the long black claws sticking out of the little hands, and the sharp teeth poking out between its closed lips. It was as tall as my waist, and it looked like an experiment gone wrong.

I moved away from it as the monster's black eyes stared blankly at me. Before I had time to examine it more, it crouched as if it was about to pounce. I didn't stick around to find out what it was about to do to me. I quickly turned and sprinted down the trail without looking back. I heard from behind what sounded like the monster, not running, but leaping after me. I kept hearing it make a grunting noise and then a thud, as if it was hitting the ground. The sounds kept repeating over and over again.

I didn't dare look back. Every time someone looked back in the movies, they would trip and instantly become monster chow. My heart hammered painfully in my chest from fear and exertion. The sound of my pursuer grew more distant, but I still didn't dare slow down or turn to look. I continued to sprint through the white trees, following the little trail.

As I ran, I began to hear muffled voices up ahead. My lungs burned and my legs ached, but the sound of people kept me going. Through the trees, I could make out a large brick building. I also saw people dressed in funny clothes and what looked like knights on horses. Well, it was a dream, so why not?

I no longer heard anything behind me. I finally risked a quick look back and saw no monsters chasing me. My body begged for rest and my lungs felt ready to explode, so I slowed to a jog as I neared a clearing. Maybe the monster was just trying to trick me so it could sneak up and get me once I let my guard down. But I wouldn't do that just yet, that's when people usually die. They think the bad guy is long gone or dead when all of a sudden, he's actually right behind you about to bite your arm off.

As I passed the last few trees, I entered a spacious field with dark green grass almost to my knees. Scattered throughout the field were people wearing all kinds of medieval clothing. Some were dressed as knights in full suits of armor, but some were dressed like normal villagers in their homemade, plain-looking clothes. They stood around conversing and laughing, while others gathered wood or rocks. Some were fencing with swords and some looked to be patrolling the border of the woods.

In the center of the field was a large brick building that closely resembled a castle, but my guess was that it was a fortress of some sort. It had large towers on all four corners with tall walls that men patrolled. On each tower was a white flag with the same image printed on it. The image was a bunch of clouds clumped together with the sun just peeking through the center and over the top, a couple of its rays shone above. If that was supposed to be the royal insignia or something, then I was disappointed. It should be a fierce animal like a lion or a bear. Or even a dragon. There had better be dragons here.

I noticed a wide moat surrounded the entire structure with a drawbridge lying over it, granting access to the entrance. Castle or fortress, the structure was certainly impressive. I had never seen anything like it in real life, which made sense because this was all a dream. Maybe I could fly if I wanted to. I jumped into the air and willed myself to fly away. Nothing happened. At least I tried.

"Hail, Young Sir!" A voice yelled from the distance.

I turned to my right to see two knights on horseback trotting toward me. I stood there, unsure of what to do as they quickly closed the distance between us and slowed their horses to a stop. The horses were both large and black with rippling muscles covering their legs. The knights astride the horses dismounted. They were both about the same height as me and on the chest of their armor was the same picture of the sun peeking through the clouds.

"Judging from your strange apparel, this must be your first time here," the knight on the left said with a light-hearted voice.

"Yeah," I replied. "I've never dreamed up anything like this before."

The same knight who spoke chuckled before removing his helmet. The other took his off as well. The knight who spoke to me had long black hair that hung just above his shoulders. He was clean-shaven and had a face that belonged on the cover of a magazine. I knew if he was real then every girl in the world would probably be in love with him. He looked a lot like Aragorn from the *Lord of The*

Rings movies.

The other knight had red hair pulled up in a manbun, thick eyebrows and green eyes. They both grinned at each other like there was some inside joke between them.

Okay, Aragorn and *Faramir now*, I mused. What a random dream! If I ended up getting chased by orcs or another demonic balloon, then I was going to jump off a cliff and wake myself up.

"I'm Fynn," the dark-haired man said, holding out a gloved hand for me to shake. "Son of Albor Kraft, and First Captain of Kellamare's Army."

"I'm Garriton Warner," 'Mr. Manbun' said, shaking my hand as well. "Right-hand man to the First Captain." He shared another grin with Fynn.

"I'm Chaz," I said. "Son of Robert and rightful heir of the Ring of Doom."

"That's not the first time someone has tried to fool us with Lord of The Rings references, young sir," Fynn said, still smiling.

"Really?" I questioned. "How do you know about the Lord of The Rings? Isn't this a dream?"

"It is a dream, but not like any other dream you've ever had before."

"What do you mean?"

"It's really not our place to say," Fynn replied, apologetically. "All I can tell you is that this is the most realistic dream you will ever experience. And it is also the only dream you are going to have from now on."

"Okay . . ." I wasn't convinced. "What if I go throw

myself off a cliff or something? Won't I wake up?"

"I wouldn't do that if I were you, my friend," Garriton answered. "Trust us, you don't want to go throw your life away here. You will wake up, but the consequences are not nice."

"Right." I didn't believe a word of it, but maybe it would be fun to play along. "So why am I here?"

"Chaz, I know this is all confusing," Fynn said. "But I can promise you that this is all real, and all your questions will be answered soon. Right now, you probably don't believe it, but pretty soon you will. For now, just know that this place you are in is called the *Dream World*. Every now and then, we get people like you who come from a place we call the *Waking World*, which is reality for you.

"From now on, you will probably hear many people refer to you as a *Waker*, that is simply what we call people in your situation. Currently, your body is back in bed at home, and at the same time, your mind is here. It will remain here until you wake up. But please wait until everything else is explained to you later before you try to get yourself killed."

I looked from Fynn to Garriton. "So, how do I wake up then?"

"You go to sleep," Garriton answered.

I raised an eyebrow in response.

"I know it sounds ridiculous, but you will understand later. You need to meet the Archduke before any more is revealed."

Fynn whistled loudly, catching the attention of a man in the distance walking a set of horses. Fynn waved him over.

"The Archduke?" I asked. Where in the world was that title on the totem pole of royalty?

"You'll come to find over time that our government system is quite unique," Garriton said. "The Archduke is the highest authority in the land. You can consider him the king."

"Oh. Why would he want to meet with me?"

"Because you're a Waker," Fynn said.

The bald man with the horses finally reached us. "You in need of another mount for the young lord?" He asked.

"Yes," Fynn replied. "Thank you, Rick."

Rick handed me the reins and did a small bow. "This is Fisher. He's an excellent horse."

"Thank you," I said, gazing nervously at the large brown stallion.

Rick began singing as he guided the other horse away.

"You all ready to go then?" Fynn asked.

"One quick question," I said. "Are there . . . like elves and dragons here? Or creatures like orcs or goblins?"

"No, but there are unicorns."

"Really?"

"I'm jesting, of course. There are no mythical creatures here."

"But what about that ugly fat black thing that chased me?"

Fynn and Garriton shared a look.

"I'm sorry you had to experience something like that your first day here," Fynn apologized. "But the answer to that question will have to wait until later. Let's be off."

I turned my attention to the horse and eyed it warily. I wasn't really sure of the best way to hop on. Plus, I didn't want to make a fool of myself in front of these two cool guys I just met.

"Have you ridden before?" Garriton asked.

"Yeah, but not for a couple of years," I said, finally putting my left foot into the stirrup and swinging my other leg over the horse. Well, I was glad I was able to do that right. Now I just had to figure out how to make him move. I had ridden horses a few times during summer camps, but my leaders always grabbed the reins and walked it around while I rode. I could try to kick his sides like they did in the movies, but I was terrified of making him bolt.

"I'm not sure how to steer this thing." I admitted as they hopped onto their own mounts.

"Just put tension on the reins and squeeze with your legs to tell him to go forward," Flynn instructed. "This will be a short trip and Fisher is good at following, so you won't need to worry about steering him."

"Okay . . ."

"You ready?"

"I guess so. Where exactly are we going?"

He pointed down the road away from the fortress. "To Kellamare, the capital of Elegit Terram." His words were gibberish to me, but I didn't bother asking.

We started off through the tall grass in a canter and

quickly found ourselves on a wide dirt road that led away from the fortress. My horse really was great at following once I had nudged him to go. Once on the road, we followed it through the field, away from the forest. As we passed, I noticed that many of the people around the fortress would stop what they were doing and wave or point excitedly at us. Maybe Fynn was some sort of celebrity or supermodel here. He seemed like the type.

"What is this building here?" I asked Garriton, pointing to the fortress.

"We call it the Portal," Garriton replied as he rode next to me. "It is the gate that connects the Dream World to the Waking World."

"What do you mean?" I noticed I was already starting to feel a little sore from the horse. This was going to be a very long ride.

"When people from the Waking World first appear in this world, they always end up somewhere around here. We don't know why, it's just where we always find them. At first, there was nothing here, but after a awhile we decided to make a fortress and station knights here to welcome and keep new Wakers and Dreamers safe."

"Dreamers?"

"We'll get into that later."

As we reached the peak of the small hill, I found out just how high we were as I stared at the beautiful valley far below. Gazing down at the fields of green, I could see for miles. There was a city that looked like it was many miles away. It was hard to tell, but I was pretty sure I could see a castle standing tall above the rest of the city. Even further past the city was an endless expanse of blue. It was the ocean. I hoped they had a nice beach.

"Is that where we're going?" I asked.

"Yes," Garriton said. "That's Kellamare."

"Kella-mare," I said, trying the word out.

We continued to descend steadily into the flat valley below onto the dirt road, passing travelers here and there. Some were on horseback, some were pulling handcarts, and others simply walked. Every now and then, the people we passed by would stop and cheer or say something like, "Welcome to Kellamare, young sir!" or "Hail the Waker!"

"Why are they all so excited?" I asked.

"You'll come to find that Waker's are very popular here," Garriton replied.

It didn't take long until we reached the valley floor. The city still looked to be a good distance away, but now we could move a bit faster. It took maybe an hour to reach the wall that surrounded the city. It was made from large gray bricks and the whole wall was about ten feet tall with even taller guard towers. We followed the road straight to the city entrance. Two knights wearing the same armor as Fynn and Garriton stood guard, though people entered and left the city without a pause.

As we passed the guards, they both saluted by raising their fisted right hand and placing it over their hearts. I was impressed by how in sync they were. They probably got so bored standing there that they practiced it often.

"Captain, Fynn." The knight on the left addressed

him. Fynn nodded to him as we passed.

The city was unlike anything I could have dreamed up. There was so much detail, I couldn't believe it. Brick buildings lined both sides of the street. All were the same color and structure, though they each housed different kinds of shops. Most had large windows displaying various items. I noticed many inns and taverns as well. The streets were so crowded with people that it was hard moving very fast on a horse, but most were smart enough to move out of the way. The street was connected to many smaller streets that branched off in different directions, but we continued straight down the main road we were on.

As we trotted by, many people took notice of us and cheered or waved. The streets were so noisy that I didn't bother trying to start a conversation with Fynn or Garriton. We continued through the crowded streets and I watched the scenery shift as it changed from shops and inns to half-timbered homes and larger brick buildings. The area started to feel like a fancy HOA from back home with its matching houses, nice archways, and perfectly trimmed hedges. The further along we went, the cleaner the area looked.

The road started to slowly veer left and we continued to follow it. As we followed the bend in the road, a castle came into view. We were still pretty far away but I could already tell it was massive.

The road opened up to an intersection with a large fountain in the center, spraying water high into the air. It was so big, I thought it would be fun to swim laps in. The area around the fountain was filled with children running and playing, and people dancing to bluegrass-sounding music being played by a four-man band.

"I see you found another Waker," a young man said as he approached.

"Ah, Chancellor Kaden," Fynn said, stopping his horse. "Good timing. This is Chaz, he just arrived here only an hour or two ago."

Kaden didn't introduce himself to me, he just stared at me like he wasn't sure what I was.

"Kaden is a Waker as well," Garriton said, breaking the awkward silence.

"Oh, nice," I said, a little excited to meet someone who was supposedly like me. When I first saw his brown hair trimmed short on the sides, I had a feeling he wasn't from the Dream World. I had yet to see anyone else with hair that short or neatly trimmed. "Where are you from?"

"It doesn't matter," Kaden replied, sounding slightly annoyed. "Just know that this world is as real as the other one you know back home. Don't go doing anything stupid. See you at the feast."

As Kaden walked away, I turned to Garriton and whispered, "What's his deal?"

"He's not much of a people person. I'm sure once you get to know him, you two will have much to talk about."

I doubted it. He seemed like the type that was into poetry, modern art, and other boring stuff like that.

"What was he saying about a feast?" I asked, hopeful.

"The Archduke always throws a feast when a Waker

comes to our world," Fynn explained.

"Oh, heck yeah!"

We made our way past the intersection and came to a drawbridge stretching over a moat that surrounded the castle grounds. As we crossed the bridge, I took in the majestic beauty of the castle. It was constructed from a sparkly gray stone and rose hundreds of feet in the air with its enormous towers and battlements. The whole structure was square shaped with towers on every corner. Many flags with the familiar symbol of the sun peeking through the clouds hung around the castle.

"How old is this castle?" I asked.

"Just a little over three hundred years old," Garriton answered. "Not very old compared to the other castles."

We passed under the portcullis and through the towering walls into the castle courtyard. The courtyard looked as fancy as you would expect it to; it had a cobblestone path that led through the perfectly clipped lawn. There were many bushes and trees trimmed to perfection, and there were fountains that all rose and fell in unison. A few children played in the grass, and I glimpsed a short distance away what looked like a man proposing to a woman as he held out a ring while he rested on one knee. Most of the other people around the courtyard were knights.

Fynn and Garriton stopped and dismounted from their horses. I did as well, almost falling right off. A man wearing overalls with big muscly arms and short hair came over to retrieve two of the horses with a smile. A small boy followed and grabbed the reins of the third horse.

"Thanks, Heg," Fynn said. He handed the man a silver coin.

"Anything for you, Captain Fynn," The man replied in a deep voice.

He turned and guided the horses to the stables as the young boy followed behind.

"Are you ready to meet the Archduke?" Fynn asked.

"I guess so," I said with a shrug. "I have no idea how I'm supposed to act. Do I bow or anything like that?"

"Good question. We do bow when we first greet him to show our respect. We also always refer to him as *Lord* or *Archduke*."

"What kind of bow? Like this?" Trying to be funny, I did a little curtsy.

"If you want us to start calling you *Lady* Chaz, then I suppose that will do," Garriton said with a laugh.

I laughed. "Yeah, I'm just messing around."

"A small bow will do," Fynn said. He demonstrated by putting his arms straight at his sides as he tilted his head forward and slightly bent his body at the waist. "You try it."

After I copied his quick bow, they both nodded.

"I think he's ready," Garriton commented to Fynn.

"I agree," Fynn said with a smile. "Let's be on our way."

I followed the two men through the courtyard to the castle doors which also had guards stationed before them. The guards opened the tall black wooden double doors for us, and we headed inside. Through the doors was a large spacious hall with white walls and a high ceiling. There were so many closed doors on each side of the hall that I wondered how anyone knew where they were going. Near the doors we entered, on each side of us was an identical scene of fancy-looking floral couches with a light wooden table centered in front.

At the end of the hall, there was a woman sitting behind a wooden desk writing on paper with a feathered pen. To her left was another set of large doors where four knights stood guard.

"Welcome to Kellamare City Hall," Garriton said, slapping my back.

"City hall?" I asked. "Isn't this a castle?"

"Yes, it is, but ever since the structure of our government changed, Kellamare is no longer considered a kingdom. It is now a city. And every city needs a city hall. The people decided the castle would be the perfect place."

"Well, I guess that makes sense."

We proceeded through the hall and approached the lady sitting at the desk.

"Good afternoon, Lord Fynn," the woman greeted, her blue eyes studying each of us in turn. Her blond hair was tied at the top of her head in a neat bun and she was wearing a sky-blue dress.

"Good to see you, Grace," Fynn said. "We need an immediate audience with the Archduke."

"I will make that happen." She got up from her chair and asked, "Who is requesting the audience?"

"Captain Fynn, Garriton of the knights, and Lord

Chaz of the Waking World."

"One moment please."

Grace walked over to the guarded doors and knocked softly. She opened one of the doors without waiting for a reply and stepped in, letting the door shut behind her.

As we waited, Garriton leaned over to me and said, "You are about to be the center of attention in an important meeting with many government officials. No pressure."

Great. I hoped they weren't expecting to hear some wise words or something. The only thing I knew how to talk about was video games and movies.

One of the doors opened and Grace stepped back into the room.

"The Archduke will see you now," she said, holding the door open for us.

Chapter 6

So . . . I'm Pretty Much a Superhero

I followed Garriton and Fynn into the room. Inside, there were a few people sitting at a long rectangular table, and all of them were staring at us. The room was very bright due to the skylight above letting in the sunshine. The walls were white, and the floor was a gray marble.

I counted five people at the table, the Archduke most likely at the head. The man I thought was him looked to be in his mid-fifties, he had wavy gray hair and a neatly trimmed beard. His hazel eyes stared right into mine, and his friendly face helped me feel a little less tense. He looked like the leader type. He also looked like he would be the old guy in the movies that always surprised everyone with his insane fighting skills.

Fynn and Garriton bowed to the Archduke so I did as well.

"Welcome, friends," he said in a soft, yet commanding voice. "It sounds like you brought some good news."

"We have, my lord," Fynn said.

"First, tell me about your assignment in Ausidor, then you can introduce us to this young man."

"Of course." Fynn stepped forward. "My men and I escorted Lord Brevan to the city of Ausidor where he was received with open arms and a grand celebration. Duke Brighton acted pleased with the young man, and he recognized Brevan's titles of Lord and Dreamchaser, rightfully bestowing upon him his inheritance. Neither on the way there or back were we troubled. The land was very quiet."

"Not even a sign of the enemy?" the Archduke asked.

"Nothing. It was as if they wanted us to come."

"Interesting. If that is true, then we had better keep a close eye on Lord Brevan."

"And the forest surrounding the Portal," Fynn added, looking at me. "Lord Chaz had a very rude awakening."

Every eye in the room shifted to me.

"I'm sorry to hear that," the Archduke apologized. "Young man, will you please introduce yourself and fill us in on your unfortunate encounter."

Okay, first impressions are always very important. It was time to let them know if I was the funny guy, the wise guy, or just the plain, boring guy. I wasn't very wise, so maybe I could be the funny guy. That would probably only last so long though. My jokes made my own Dad cringe.

I stepped forward and did an awkward little wave. "Hello." I said. "My name is Chaz, son of Robert. I hail from the great mountains of the Utah valley. I'm fluent in Elvish and Wookiee, and I am a master in the art of the yo-yo. Wanna hear a joke about construction? Never mind, I'm still working on it."

It was silent for almost a full minute until someone at the table snickered. It was a really cute girl who looked to be about my age. How had I not noticed her until now? Her blond ponytail alone made her stand out from all of the guys in the room. She looked at me with her brown eyes full of amusement as she covered the smile on her face with her hand.

"Anyway," I continued, "I went to bed last night and when I woke up, I was in the forest with the white trees. I had no idea where I was. I walked around for a couple of minutes until an ugly, round black monster jumped out of the bushes and chased me. I ran for a long time until I found the fortress. By then, the monster had stopped chasing me and that's when I ran into Fynn and Garriton."

"We are all glad you made it here safely, Chaz," the Archduke said. "A lot of your questions are about to be answered." He turned his attention to the whole group. "We will adjourn our meeting so that Constable Darven and I can visit with Chaz. Please introduce yourself to him on your way out. And Juliet, would you wait for us outside the room?"

The girl who snickered turned her head in surprise as if she'd been caught off guard. She nodded with a frown.

"Excellent. You are all dismissed."

Everyone stood up and began conversing with one another as they made their way out of the room.

"We'll be seeing you later," Fynn said, patting me on

the shoulder.

"Don't make him angry," Garriton said with a wink and a small smile as he followed Fynn out the door.

I turned my attention to the girl named Juliet as she approached.

"You were the only one that laughed." I said.

"Well, it sure wasn't because of your joke," she said bluntly. "You were really awkward; I couldn't help it. I'm Juliet by the way. I'm also a Waker like you."

"Really? Where are you from? How long have you been here?"

"I'm from Los Angeles. I've been here for almost a week, so I was just barely in your shoes."

"Is this all even real?" I questioned, more to myself than her. "You could be part of the dream too."

"I don't think I really believed it until the third time I came back," Juliet said sympathetically. "Trust me, it's real. Don't go do anything stupid."

"That's what that Kaden guy said too."

"Ugh! Kaden is the worst. Please don't compare me to him. Anyways, we'll talk later."

Juliet headed out the door and a tall, dark-skinned man stepped in front of me. He had long dreadlocks and arms bigger than my thighs. He looked like he could crush a skull with just two fingers.

"Good to meet ya, bruddah," he said in what sounded like a Jamaican accent. He shook my hand in a crushing grip. "My name is Akoni, Duke of Beckstead and son of Jelani. I'm very glad dat dere's finally someone else who speaks Wookiee." He opened his mouth and made a very impressive Chewbacca noise.

"Cool!" I said, already deciding that he was going to be my favorite person in the Dream World. "You're gonna have to teach me how to do that."

"As long as you teach me to yo-yo."

"Sounds good to me."

"I'll be seeing ya later, den."

Waving, he walked away. The next man that stopped in front of me had long black hair that hung past his shoulders and a neatly trimmed beard. His face was very rough and unfriendly.

"Grayson Hammer," he said in a gruff voice. "Weapons Master and High Strategist of Elegit Terram."

"Nice to meet you," I said. "What exactly is a High Strategist?"

"In the time of war, it is my job to figure out the most effective and efficient way to take down the enemy."

"Sounds stressful."

"It can be. I will certainly be seeing you later." He turned and walked away.

I looked over and saw that the only two people left in the room were the Archduke and another older man. The other man made his way over to me. He had short gray hair and a friendly face.

"Good to meet you, Lord Chaz," the man said.

"Constable Darven at your service."

"Good to meet you too," I replied. I didn't know why, but I was already getting a friendly grandpa kind of vibe from him.

The Archduke came over and shook my hand as well. "I just wanted to formally introduce myself," he said. "I am Archduke Bradford. Welcome to the Dream World."

"Thanks."

"Well, let's get started. Go ahead and take a seat at the table."

I sat down on the closest chair before Bradford and Darven sat down across from me.

"We have many things to talk about," Bradford said. "Sadly, we don't have time to go over everything, but I will hit on all the key points. Darven will be sure that I don't leave out anything important."

I leaned forward on the table. I was actually a little excited to learn more about this place. Sure, maybe it was my own dream making things up, but it was still interesting. I especially wanted to learn more about that monster that chased me. Maybe my mind had decided that was what a Sasquatch looked like.

"It will make most sense if we start from the beginning." Bradford began. "You see, as far back as we know, the Dream World has co-existed with the Waking World. The Dream World exists in the mind, just as the Waking World exists in the body."

"What do you mean, *the Waking World exists in the body*?" I asked, hoping his whole spiel wasn't going to confuse me.

"If you didn't have a body, would you be able to exist on earth?" Bradford asked.

"Well, no . . ."

"That is exactly why the Waking World exists *in* the body," Bradford explained. "And it explains why the Dream World exists in the mind; you can't exist here without one. But unlike the Waking World, not everyone can access the Dream World. Only those with a special heightened awareness and a fully cognitive mind can find their way here. These particular people possessing those special minds are the extra creative ones, the ones who tend to daydream a lot. Because of the way their brain works, they can do things that others can't do."

"So, I'm confused," I interrupted again. "Are you saying that because I'm here, I have one of those special creative minds?"

"Yes, you do. I will get to that soon. But first I must continue where I left off. The only minds that exist in the Dream World are those with special minds, whether they currently live in the Waking World or have passed on." Bradford held up a hand to stop the question he saw forming on my lips. "Yes, I mean those who have died.

"Most of the people you see here in this world no longer have living bodies. Once upon a time they lived on the earth, some for a few short minutes and some for a whole lifetime. We call them Dreamers. It seems that the mind continues to live on after death, though it doesn't stay here forever. Even for the dead, the Dream World is just another temporary state.

"The only way to get to the Dream World is through dreaming, which is why you can only get here when you go to sleep. To go back to the Waking World, you also have to go to sleep, during which time you would actually be waking yourself up. When we sleep, our mind enters a unique creative state that allows us to bend reality in a way. We can also access that creative state while awake through different means such as daydreaming."

"What do you mean?" I asked, my interest building.

"Darven, I think it's your turn," Bradford said, looking to the Constable.

"Ah, yes," Darven said, straightening in his chair. "Have you noticed a lot of odd coincidences lately? Maybe a lot of Deja vu moments?"

"Yeah!" I said excitedly. "There were a few times over the last day or two where I would imagine something happening before it did."

"That is because you have been accessing the creative state while awake," Darven explained. "Chaz, because of the special mind you possess, you can use the creative state to bend reality in a way that allows you to see the future."

"Are you serious?"

"Very serious," Darven said. "If you don't believe me now, you will when you continue to glimpse the future."

"I still don't understand how it works, though. How can you bend reality in a way to see the future?"

"Maybe this will help." He pulled out a white piece of yarn. It was about a foot long. He laid it out flat on the table so it made a straight line. "So, this string represents time and reality." He put his finger on a random spot toward one end of the string. "This is where you are. You can only see this one point in time where you are at the moment. You can't see forwards or backwards. But when you bend reality–" He pulled the other end of the string into a loop so now it overlapped where his finger was. "You literally bend the timeline. You can now see this other point in time further down the line because it is now crossing the point where you are. Does that make sense?"

"It does," I replied. My mind was blown. "But how is that even possible?"

"No one knows. The Dream World is a mystery that logic nor science can explain. You'll find that many laws of the universe can be broken here. And because they can be broken here, they can also be broken in reality when you access the Dream World by activating the creative state. Seeing the future isn't the only way to bend reality."

"What else can I do?" I asked, on the edge of my seat. I hoped so badly this was all real. I could literally be a superhero if I wanted to. What if I could bend reality in a way that would make me fly or have super strength?

"You will have time to explore the possibilities of your gift later," Darven said with an amused smile. "We still have more to discuss."

"More?" I complained. "Like what?"

"The monster you ran into," Darven said seriously.

Chapter 7

Now There's a Villain Too

"Chaz," Darven said, "why do you think some people choose not to chase their ideas or dreams?"

It seemed like a random question, but I still answered it. "Well . . . probably because they're scared it won't work. Or maybe because others tell them it's crazy, so they start to think it's crazy too."

"That's right," Darven agreed. "That creature you saw is what some call *Somnum Exterreri*. It is Latin for *Nightmare*, which is what we prefer to call them. When people in the Waking World listen to their doubts and fears by choosing not to chase their dreams or ideas, without even realizing it, they are breeding one of those monsters you saw in the forest. After a Nightmare is created by the doubts of someone in reality, it will then continue to grow bigger here as it feeds off the negative emotions of anyone it comes in contact with. It no longer only feeds off the host."

"So . . ." I said, thinking out loud, "that would mean

there are thousands of those monsters, because there's gotta be thousands of people who are too scared to chase their dreams."

"Millions actually," Darven said sadly.

"Well, that's pretty scary."

"That's not even the scariest part. They get much worse if they continue to feed off of heavy amounts of negative emotions from the host. If a Nightmare is not destroyed, eventually it will evolve into something much worse. The creature they evolve into is called a *Mors Somnia*, which means *Death of Dreams*. But we prefer to call them by their Latin name, and we just call them *Mors* for short.

"A Mors is at least a hundred times worse than a Nightmare. They are faster, stronger and almost as smart as humans. They are also easily distinguished from the Nightmares. They look almost identical to the host they are feeding off of–not exactly the same, but a shadowy and darker version of them. They are formidable opponents in battle, and one of them could easily slay a hundred knights."

I imagined a dark shadowy version of myself swinging a giant sword around as it mowed down dozens of knights. That would be terrifying.

"Is there a special way to kill a Mors . . . soma?" I asked.

"Not a special way," Darven said. "But a special person–someone like you."

"Someone like me? I'm just a teenager."

"You're also a Waker. Wakers have the potential to be more powerful than any Dreamer could ever imagine. No one knows why. It's another mystery of this world. Wakers have always been the mightiest of leaders among us. They are our brightest hope during dark times. We always eagerly wait for the next Waker to show up and join our forces. You've probably noticed that you are already treated like a celebrity around here."

"Yeah," I said. "I've been wondering about that."

"It's because Wakers have been scarce lately. We used to have a few of you show up every year. But until Juliet showed up, and now you, we hadn't had any newcomers for about a year and a half. On top of that, many Wakers have been either disappearing, or joining The Quin Anulus."

"The what?"

"The Quin Anulus is the reason new Wakers are to be brought to me immediately," the Archduke interjected. "Almost twenty years ago, a Waker named Victor arrived in the Dream World. He was a great kid with great aspirations, but he quickly went down a dark path. The short version of the story is that one night we caught him making deals and promises with a Mors Somnia in exchange for power.

"Well, for whatever reason, he decided to join forces with the Nightmares and Mors and has been an annoyance ever since. Over the years, he has also gained many human followers, most of which have been young and naive Wakers who hadn't been in our world long enough to know better. He calls his group of Wakers the Quin Anulus, which means *Ring of Doubt*. Now, we not only fight monsters, but this group of foolish men as well."

"So now there's a villain too," I said.

"There usually is," Darven replied.

"Well, what do you want from me?"

"We want you to join our team," Bradford said. "We need you to fight for us. And not just for us, but the people in the Waking World as well."

"Sounds good to me," I said. I was still mostly convinced this was all a dream. Mostly. "We need a team name though. Something a lot better than the Clean Amulet or whatever their name was."

Bradford and Darven shared an amused smile.

"We actually have a name for our team," Bradford said. "I know it doesn't sound very intimidating, but we call ourselves the *Dreamchasers*."

"Team Dreamchasers?" I laughed. "Why not something cool like *The Reality Breakers* or *The Future Benders*?"

"Dreamchasers has always been what we call those who choose to actively oppose the Nightmares. I can only speculate why they chose that name. Either way, Chaz, will you join the Dreamchasers?"

"Heck yeah! As long as I get a sword. Maybe two?"

Both men laughed as they stood up. I stood up as well.

"I'm sure you will get your own sword soon enough," Bradford said, chuckling. "Thank you for your willingness to serve, we will forever be grateful to you. During the feast tonight, we will officially introduce you as our newest Dreamchaser. And just so you know, as a Waker, when you become a Dreamchaser, you are then given the title of Lord, classifying you as a noble. When you finish your training here at Kellamare, you may receive a house and land as your rightful inheritance as a Lord."

Me, a Lord? It was crazy, but cool at the same time.

If only my friends could see me now! I mused. Jake and Isaac would be so jealous. It was too bad that if I told them about this place, they would think I was a psycho. Maybe I was.

"The rest of the time is yours to do whatever you want until the feast," Bradford said as he and Darven ushered me toward the door. "I had Lady Juliet tarry outside in case you wanted a tour. Or if you'd rather, I can have her help you find where your quarters will be so you can rest and ponder."

"It'd be fun to talk and see more of the city," I replied.

"Wonderful."

Out in the waiting room, we found Juliet sitting on one of the couches looking bored. The three of us made our way over and she stood when we approached.

"Lady Juliet, let me introduce you to our newest Dreamchaser," Bradford said, gesturing to me.

"Decided to join the good guys, huh?" Juliet asked.

"I don't want to be on the same side as a bunch of ugly demons," I replied.

"Juliet, would you be so kind as to give Chaz a tour of the area until the feast?" Bradford asked.

"I would love to." Her voice was thick with sarcasm.

"Excellent. We will be seeing you in a few hours."

Suddenly, the front door opened and Captain Fynn rushed inside followed by Garriton and a really cute girl with big blue eyes.

"My Lord!" Flynn said excitedly as he and Garriton bowed. "We were just on our way back to the Portal when a couple of my men stopped us right outside of the city. They introduced us to this young maiden here and told us she arrived not too long after Lord Chaz did." He stepped aside. "May I introduce you to Lady Autumn of the Waking World."

As he spoke, I couldn't help but stare at her pretty face. I had never seen someone with eyes so big and blue before. She had very light blond hair and was wearing black pants and a white striped shirt. It was nice to finally see someone else wearing 21st century clothing in a medieval world. She glanced in my direction and noticed my normal clothes as well. A big smile spread across her face as we made eye contact.

Oh yeah! I cheered inwardly. There was another cute girl to hang out with. Hopefully she was nothing like Juliet though, that girl was too sassy.

Chapter 8

I'm Not Ready to Be Assassinated

Autumn seemed a little embarrassed. She stared at the ground as every eye in the room rested on her.

"Three?" Bradford said with a bewildered look. "In one week?"

"This has to mean something!" Darven said excitedly. The Archduke stepped closer to Autumn and held out his hand. "Hello. I am Sherman Bradford, Archduke of Elegit Terram. It is so wonderful to meet you."

"It's nice to meet you too," Autumn said timidly, shaking his hand.

"I'm sure you are very confused and maybe a little frightened, but I assure you, you are safe. All of your questions will be answered soon." He turned to me and Juliet. "Lady Juliet and Lord Chaz, would you please introduce yourselves?"

I looked to Juliet and she stepped forward first.

"I'm Juliet," she said. "I'm from California and I got here almost a week ago."

Autumn's face lit up with a big smile. "I'm so glad I'm not alone. This is all so crazy. I feel like *I'm* going crazy."

"You're definitely not going crazy. It took me a couple of days to believe this was actually happening. We'll talk a lot more later."

Juliet stepped back and I stepped forward, raising my hand to shake hers.

"Hey, I'm Chaz," I said, trying to sound smooth. "I just got here today too, so I know how you're feeling."

"Really?" Autumn asked, even more excited. "Has it been really scary and confusing for you too?"

"Yeah, it was pretty scary when I first arrived. But so far, everyone has been really good to me, and most of my questions have been answered. Since we're both new here, we'll have to make sure we stick together."

"Yes, we will," Autumn agreed. "I'm glad I already have some friends I can talk to."

Next, Darven took a turn to introduce himself.

"Lady Autumn," Bradford said, "if you would please follow Darven and I, we will explain everything that is going on and hopefully answer a lot of your questions." He turned to the rest of us. "Captain Fynn, you are dismissed. Juliet and Chaz, you may also be on your way. After we are done briefing Autumn, we will come find you."

Fynn and Garriton bowed to the Archduke, then Juliet and I did as well. I watched Autumn and Darven follow him out of the room. At the same time, Fynn and Garriton headed out the door. I turned to find Juliet grinning at me.

"You're crushing on her already?" Juliet teased.

"No way," I stated. "I just barely met her."

"We'll have to make sure we stick together," she quoted. "You're such a flirt. I'm pretty sure you're one of those guys who falls in love with every cute girl he meets."

"Whatever. I just try to be friends with everyone."

"We'll see about that."

"Well, are you going to show me around?" I asked.

She sighed. "I guess. What do you want to see?"

"I don't really care. I don't know what there is to see."

"How bout for starters we find you a room and then I'll also show you where the training grounds are?"

"Sounds good to me."

Juliet led the way to a door in the left corner of the room. Inside was a long, gray brick hallway that was lit by torches. There was a row of doors on the left, and at the end of the hall were stairs.

"All of these doors are bedrooms," Juliet said. "There are more upstairs too. I'm pretty sure you can pick any one you want. That's what they let me do."

"How am I supposed to know which ones are taken?" I asked.

"If it's locked, then it's taken. But I've been told that Wakers in training are the only ones who stay in these quarters, and as far as I know, that's just us two. And soon, Autumn."

"Have you met any other Wakers?"

"A few, but they've all been here for years. The

newest one was Brevan, and he just finished his training right before I got here. I didn't really get to talk to him much."

"And now there's three more of us," I commented.

"Yup. Now hurry up and choose a room."

"Okay." I moved down the hall. "Which one's yours?"

"The last one. And no, I'm not going to show you inside."

"I wasn't even going to ask. Why not choose one of the first rooms?"

"Because if someone breaks in and tries to assassinate me, then they will have to search the other rooms first." She said it like it was obvious.

"Good point. Hopefully that doesn't happen though."

I walked to a door that was two doors down from Juliet's and tried the doorknob. It was unlocked so I pushed it open and stepped inside.

"Good choice," Juliet commented as she followed me inside. "It would've been weird if you chose the one right next to mine."

The room was gray and boring like the hallway we had just come from. It had brick walls and a brick floor that was covered by a red rug with gold embroidered patterns. There was a large window on the opposite wall, and the thin drapes let in a good amount of light.

On the right was a small bed about the size of the one I had back home. It was covered with a thick maroon blanket, and the king-size fluffy white pillows made it look comfortable and inviting. On the left of the room was a cherrywood dresser with a large oval mirror. The only other furniture was a wooden chair in the corner. And though the room didn't ooze coziness, it was clean, and that was all that mattered to me.

"Looks exactly like mine," Juliet commented as I made my way over to the curtains. I pushed them aside, the view revealing a large field that looked well-trodden with very little grass. I observed various people out there doing silly-looking exercises or sparring with swords.

"That's the training grounds," Juliet said as she pulled open a dresser drawer, took out a key and handed it to me. "This is the key to your room. I don't think they have spares, so don't lose it."

I took the key from her and said, "I'm not really ever going to be in this room, am I? Just when I go to sleep?"

"And when you wake up," she added. "And when you need to change, or just relax."

"I won't be waking up near the Portal every time I come here?"

"Nope. You wake up where you last went to sleep."

"Well that's good," I said, feeling relieved. "I don't want to get chased by a Nightmare every time I wake up."

"Are they really as terrifying as they say?" Juliet asked curiously. "I still haven't seen one."

"Really? You've been here a week and you've never seen one?"

She shook her head.

"Well, that makes me feel a lot better about being here. Yeah, they really are scary. I mean, at first it was.

Now, it almost makes me laugh thinking about how ridiculous it looked."

Juliet nodded, heading to the door. "Let's go to the training grounds."

I followed her out and used the key to lock the door.

"How long will we be training for?" I asked. "You know, until we graduate?"

"Grayson told me it all depends because some people are ready before others. He said on average it takes a couple of years."

We exited the Waker's hall of bedrooms and headed straight to the big doors leading out to the courtyard. The moment we stepped outside we were met by a large crowd. They began to cheer and clap as soon as they saw us. I was a little startled by the sudden noise and attention.

"Hail the Wakers!" someone yelled.

"Hail the Wakers!" the crowd repeated in unison.

I stood there awkwardly, unsure of what to do until Juliet grabbed my arm and pulled me through the crowd. As we passed, many people patted us on the back and thanked us. After we made our way through the crowd, Juliet let go of my arm and we headed around the castle.

"Get used to that," Juliet said. "It happens almost every time I come out of the castle."

"Really?" I asked. "They just wait for us to come out?"

"Yup. It's like they got nothing better to do. This is probably exactly what it feels like to be a celebrity. I'm not gonna lie, I kinda liked it at first. But now, it's just annoying."

To the side of the castle was a tall hedge that stretched from the castle to the walls surrounding the courtyard, completely blocking the other side from view. The only way through the hedge was an opening near the middle where two knights stood guard.

As we passed through the hedge, the knights acknowledged us with a nod. On the other side of the hedge was the training field I saw from my bedroom window. There was a simple wooden fence surrounding the trodden area, and on the outside were a couple pergola-type structures with benches underneath. Inside the fence, there were multiple one-on-one matches going on at once, their wooden swords clacking against each other. Two other men watched as they sat on the fence.

"So, what kind of training do we do?" I asked as we made our way in the direction of the fight.

"Weapon's training, like swords and bows," Juliet replied. "And also mind training."

"Mind training?"

"Yeah, so we can learn to daydream in battle." We stopped at the fence near the other men who sat watching the duel.

"Why would we want to daydream in battle?" I asked.

"So, you can see the future and know your opponent's moves before they make them."

"I guess that makes sense."

"Watch those two," she said, pointing to two of the men locked in combat.

At the moment, the two men were a couple feet away from each other with their wooden swords raised, slowly circling each other as if looking for an opening. One of them wore blue padding while the other wore red. The padding consisted of thick leather helmets and vests that covered their chests. It looked like they were in the middle of an intense staring competition. Their eyes were locked onto each other's without blinking or focusing on anything else.

After a few seconds of circling each other, the man in blue struck so fast, I barely had time to register it. Blue attempted a few quick jabs at Red, who blocked them with ease. On the last jab, Blue swept his right leg as if trying to trip Red. It seemed as if Red had known the kick was coming, and while Red blocked Blue's last attack, he also jumped back out of the way and then smacked Blue's leg with his sword.

Blue stumbled, but he didn't fall. They started to slowly circle each other again. Blue attacked first again. He swung so fast that I could hardly believe it. But Red was able to block every single swipe like before. It looked like he knew exactly where Blue was going to attack. After another failed attempt by Blue, they went back to circling each other. I watched the pattern repeat over and over again for a few minutes. Red quickly started to gain the upper hand. He was able to land a couple of blows to Blue's body, but Blue had yet to land a single one.

"Why do they keep pausing to circle each other?" I finally asked Juliet.

"To us, it looks like they're not doing anything," Juliet said. "But they're actually Dream Fighting."

Who came up with names here? *Dreamchasers* and *Dream Fighting? Really?* I chuckled inwardly. *That was so lame.*

"Yup. Dream Fighting is where two skilled daydreamers pretty much fight in the future. As they circle each other, both of them are trying to see further into the future than the other to know how to attack or how not to attack."

"Then how is the blue guy losing if he can see where red guy is going to attack?" I asked, still confused.

"It's because the red guy is seeing further into the future then blue. Blue sees a future where he lands his attack, but right before he attempts that possible future, Red also sees it and then looks further. Grayson can explain it to you better when you start training with him."

"No, it's okay. I think I got it. That sounds really intense. Are you good at it?"

"Dude, I've only been here less than a week." She turned away from the fight. "Let's go back into the castle, I bet they're almost done with Autumn."

I continued to watch the fight for as long as I could as I followed Juliet away from the fence. Outside of the training grounds, just past the hedge, there was another crowd waiting for us. They were just as enthusiastic as the one before, and I thought it would be cool to stay and sign autographs or something. Sadly, Juliet wouldn't have it. She pulled me away and we headed into the castle.

"Don't let it all go to your head," she said, sitting down on the couch in the waiting room. "You'll probably end up worse than Kaden."

"Impossible," I said as I sat down on the opposite end of the same couch. I made sure I sat as far away from her as I could. If I sat too close, she would probably make fun of me or think I had a crush on her. She was probably the one crushing on me though.

As soon as we sat down, the boardroom door opened and Autumn and Darven walked out. Autumn looked a little stressed. Or maybe worried?

"How did it go?" I asked to neither of them in particular.

"Lady Autumn needs some time to think before she decides if she wants to join the Dreamchasers," Darven explained, without any hint of negativity. "I told her it would help if she talked with you two about it."

"There's just so much to think about," Autumn said. "If this is all real, then that's a really important decision to make."

"It's okay, Autumn," Juliet said as she walked over and put an arm around her. "I understand how you're feeling, and so does Chaz."

"The Archduke hopes she will have a decision before the start of the feast," Darven said. "That gives you a couple hours to talk about it. And while you do that, Lady Juliet will you please help these two get outfitted for the occasion?"

"I will."

"Great. I will see you three in a short while."

Darven walked away and we all stared at each other for a minute.

"Let's get you two some clothes and then we'll talk," Juliet said. She led us through one of the many doors on the left side of the room. Inside was a barren short hall lit by torches. At the end was another set of stairs.

"How do you know your way around here so well?" I asked as we ascended the stairs.

"I don't," Juliet responded. "I just know the few areas I use every day–the bedrooms, the training grounds, the dining hall, and where we're going now. Up here are the baths and dressing rooms. They're stocked with clothes and armor for us. You can leave your dirty clothes here and they'll wash them for you."

"Do they cook every meal for us too?" I asked, mostly joking.

"Yeah. They pretty much treat us like royalty."

"Everyone is so wonderful here," Autumn said. "I really do want to help. I just wish I didn't have to fight."

We walked through the doorway at the top of the stairs to find a long, white hallway with a few skylights overhead where the sun shone through. To our right was a green carpeted room full of shelves stacked with various clothing, armor, and boots.

"There are other ways to help besides fighting," Juliet said, walking into the room. We followed behind her, and once inside, I noticed an older woman to the left sitting on a chair sewing what looked like pants. To the right of her were a couple of changing stalls that looked just like you would see in a clothing store. There were even mirrors inside.

"Lady Juliet!" The woman exclaimed in a squeaky voice. She waddled over to Juliet and gave her a hug. She wore a plain green dress that resembled a nightgown. Her gray and black hair was pinned up in a bun and she wore large round glasses. "It's wonderful to see you, as always." She grabbed Juliet's hands.

"Thanks, Gretchen," Juliet said before turning to us. "I brought some new friends."

Gretchen squealed in delight as an even bigger smile covered her face. She quickly hobbled over and grabbed my hand in one of hers and Autumn's hand in the other. "What's your name, beautiful?" Gretchen asked Autumn.

"It's Autumn," she replied, the big smile I had seen on her earlier appearing once again.

"Oh, what a gorgeous name for a gorgeous girl! And you have one of the most wonderful smiles I have ever seen!"

Autumn blushed. "Thank you so much."

Gretchen turned her attention to me and squeezed my hand tightly.

"What about this good-looking lad?"

I smiled. "My name is Chaz."

"Chaaaaz." Gretchen repeated, drawing it out. "Chaz. That is also a gorgeous name!"

"Hah, thanks," I said. It was the first time someone had ever said *anything* about me was gorgeous. What a crazy lady.

"Let me guess, you two are here to get new outfits?" Gretchen asked. Before either of us could respond, she turned away and walked towards the shelves of clothing. "No, those tacky modern clothes won't do for sure."

Autumn and I shared an amused grin.

"*Tacky*?" she whispered.

"She probably doesn't even know what it means," I said back.

We both shared a laugh. We smiled at each other for a few more seconds before I turned to Juliet and found her giving me a knowing smile.

"What?" I asked.

"Oh nothing," she said before turning away, grinning to herself.

I turned to Gretchen and watched her rummage through the clothing on the shelves, making two neat piles on the ground.

"What size shoes do you two wear?" Gretchen asked as she moved over to the racks of boots. We both told her our shoe sizes and she topped each pile of clothing with a pair of boots. She handed a pile to me and the other to Autumn.

"That should do it. Now go and change. I can't wait to see how noble you two will look!"

"But you didn't ask for my size of clothing," I pointed out.

"I don't need to ask," Gretchen said with a wave of her hand. "I've been doing this for longer than you've been alive."

Autumn went into the stall on the right and I went to the one on the left, shutting the door behind me. I stripped down to my boxers and pulled on the black leather pants. They fit perfectly, but they were a lot skinnier than I was used to. They looked like the kind of pants an 80's rock star would wear. There were two shirts; the white frilly one I guessed was supposed to go underneath, so I put it on first. The overshirt was a blue jerkin, which actually looked pretty cool. It took me at least five minutes to slip on the tall black boots and tie them tight.

I examined myself in the mirror and grinned. I looked really good. I *did* look *noble*. Maybe I could be a medieval model, if there was such a thing. I started to imagine myself going into battle with a sword strapped to my hip, riding on a horse at the head of a massive army. I was startled when my vision suddenly went dark.

I found myself in my room at the castle. I held a bright gleaming sword in my right hand. I looked into the mirror and noticed I was wearing the same clothing I just put on. The only light in the room came from three candles placed around the room. Outside my window was dark and I assumed it was nighttime. For some unknown reason, I felt restless. I knew I wouldn't be able to sleep even if I tried, and I was sure I needed to be awake and ready for something. For what, I didn't know, but I felt anxious.

Eventually I decided I would practice the offensive and defensive sword exercises I had done so many times. Sure, my room wasn't very big, but it would work if I was careful. I held my sword out in front of me and began blocking the attacks of imaginary foes while shuffling my feet. I spun and jabbed, I sidestepped and parried, I lunged and swept. It felt good to be using my sword, even if it was only for practice. As I continued to practice, I felt even more confident in my swordplay. I wanted desperately to prove how amazing I was in battle. No one would be able to stop me.

I heard faint noises coming from out in the hall. It sounded like shuffling and . . . grunting? It definitely sounded like faint grunts. I lowered my sword as I crept closer to the door and listened. There was a 'click', and then the sound of a door creaking open. The shuffling and grunts increased for a couple seconds, as if people were struggling past each other to get into the room. Then I heard the sounds again, the shuffling and grunting getting closer. Another door creaked open.

This couldn't be good. That fact that someone was sneaking into the Wakers' hall this late at night was already a bad sign. It probably wasn't the paparazzi.

Unsure of what to do, I looked around the room for a couple seconds before I looked to my sword. Seeing my polished sword reflect the candlelight sent waves of courage through my body. Maybe it was finally time to test myself. I took a deep breath, pulled open the door and stepped into the dim hallway. It was lit by a single torch near me, the rest of the torches down the hall were out.

I turned to my right and saw figures rush into a room a few doors down from mine. Because of the dimness of the hall, I didn't recognize the dark figure at the head of the group, but it was easy to recognize the round shadows behind him. Three Nightmares followed behind the figure, grunting as they leaped into the room after him.

It would have probably been a good idea to go and wake Juliet and Autumn before the creatures saw me. But then again, I didn't want them to get hurt. I felt like it was my duty to protect them. They were probably asleep anyway. And I could see the future, the monsters couldn't. Hopefully, it would be a quick fight.

I readied myself as the figure and their Nightmare henchmen came rushing out of the room. They all slowed to a stop as they noticed me standing in the hallway. The figure held out a hand to the Nightmares, as if telling them to stay as he walked toward me. Once the torch light illuminated the figure, I froze in fear. I had never seen a Mors Somnia before, but I knew it had to be one.

The figure looked like the pitch-black silhouette of a man covered in fur. I was surprised to be able to even make out a face because of how black it was, but it certainly looked like a man, a man who had a psychotic look on his face. His tongue poked out the side of his mouth and he held a black sword in his right hand.

As the Mors came closer, my confidence slowly started to drain, and instead, doubt and hopelessness started to creep in. The Nightmares must have sensed it, because as soon as these feelings entered me, they went wild. They growled and stomped their feet restlessly. The Mors just kept walking toward me at an even pace, and once he was close enough, he lashed out with his sword. I block the attack, surprised by the force behind the blow.

The Mors continued to reign down upon me blow after blow, and as I successfully blocked each one, my confidence started to return. After being completely on the defensive for a minute, I started slowly taking the offensive by slipping in a couple attacks here and there. The Mors was able to easily block my attacks, so I decided it was time to use my gift. I focused on seeing the future as I blocked the monster's attacks, and I was quickly able to see a few possibilities of breaking his defense.

I began moving and attacking the same way I saw in my future vision, and surprisingly, my sword began to connect. I took out a chunk of the monster's leg, a slice off of his shoulder, and then his whole left hand.

Before I could finish him off, the Nightmares behind him charged me. I tried to find a future fast enough where I was able to quickly dispose of all three, but before I knew it, one crashed into me and knocked me to the ground. Another began chomping painfully on my arm, and then the other began raking it's claws deep into my chest. It was unbearably painful, and I knew I wouldn't be able to get out of the situation alone.

"Help!" I screamed. "Please! Help!"

The pain became too much. I closed my eyes and quit fighting. My life was over for sure. Why did I think I could handle them on my own? I was stupid. So painfully stupid.

Chapter 9

What Did I Get Myself Into?

Chaz. Chaaaaaaaz."

Was that Juliet? I opened my eyes and realized it had all been in my head. I was still standing in front of the mirror in the changing stall. My hands were shaking, and I was breathing pretty hard. It had felt so real. If I really could see the future, then I was going to die in this place, and It would be soon. I didn't look any older in that daydream. What did I get myself into? Was there even a way out? I desperately hoped this whole day was nothing but a bad dream, one that I wouldn't come back to.

"Chaz, are you okay?" Autumn's voice rose from outside the stall, instantly pulling me out of my thoughts.

"He's probably embarrassed because his pants are too tight," Juliet said.

"I'm coming out," I finally said.

I opened the door and stepped out of the stall to find Juliet, Autumn and Gretchen all staring at me.

"Oh! You look so handsome!" Gretchen exclaimed.

"You look depressed," Juliet stated. "Were you crying in there?"

"No, I wasn't crying," I insisted. "I just kind of zoned out for a second."

"Did you have a vision?" Gretchen asked excitedly. "If you did, make sure to remember it. They are very sacred."

"Okay." I didn't want to talk about it at all. I looked at Autumn, just barely noticing her blue and brown knee-length dress. "Autumn, you look good in medieval clothing."

Juliet's eyes went wide, and she made an 'O' shape with her mouth. I instantly regretted complementing Autumn. She wouldn't let me live it down.

"Thanks, Chaz," Autumn replied, her face turning a little red. "You look great too."

Gretchen handed me and Autumn each another pile of clothing. "Here is an extra change of clothes and some sleepwear. If you need any of your clothing mended or a better variety, make sure you come straight to me."

"Thank you so much," Autumn said.

"Yeah, thank you," I added.

"It's my pleasure," Gretchen said with a small bow. "Anything for the future heroes of our world."

"Well, we need to go now," Juliet said, already walking away. "See you later, Gretchen."

"See you, sweet darlings later," the woman called after us as we followed Juliet out of the room.

After we entered the stairwell, Juliet said, "You kind

of have to just leave or else she won't stop talking."

When we reached the Wakers' hall, Juliet showed Autumn where our bedrooms were and had her pick one. Autumn chose the one in between mine and Juliet's. Once inside Autumn's new room, she and Juliet took a seat on the bed and I sat on a chair in the corner.

"All right, it's time to come clean and share what you're feeling," Juliet said. "Why are you scared of joining the Dreamchasers?"

"There's a lot of reasons," Autumn answered sadly. "I just feel like I'm going to let everyone down, you know? I'm just a normal high schooler. I'm not a warrior, I can't fight monsters. How am I supposed to be the hero they need?" She started to tear up a little bit. "I'm so scared. I didn't ask for any of this. Why can't I have more time to decide?"

I knew exactly how she was feeling, I was scared too. I just wanted to go back to my normal life and pretend like this never happened. And maybe I would after I woke up and realized it was all a dream.

"Don't worry, Autumn," Juliet said, rubbing her back. "We're all scared. Me and Chaz are in the same boat as you. We didn't ask for any of this. We're both just normal kids too." She turned to me. "Chaz, what made you decide to fight for the Dreamchasers?"

I felt like I'd got caught with my hand in the cookie jar and now I had to explain myself. I didn't want to say what I was about to say for Autumn's sake, but I knew it would be better if I didn't lie.

"Actually," I said slowly, "I don't think I want to be a part of this anymore."

"What?" Juliet said in an icy tone, giving me an even colder glare. "And why is that?"

"I had a daydream while I was changing . . ." I rehearsed to them everything I saw in my daydream and made sure to point out that it wasn't too far in the future. "I don't want to die," I said, finishing my story.

The girls were both silent for a few seconds.

"That wasn't the future, Chaz," Juliet said.

"What do you mean?" I asked. "How do you know?"

"I know because of what Grayson told me. He said that even the most powerful daydreamers can only see about a day into the future, and to even see that far ahead it takes years and years of practice. From the way it sounds, your dream was a lot more than a day away."

"You're sure? I've had a few daydreams happen the way I saw them the very next day."

"Then they were probably visions. When visions happen, they are out of our control, and they can give us a glimpse of a few days in the future as well. You can ask Master Grayson more about it later. And even if it was the future, you now know what *not* to do. But I could have told you that fighting four monsters on your own is a stupid choice. You're not getting out of this that easy, Chaz."

"No, no," I said. "I'm not trying to get out of this, I was convinced I was going to die soon. Also, I never thought of this until now, but what actually happens when you die here?"

"That's the other reason why I'm scared," Autumn said. "The consequences for dying are real."

"Well," Juliet began, "because our bodies aren't actually here, they say if you get killed, you won't die, your mind will just get hurt. From what I understand, dying here usually causes you to develop something like cerebral palsy. Grayson said that some people have died and woke up in their bed and they can no longer move their legs, or their arm, or maybe just a couple fingers. Some cases have been so severe that they can no longer move or talk at all, then there are others who are completely fine."

"Okay, that's pretty intense," I said, understanding a little more how Autumn felt.

The thought of coming to this place every night to fight monsters was starting to freak me out. Again, I hoped it wasn't real. But if it was, then I might as well join the good guys because I would be stuck coming here either way.

"I've made up my mind." I said, looking to Autumn and then Juliet. "I made a choice to join the Dreamchasers and I'm going to stick with it."

For once, Juliet smiled at me. "Why is that?" she asked.

"Because I know it's the right thing to do. And helping this world is going to help the real world too, right? That's good enough for me."

"Good answer. It's pretty much the same for me. I know I'm not a warrior, I know it's going to be dangerous, and I might get hurt. But if I have a chance to make a difference in this world and ours, then I'm going to take it. Autumn, whatever you choose to do, Chaz and I won't judge. I just want you to know that we would both rather have you here with us."

"Well… If you two are going to be brave," Autumn said, "then I'm going to be brave with you. I will join the Dreamchasers."

The girls stood up and hugged each other, and I just sat there awkwardly, pretending I wasn't there.

"I'm so glad I already have good friends here," Autumn said.

"Yeah," Juliet agreed. "It will be nice to finally have someone to hang out with. Maybe not with Chaz though."

I glared at her and she smiled back.

Together the three of us roamed around the castle in no particular direction. We got to know each other better as we talked about our lives in the real world. Not surprising to me at all, Juliet was a cheerleader. She was also on the school's dance team, and after school she taught dance to toddlers.

Autumn also did a little bit of dance. She was on the ballroom team. She was very smart too; she was taking all honors classes and was on course to graduate a year early. In her spare time, she liked to go on hikes with her dog, Ralph.

After hearing all about their busy lives, I was a little embarrassed to tell them about mine. I didn't really do anything. I went to school, but I wasn't in any honors classes or on any teams. I liked playing sports for fun, but I had never had a desire to play competitively. My only hobbies were hanging out with my friends and playing video games with my little brother. The only other thing I spent time doing was daydreaming. I was really good at that.

Exploring the castle was fun at first, but it quickly got boring. Most of the rooms were either empty or they were full of junk. It seemed the building was hardly used anymore. After wasting about an hour, we decided it would be a good idea to find the Archduke so Autumn could tell him her answer. We entered the waiting hall and walked over to Grace, who was sitting at her desk scribbling away on some paper.

"Hey, Grace," Juliet said. "Is the Archduke in?"

"Yes, he is," Grace answered without looking up. "He told me to send you right in."

"Thanks."

Autumn and I followed Juliet inside. Archduke Bradford and Master Grayson were sitting at the table. Their conversation stopped abruptly when we entered.

"Ah, just the three I was hoping to see," Bradford said with a welcoming smile. "Thank you, Juliet for being their host and getting them ready for the feast."

"You're welcome," she replied. She then quickly bowed like she'd just remembered she was supposed to. Autumn and I did as well.

"Have you made your decision yet?" he asked Autumn.

"Yes, I have," Autumn replied. She took a deep breath. "I'm going to fight with the Dreamchasers."

"Thank you so much, Lady Autumn," Bradford said sincerely. "I promise you that we will do everything we can to protect you. We will make sure you're ready for whatever the future brings."

"Thank you, my lord," Autumn said with another bow.

"And you two should know that Master Grayson here will be in charge of your training."

"Training will begin first thing tomorrow," Grayson said in his gruff voice. "We have a lot to prepare for."

"Especially with all of these claims of Victor being at large," Bradford added.

"What do you mean?" Juliet asked.

"There have been a few reports that he has been seen in Calverstone and Ausidor. If it is true, then it is the first time he has left Dolorem Terra for almost a decade."

"What are you going to do if it is true?" I asked.

"It all depends, Lord Chaz. If he was invited by the Dukes over those cities, then he is justified in being there. If not, then he will be arrested and interrogated. I will personally visit Duke Brighton and Duke Alvered to find out what's going on."

"Nice," I replied. "Can we help you arrest him?" I couldn't lie, I did want to meet Victor. I mean, he was pretty much the Sith Lord of the Dream World. It would be interesting to talk to someone like that. And it would be so cool to be there when the good guys took him down.

There would probably be an epic fight.

"I don't think you're ready for something like that," Grayson replied. "You can help by training hard until you're ready to go on missions."

"Okay, that's fair."

"You three should head on over to the feast," Bradford said. "Grayson and I will be there soon. Grace will escort you to the dining hall."

We bowed to the Archduke and headed out the door.

• • •

"Who knew a feast could be so boring?" I commented as we made our way through the empty halls of the castle.

The feast wasn't anything like I was hoping it would be. I was expecting a fancy ceremony where the Archduke would tap my shoulders with his sword and dub me a Dreamchaser, and then everyone would cheer and light fireworks and stuff. Or at least something like that. Instead, he had Autumn and I come to the front of the room where he introduced us as the newest Wakers, and that was it. Once the feast started, no one paid attention to us. The food was pretty good, but I expected better.

"I should have told you not to get your hopes up," Juliet replied.

"I thought it was nice," Autumn commented. "It made me feel special."

We continued down the hall in silence for a few minutes.

"So how exactly does it all work?" I asked.

"What?" Juliet replied.

"The traveling back and forth between worlds. How much time will have passed when I get home?

"Yeah," Autumn chimed in. "I've been wondering about that all day."

"Time passes the same here as it does back home," Juliet answered. "If you spend eight hours here, when you wake, up eight hours will have passed. But even though time passes at the same rate, it's lined up differently. 12 PM here would be 12 AM back home in Central American time. That's why it was night back home, but when you woke up here, it was morning."

"Ooooohh," I said, understanding. "No way. What time is it here now?"

"I don't know, I don't have a watch. The feast started at 6, so it's probably almost 7."

"That would mean it's almost 6 AM for me," I said. "Which means my alarm is going to go off soon."

"And that's why we're heading to bed. You have to make a habit of going to bed early because once your alarm goes off, you'll be out cold just like that."

"That's crazy."

"I wonder if I'll believe this all happened when I wake up," Autumn said.

"I didn't," Juliet replied. "I was convinced it was just a dream."

"Well, technically it is a dream." I commented.

"Well, technically you're a nerd."

"I have an idea," Autumn said before I had a chance to send an insult back. "What if we exchange phone numbers? Then we can text each other tomorrow and we'll know that it's real and we're not crazy."

"I think that's a good idea," I replied with a nod.

"Of course, you think it's a good idea," Juliet retorted with a knowing smile. "You would love to add the numbers of two cute girls to your collection."

Autumn giggled. I didn't have a good comeback, so I just shook my head in response.

When we finally reached the Wakers' hall, we stopped in front of my door.

"So, should we write them down on a piece of paper?" Autumn asked.

"That won't work," Juliet replied. "I can't bring the paper back with me to the real world."

"Oh. What do we do then?"

"I guess I'll just have to memorize them real quick," Juliet said, like it was nothing.

"You think you can memorize two phone numbers that quick?" I asked, doubtful.

"I've always been pretty good at memorizing things. Trust me, I got it."

We told her our numbers and she repeated them to herself a few times. After she was confident that she had then down, Autumn quickly gave her a hug. I was surprised when she gave me one next. After she pulled away, she said, "I'm so glad I met you two. Juliet, text us as soon as you can."

"I will," Juliet promised. "See you guys tomorrow."

We all said goodnight and I headed to my room. The room looked exactly how I left it earlier, only there was an unfamiliar set of clothing on my bed and the candles around the room were lit. Must have been the servants or whoever did everything here. I unfolded the dark blue silky clothes and realized they were pajamas. There was a button-up top and some pants. I closed the curtains to my window and slipped them on. They were so soft and comfy that I knew I wasn't going to ever want to take them off. Would they care if I wore this to training tomorrow? Who cares, I was a celebrity. I set the fashion trends now.

I blew out the candles and got under the warm bed covers. My bed at home was a lot more comfortable than this one. Hopefully what Juliet said was true about me falling asleep as soon as my alarm went off back home. I wasn't tired at all. I had so much on my mind, it was hard to focus on one thing at a time. I sorted through my thoughts for who knows how long, when out of nowhere I felt a heavy drowsiness take over.

Chapter 10

There Goes My Good Grades

I woke to the sound of my alarm clock blaring. I quickly turned it off and laid in bed for a few more minute as memories of the Dream World slowly came back to me. What a crazy dream that was! It had been so real, I wanted to believe it really happened, but it was impossible. Things like that didn't happen. It was too bad though; Autumn was pretty cool.

Getting out of bed, I went through my normal morning routine of getting dressed and fixing my hair. After I was ready to go, I headed into the kitchen to find Mom leaning against the counter reading a book.

"How was last night, Chaz?" Mom asked as I grabbed a bowl and dumped some cereal into it.

"It was kind of crazy. There was a fire at the fun center."

"What?" Mom asked in surprise. "Really? How did that happen? Did anyone get hurt?"

"I heard it was some messed up wiring or something.

I think everyone was okay though."

"I hope so."

My brother Garrett entered the kitchen looking like he'd just woken up. His hair was matted against the side of his head. He plopped down beside me and poured some cereal into his bowl.

As I waited for my brother to finish eating, I thought back on my birthday, remembering the daydreams that had come true. It was so weird that my mind had come up with a crazy, supernatural explanation for it when I went to sleep. It would've been kind of cool to be a hero and learn to fight with a sword, but real life was too boring for that.

After Garrett finished eating, the three of us got in the car and headed off to school. Right after we dropped Garrett off, my phone buzzed and I found a text from a random number.

Hey Autumn and Chaz, I told you I am THE BEST at memorizing things. ;)

I couldn't believe it. How in the world was that even possible? They were both real! I really did go to a secret dream world where people fight monsters with swords. I really did have superpowers. My mind was blown. My life was about to change drastically, and I wasn't sure how to feel about it. A smile crept into my face as I read the text over and over again.

Before I could reply, I got another text that I assumed was from Autumn.

Holy cow! I can't believe it's all real! I was sure it was just a dream! :O :)

Next, I sent my reply.

Well, there goes my good grades this term. Say goodbye to paying attention in class. ;)

We arrived at my school and I quickly hopped out. I was so excited, I felt like I wouldn't be able to sit still.

"See ya, Mom!" I said with a wave.

"See ya. Have a good day at school."

I headed straight to my English class, my thoughts buzzing the whole way there. I passed by Presley's locker but didn't see her. She must have already left for class. When I got there, I found her there with Jenna and a few other students who usually show up early. Presley smiled at me and I waved back. Once I sat down, both girls turned their attention to me.

"We were just talking about Prom," Jenna said. "We think it would be cool if we were in the same group."

"That would be cool," I agreed with a smile, while secretly cringing inside. I really didn't want to be in the same group as Quinn and his wannabe cowboy friends. They would probably want to lasso chairs or something like that for the group date. But Presley was really good friends with Jenna, so If it would make her happy, then I would do it. "I'll talk to Quinn about it."

They both smiled at me before returning to their exciting conversation.

I pulled out my phone and found two more unread texts.

The first one was from Autumn.

I'm with you, Chaz, it's all I can think about now! :)

The other text was from Juliet.

It might take a few days, but you'll get used to it.

The phone buzzed again with a text from Autumn.

I'm just glad I'm not crazy, and I've made two new friends. :)

I sent a reply.

Me, too. :)

Next came Juliet's reply.

You two better not blow up my phone with flirty texts to each other. ;)

Yeah, that was definitely the same Juliet I met in the Dream World.

I put my phone away as the last few students filed into the room and Mr. Oakland pulled down the screen for the projector. I immediately zoned out, thinking about the Dream World and my reality-bending powers. I couldn't wait until I could see the future on command. Life would be so much easier. I could know if a girl was going to reject me before I asked her out. Maybe I could even get a job as a professional psychic or something. But there was always a chance that the government would take advantage of my powers and make me their slave or lab rat. I would have to keep it a secret for now.

I was startled out of my thoughts when the bell rang. As everyone packed up their things and headed out the door, I approached Quinn.

"The girls think it would be a good idea if we were in the same prom group," I said, trying to sound enthusiastic.

"Yeah, that'd be cool," Quinn replied with a grin.

"Danny and one of my other buddies are going to be in my group as well. That cool with you?"

"Yup, as long as Jake and Isaac can join too."

"Yeah. We can talk about it some more next week in class."

"Sounds good," I said. Just then, I realized that it was Friday and I didn't have any plans. I joined up with Presley and together we headed out the door.

"You doing okay, Chaz?" Presley asked as we moved through the halls of the school. "You looked kind of out of it the whole time."

"Yeah, I was just thinking."

"Thinking about all that happened yesterday?"

"That and how I don't have any plans for tonight." I couldn't believe how casually it came out. Smooth Chaz was at it again!

"Me either. We should do something."

"Okay. I'll text you."

"Okay." She smiled.

I walked away grinning from ear to ear.

During math class, I tried really hard to glimpse the future. I tried to see what people were going to say before they said it, and I tried to predict things that would happen during class. I wasn't successful at all. I didn't see the future even once. It made me a little disappointed, but I wasn't going to give up. Once class was over, I met up with Isaac in the hall and we headed to geology together. After we took a seat at our desks, he asked, "Do you want to help me ask Jamie Harper to prom tonight?"

"Well…" I hesitated. "I was planning on hanging out with Presley tonight."

"Ohhhh, nice dude. What if you both help me and then you two can go do your own thing?"

"Alright. That's fine. How are you planning on asking her?"

"Well, Jamie really likes chickens, so I'm going to borrow one of my friend's chickens and tie a note to its leg and leave it in a box on her porch."

I stared at him, waiting for him to tell me he was joking, but he didn't.

"You're serious?" I asked.

"Yeah." He grinned. "She'll think it's hilarious."

"Why don't you just get her a fake chicken? Or some barbecued chicken?"

"It's an inside joke between the two of us. You wouldn't really understand. Trust me, it'll be hilarious."

"Okay . . . why do you need me for this?"

Just then, the lights went out and Mr. Durham was pulling down the projector screen.

"A lot of reasons," he whispered. "Well, mostly to go get it after I drop it off, but it would also be nice to have someone there for moral support too."

"Okay dude, if that's really what you want to do."

After he turned away, I slipped right into my thoughts about tonight. Isaac could be so interesting sometimes. Once he got an idea in his head, he was going to carry it out no matter how ridiculous it was. I began to play out that night in my head like I already knew what was going to happen.

The evening was getting dark, but it was the kind of dark you get right after the sun sets. Presley and I both sat in the backseat of Isaac's car as we watched him through the back window. He was carrying a tall cardboard box that had Jamie's name written on it. Inside was the live chicken that squawked loudly the whole way here. The house he was carrying it toward was navy blue with white trim. We were parked just two houses away, so Isaac's car wouldn't look suspicious.

"Isaac is so funny," Presley said, gazing out the window. "I've never heard of anyone getting asked to prom this way."

"Yeah, he's hilarious," I agreed as I sat next to her, looking out as well.

We both watched as he set the box in front of the door, rang the doorbell and booked it toward the car. He made it back quickly and squatted down by the car, peeking his head around the bumper to see the house. A younger girl who must have been Jamie's little sister opened the door and looked in the box before running back into the house.

A moment later, Jamie came out and peered into the box. We couldn't hear her, but we could easily see that she was laughing. She grabbed the box and carried it inside. I was surprised that she actually took the box inside considering the fact that it had a live chicken in it.

Isaac opened the car door and got into the driver's seat. He looked back at us with his signature grin. "She was laughing so hard. I told you guys she would think it's hilarious.”

“I will never doubt you again,” I said with a laugh.

“Let's wait about ten minutes before you get the chicken.”

We sat in the car without much conversation, listening to music for a little bit until Isaac said it was time. Presley offered to come with me so we both got out of the car and headed to the house. On our way over, I noticed there was a weird smell in the air. I had no idea what it was. Once we reached the front door, we rang the doorbell and Jamie answered.

“Hey.” I greeted. “We were sent here to pick up a chicken.”

She laughed. “Okay, hold on.” She walked away and promptly returned, pulling the box behind her. “You two are good friends with Isaac, right?”

“Yeah,” I said.

“It makes me sad, but I'm going to have to tell him that I've already been asked. I would've really loved to go with him, but I can't. I'll text him and let him know, but could you also tell him, and let him know how sorry I am?”

“Yeah, It's no big deal. He'll find another girl to give this chicken to.”

We all laughed and then said goodbye. As Presley and I started walking back to the car, I felt someone shaking my shoulder.

I turned to look at Isaac as he removed his hand from my shoulder.

"You zoned out?" he asked, like he already knew the answer.

"Yeah."

What a random daydream. It felt so real, though. Just like the other ones that actually happened exactly how I saw them. Was it the future? If it was, why would I need to see something like that? Maybe just so Isaac doesn't waste his time asking her out?

"Do you know if Jamie has been asked or not?" I whispered to him.

"Yup." He nodded. "I was texting her about it earlier today. She hasn't been."

"Okay," I said.

Maybe it wasn't the future then. Well, whatever the case, it probably wouldn't matter too much.

Chapter 11

The Stinkiest Night of My Life

So, are you in?" Isaac asked. He had just finished explaining his chicken mission to Presley, and judging by the look on her face, she probably thought it was as ridiculous as I did.

"That's seriously how you're going to ask her?" Presley laughed.

"You know it."

"Okay, I'm in. I wouldn't want to miss out on something like that."

"Thanks, guys," Isaac said.

"What did Jake think about your idea?" I asked. I had just found out that Jake was sick, so he wasn't able to make it to school today.

"Oh, he loved it," Isaac replied. "He wants to do something like it to ask out Lindsey."

"Of course, he does." Presley replied with a small smile.

When I got home from school, I was just a little

disappointed that I hadn't glimpsed the future yet. I didn't worry about it though. Heading to my room, I started on my homework. I also texted Autumn and Juliet for a bit, just talking about school and how hard it was to pay attention.

During a quiet dinner with my family, I couldn't help but think about my Dad. Supposedly, he had a Nightmare somewhere in the Dream World, and if I killed that Nightmare, it would help him be more motivated. He would stop being so lazy and negative. But how in the world was I supposed to find his Nightmare?

And even if I did find it, I wasn't ready to kill it. I needed to train first. I needed to get some mad sword skills before I attempted something like that. But I didn't want to have to deal with this problem for another year or two. Hopefully, someone else would get to it before then. Wouldn't that be wonderful?

• • •

Later that evening, Isaac came to pick me up, and together we drove to Presley's house. I gave her the front seat so she didn't have to sit in the back with the noisy chicken in a box.

"Thanks, Chaz," Presley said as she buckled her seatbelt.

"No problem," I said. "I figured It would be better for me to be back here because I'm actually a trained chicken whisperer."

Presley and Isaac both chuckled and we set off towards Jamie's house. Surprisingly, she only lived about five minutes away from me. We slowed to a stop behind another car parked along the curb. Isaac pointed to a house across the street that I recognized. It was navy blue with white trim.

"The blue one is hers," he said.

Interesting. Maybe I did see the future. I guess I would find out when it was time to get the chicken back.

I took in my surroundings, trying to find anything else that was familiar to me. The area looked like a small HOA, all the houses similar to one another, only differing in color. The whole street was very clean, and all the lawns looked tidy with recently planted bushes and little pine trees everywhere.

"Okay, I'm going to drop the chicken off now," Isaac said. "I'll ditch it on the porch and hide behind the car so they don't see me." He got out of the car, and I opened my door and handed him the box.

"I'm going to come back and sit with you so I can see better," Presley said, getting out of the car and joining me in the back seat.

She scooted close to me and I instantly felt a sense of Deja vu. I looked out the window and saw Isaac walking towards the house with the box.

"Isaac is so funny," Presley said as she watched him through the window. "I've never heard of anyone getting asked to prom this way."

Okay, I was finally convinced of my psychic powers.

I definitely saw this exact moment. We were going to go get the chicken and find out that Jamie had already been asked. It would probably be a good idea to start coming up with superhero names.

"Yeah, he is," I said.

We both watched as Isaac set the box on the porch, rang the doorbell and then sprinted back to the car and hid. Just like I saw before, a younger girl opened the door, saw the box, and ran back inside. Jamie came out, looked in the box, laughed to herself, and then brought it inside. Isaac hopped in the driver's side and grinned back at us. "She was laughing so hard," he said. "I told you guys she would think it's hilarious."

"Nice job, dude," I praised. Hopefully, he wouldn't be too bummed out when he found out she had already been asked.

"Let's wait ten minutes before you guys get the chicken," Isaac said.

"Sounds good." I nodded. "What are you going to do if she's already been asked?"

"She hasn't though. I already checked."

"Well, you never know. Maybe she got asked after you checked."

"Don't jinx it, man. But if she has, then I'll ask someone else. I have a few others in mind."

We chatted about prom for a few minutes until ten minutes had passed. Presley and I got out of the car and headed to the house. Once we got out of the car, I noticed an awful smell in the air. It was familiar, but it was so faint,

I wasn't sure what it was. Once at the house, we rang the doorbell and a few seconds later Jamie answered.

"Hey, we just got word about a rampaging chicken," I said. "We're here to pick it up."

She laughed and said, "Okay, hold on."

She disappeared inside the house and then came back dragging the box behind her. "You two are good friends with Isaac, right?"

"Yeah," I replied, knowing what she was about to say.

"It makes me sad, but I'm going to have to tell him that I've already been asked. I would've really loved to go with him, but I can't. I'll text him and let him know, but could you also tell him, and let him know how sorry I am?"

"But he said that you told him this morning you hadn't been," I said, trying to sound less accusing and more confused.

"That's because I hadn't until like a half an hour ago," she explained. "I was actually about to text him right before this chicken was left at my door."

"Oh, okay. No worries."

"We'll let him know," Presley said.

Jamie smiled. "Thanks. See ya."

As we walked away from the house, I noticed the horrible smell was a lot stronger. Was that a skunk?

"Something smells awful," Presley commented in disgust. "Race you to the car."

She took off running toward the car before I'd even registered what she said. I was about to run after her, chicken-in-a-box and all, but stopped when a small black and white animal moved out from under the car parked behind Isaac's. Presley screamed and jumped away when she saw it, but the skunk must have been surprised or something because it raised its tail and sprayed. It looked like the mist barely hit Presley, but she screamed again and began coughing and gagging as the skunk retreated under the car. The smell was so awful I felt just about ready to throw up. I couldn't even imagine how Presley felt at the moment.

"Stay there," I said. "I think it's still under the car."

A few seconds after I said that, the skunk came out behind the car and headed away from us towards some bushes. It was dark, but I was able to see four little skunk kits following behind it. So that must have been why it sprayed, it was just trying to protect its babies.

"Okay, they're gone," I said as I awkwardly jogged towards Presley.

Isaac got out of the car and started gagging.

"Holy cow!" He exclaimed. "That's so bad."

"At least it's not on you," Presley wheezed. "I think I'm going to die."

"I'm going to talk to Jamie and see if she can help you not stink," Isaac said, heading back toward the house. "No offence, but I don't want to give you a ride home smelling that bad. We would all probably pass out on the way."

As we waited for Isaac, I got as close to Presley as I dared, which was about ten feet away. Maybe the chicken smelled it too, it squawked loudly as I neared her. Why couldn't I have saw this part coming? I could have helped her avoid this from happening or just not invited her. What a useless daydream that was. It only showed me moments before she got sprayed. What was the point of that? Maybe it was because Isaac interrupted the vision by shaking my shoulder?

After a couple minutes, Isaac and Jamie came out and invited us inside. Isaac and I hung out in the family's living room while Jamie and her mom helped Presley get rid of the smell. I don't know what kind of home remedy they used, but by the time they were done with her, the odor wasn't nearly as bad. Sadly, it was still there though. They had to get her out of her smelly clothes, so she ended up wearing some of Jamie's in the meantime. It took about an hour and a half for us to finally leave with a less stinky Presley. She looked miserable and I felt bad for her.

Once we were in the car and heading home, I took the time to apologize. "I'm so sorry this happened to you. I thought I smelled a skunk, but I didn't say anything."

"I'm sorry too," Isaac added. "Jamie had already been asked so you got sprayed for nothing."

"It's okay guys," Presley said. "Neither of you are to blame. I was just in the wrong place at the wrong time."

No other words were spoken on the quiet drive home. We dropped her off first, and then not long after, it was my turn. After I got out of the car, I headed inside and went straight to my bedroom, feeling sad about how the night had turned out.

Chapter 12

I Might Already Be a Fugitive

I woke up in an unfamiliar and uncomfortable bed. Startled, I opened my eyes and sat up. I gazed around the vaguely familiar room, trying to remember where I was. Light shone through the thin curtains drawn over the window, revealing the soft-looking red rug on the floor with crumpled clothing lying on top. I saw the blue jerkin and black pants and then it hit me–I was back in the Dream World.

I got out of bed and grabbed the clothing on the floor. Neatly folding them, I put them in one of the dresser drawers and laid out the other pairs of clothing I had on my bed. I didn't know if it mattered, but people would definitely notice if I wore the same clothing I'd had on yesterday, so I put on something different.

I opened the curtains to let the sunshine fully enter my room, squinting as I looked out over the training grounds for a moment. Then I moved over to the mirror and took in my reflection, doing my best to fix my messy hair. Once

I was somewhat satisfied with my appearance, I left the room, locking it behind me. I looked around the empty hall, allowing my eyes to rest on Autumn's door, and then Juliet's. Were they here yet? It was the weekend, so they would probably be up late hanging out with friends and doing fun stuff.

I had no idea where I was supposed to go or what to do, so I decided I would find out if they were there. I knocked on Autumn's door and was surprised when I heard a reply.

"Just a minute," her muffled voice said from behind the door.

After a couple of minutes, Autumn opened the door. She was wearing her usual big smile. "You look nice," she said, stepping into the hall and shutting the door behind her.

"Do you think this is too fancy for training?" I asked, feeling self-conscious. "I wasn't sure what to wear."

"I'm sure it's fine. Is Juliet here yet?"

"I don't know. I haven't checked."

We walked over to Juliet's door and I knocked. There was no answer.

"Juliet, are you in there?" Autumn yelled as she took a turn knocking.

Still there was no response.

"Maybe we can go find some breakfast and then come back," I suggested.

"Okay. I like that idea."

We left the hall and entered the quiet waiting room. I

was surprised to see that it was completely empty.

"Where is everyone?" Autumn asked, looking around the room.

"Maybe it's because it's the weekend," I guessed. "They probably get the day off."

"I'm still a little confused about how the time lines up. Is it Friday or Saturday here?"

"I'm pretty sure it's Saturday."

We headed through a door on the other side of the room that I thought might lead to the dining hall.

"So, how'd your day go yesterday?" Autumn asked as we walked through the empty hallway.

"It was alright. It was hard to pay attention in school. Oh, and I had another daydream come true."

"Another? Really? How many have you had come true before?"

I briefly told her about the first two daydreams that had happened exactly as I saw them, and then in more detail, I told her about what happened with the skunk and how I didn't see that last part of the future.

"That's crazy, Chaz!" Autumn said. "It also sounds like you think about this Presley a lot."

"N-not really," I stammered, wondering how she was able to figure that out. "Why do you say that?"

"Because she was in all three of your daydreams. Do you like her?"

I thought about her question for a few seconds. I could lie and say I didn't, but what would be the point of that? "Yeah, I like her."

"Awe, that's so cute!" She exclaimed. "I'm so excited that you get to go to prom with her. I hope it's amazing!"

We reached the dining hall, and not surprising to me at all, it was as empty as the rest of the castle. And now that the room was empty, I was fully able to take in the size of it. There were too many tables to count, and it was pretty impressive that we had filled them all. There were fancy chandeliers hanging from the ceiling and a giant fireplace on the other end.

We headed to the corner of the room where the door to the kitchen was. We found it already open with people bustling around inside, preparing all kinds of foods. I saw some kneading dough, some stirring pots, some preparing pies, and others chopping veggies.

I felt bad that the bakers and cooks were the only ones in the castle who never got a day off. I didn't want to make them even busier by asking them about breakfast. I was about to tell Autumn we should go, but a short lady noticed us and stepped out of the kitchen. She was wearing a white apron over her red and white dress and her gray hair was pinned back in a bun. She had a wrinkled, sour-looking face, but when she smiled at us, her eyes twinkled.

"You two must be the new Wakers stayin' with us," she said with a southern drawl. "My name is Gina."

"I'm Chaz," I said and gestured to Autumn. "This is Autumn."

"It's good to meet you," Autumn said.

"Why don't you two go take a seat and I'll bring you out some food," Gina suggested.

"Oh, you don't need to do that," I said.

"No, no, it's my pleasure," she insisted before heading back into the kitchen.

Autumn and I took a seat across from each other at the nearest table.

"So, have you seen the future yet?" I asked her.

"Not yet. But I do have almost a sixth sense about when something bad or good is going to happen. The Archduke told me that is also a way of reading the future."

"A sixth sense?"

"That's the best way to describe it. Like, if something bad is about to happen or someone is about to make a wrong choice, I get this awful feeling inside. And when something good is going to happen, I just feel really good and happy inside. It happens all the time, and so far, I haven't been wrong about any of my feelings."

"Whoa . . ." I was amazed. "That's really cool! And really helpful!"

"Yeah, it has been helpful," she admitted. "And that's also why I chose to join the Dreamchasers. I felt good about it."

"Well, it's good that you stuck with us. I couldn't handle Juliet on my own."

She laughed. "You two are so funny. I'm glad I get to hang around you guys."

As we talked, Gina came out carrying a tray loaded with food. She set it on the table, unloading pancakes, eggs, bacon, and oatmeal with berries.

"Thank you so much!" Autumn said. "It all looks

amazing."

"Anytime," Gina said with a small bow. "Just holler if you need me. I'll be in the kitchen."

As soon as she left the room, Juliet entered. "There you two are," she said, sitting down next to Autumn. "I was starting to worry that Chaz convinced you to run away with him."

I glared at her in response.

"If anything, Chaz would be the one convincing me to *not* run away," Autumn said in my defense.

We began eating and talking about how our Friday went, which led to me again rehearsing my story about the skunk for Juliet.

"So, are we starting training today?" I asked Juliet.

"I don't think so. I'm pretty sure that Grayson said we train Monday through Friday. On Saturdays, we learn politics or something, and Sunday is our day off, so we can do whatever we want."

"Politics?" I was no longer excited for the day.

"Yeah," Juliet said, mirroring my frown. "Apparently we're supposed to be very involved."

"I hope it's not as confusing as the politics back home," Autumn said.

"We should probably go find him," Juliet said, standing up. "He's probably in the boardroom, as usual."

"We should clean this up first," Autumn said as she began stacking plates.

"It's okay. The kitchen workers will get it."

"They have enough to do. I'm sure they will feel

appreciated if we help them out."

Juliet sighed and then began helping Autumn clean up. I joined in too, and after we wiped the table, we took our plates and leftover food to the kitchen. Gina came rushing over when she saw us putting our dishes in the sink.

"Thank you very much!" She said with a small smile. "But next time don't worry about it. We'll clean up after you."

"It's the least we could do," Autumn said. "You look way too busy for us to not help out a little bit."

"Don't worry about us. This is how it is every day. We're used to it."

We all thanked Gina as we left the kitchen.

"If we really can do whatever we want tomorrow, maybe I'll go help them out," Autumn said.

"You're too nice," Juliet replied. "I honestly don't think they would let you though."

"I'll try anyway."

As we made our way through the quiet halls of the castle, I stopped in my tracks when I thought I heard someone say my name.

"Did someone say my name?" I asked.

"You're crazy," Juliet said and then paused.

There were faint voices coming from down the hall.

"No, no. It doesn't concern Juliet and Autumn . . ." A familiar voice said.

"Someone's talking about us," Juliet whispered.

She began to silently creep towards the voices.

"I don't think we should eavesdrop," Autumn said.

Juliet shushed her as we quietly followed behind.

She stopped next to a dark wood door that stood open just a crack. We sidled up next to her, and I tried to calm my breathing as I listened to the two men conversing behind the door.

"It's disturbing how much he looks like him." I was pretty sure the voice belonged to Archduke Bradford.

"Who? Chaz?" asked a deeper voice. I didn't recognize that one at all.

Juliet and Autumn both looked at me with wide eyes.

"I suppose they do share a small resemblance," the voice continued, sounding unconvinced.

"You have only glimpsed him in visions," Bradford replied. "If you had actually seen him in the flesh, then you would be uneasy about it as well."

"Well, even if he does look just like him, what exactly are you worried about?"

"Maybe he figured out a way . . . a way to . . ."

"Impossible!" the deeper voice scoffed. "Bradford, I have been around for many decades and no one has even come close. No one has even had the slightest idea how, either."

"No one has ever been as powerful as he is," Bradford said quietly. "And from what I've heard, he has only been getting stronger."

I barely heard the last part because he almost whispered it.

"Well let's not jump to any conclusions without

evidence. For now, all we can do is keep a close eye on Chaz.”

“It will be done. Since Master Grayson will be spending the most time with him, I will make sure he keeps a log on the young Lord’s day to day activities.”

“A grand idea.”

It sounded like the conversation was ending, so the three of us scooted away from the door and hurried down the hall as silently as we could.

“Nice going, Chaz,” Juliet said when we reached the waiting room. “You’re already in trouble.”

“It’s not his fault that he looks like whoever they were talking about,” Autumn said defensively. “Do you know who it is, Chaz?”

“I have no idea,” I said honestly.

I felt kind of numb inside. I didn’t know what to think or how to feel. No one had ever been suspicious of my identity before. On top of that, it sounded like they thought I might be some powerful guy they didn’t trust . . . like maybe a serial killer or something. I just got here a day ago and I might already be a fugitive. Life couldn’t get any better.

“You okay, Chaz?” Autumn asked.

“I will be as long as they don’t decide that I’m this guy they were talking about.”

“I’m sure it won’t take them long to realize you really are the immature boy you act like.” Juliet said.

“Juliet, be nice,” Autumn said. She turned to me. “Don’t worry about it. Just be yourself and things will be fine."

"I hope so," I replied. "I guess we should go to training then. It will look suspicious if we play hooky."

"Will it, though?" Juliet asked.

Chapter 13

Oran Kellamare

We stood in front of the doors of the boardroom as Juliet knocked.

"Come in," a gruff voice answered.

We entered the room to find Master Grayson and Constable Darven hunched over the table studying a large map. Their attention shifted to us immediately and they sat up in their chairs. Grayson gestured to us to have a seat, so we did. Grayson looked as grumpy as I remembered, and Darven was grinning.

"Good afternoon, Wakers," Grayson said. "How has your stay in the castle been thus far?"

"Pretty good," I said.

Autumn agreed.

"I'm sure Juliet has informed you that our training on Saturdays is a bit different than normal. Every Saturday, we will focus solely on the politics and history of Elegit Terram. I know that may sound dull and uninteresting, but I assure you it is very important."

"As Dreamchasers and Wakers," Darven began, "you will have quite an influence on what happens to our country. The majority of the people have, and always will, look to the Wakers for guidance in political matters. You are their heroes and they believe that you will never lead them astray. To the people, your tremendous power comes with tremendous wisdom.

"Even if they don't know you, they will come to you for advice. They will seek your counsel. And that is why it is our duty to make sure you are informed and well aware of everything that is going on. Also, you need to know where the Archduke stands, so we are always on the same page, so to speak."

I looked to Autumn and Juliet and saw their faces were as blank as mine.

"I know it feels like a lot of responsibility," Grayson said. "But I promise that you are not alone, you have the leaders of the country on your side. We will do everything we can to help you be what the people need. Before we start, do any of you have questions?"

"How many other Wakers are there?" I asked, hoping that the whole country wasn't only relying mostly upon the three of us. "The only other one I've met is Kaden."

"There are many more than you think," Darven answered. "There are a few, including me, who currently reside here in Kellamare. A lot more reside in other major cities of the country. Some live on the other side of the world from you, so their time lines up differently, therefore, they are usually only here at night." He paused. "Any more questions?"

No one said anything, so Grayson cleared his throat before he started speaking. "One of the most important things you need to understand is how this country and our government were formed. As far back as our records go, the land has been ruled by many kings. And with the reign of kings always comes contention and bloodshed.

"Whether he be a just king or an evil one, there is always someone who wants to dethrone him. Sometimes it's the people he governs, sometimes it's his own family. And even when a king doesn't have his own people to contend with, there are always neighboring kingdoms that want more land and more power. There is always a reason to go to war.

"And let us not forget about the Nightmares, they have been around ever since this world existed. Though the Nightmares were their common enemy, they still chose to destroy one another. Kings were too proud to unite their people together to fight the real threat, and because of this, kingdoms fell over and over again. This went on for thousands of years, and the infestation of Nightmares only grew worse.

"Man was losing the fight against darkness and they knew that if things didn't change, they would be destroyed. The kings of the land decided that the only way to stop the war and bloodshed was one last and final war. The last king standing would rule the land and the people dwelling there forever, with no one to oppose him. Well, they went through with this war. The five neighboring kingdoms met each other on the field of battle with their kings at the head.

"It was the largest and bloodiest battle that has ever happened in our known history. Hundreds of thousands were slain, including all five kings. Sadly, no one noticed that all of the kings were slain, so the fighting continued. While the battle raged on, unbeknownst to those on the battlefield, the Nightmares had taken the opportunity to swarm one of the unprotected kingdoms. They moved upon the city like a plague and attacked everyone in sight. The fears of the people only increased the Nightmare's desire to feast, and they didn't stop until the entire kingdom was destroyed. Once that kingdom was reduced to ash and rubble, the Nightmares moved on to the next one.

"There were many who escaped the kingdom before it was destroyed, and word of what happened quickly spread to those at war. Once word got out, the fighting stopped, and they finally realized all the kings were dead. No one knew what to do anymore, the kings were dead, and the Nightmares were on their way to destroy another kingdom. All was in chaos and the men on the field were without hope. A man named Oran Kellamare decided to take charge. He raised his voice and commanded all the men on the field to assemble themselves together and join the fight against the Nightmares.

"Oran was able to rally the men back into fighting spirit, and he and his legions were able to overtake the Nightmares before they destroyed another kingdom. They fought like lions until every monster in sight was destroyed. The people rejoiced and no longer desired to fight with one another. They wanted to be united as one people with one ruler. They chose Oran Kellamare as their leader. They initially wanted Oran to be their king, but he declined and convinced them that putting one man above the rest is never a good idea.

"He and a few other great leaders together came up with the structure for a new government–a government where the voice of the people decides who their rulers will be. That new form of government is the one we have now. The Archduke is the highest authority in the land, but ultimately, he has no power over the voice of the people. He has the power over the Dukes, and together, the Dukes have power over him. That way, if one of them is corrupted, he has no way of enforcing evil laws or practices among the people. Unless, of course, the majority of the people agree to it as well."

When Grayson finished speaking, Darven took over. "Oran became the first Archduke of the new system, and because of that, the city of Kellamare was named after him. And so, it was with the other four great cities in the country; they were named after the first Dukes of the new system. Oran declared all the great cities would be part of one land and one country, and he gave it the name *Elegit Terram*, which means *Chosen Land*. The castle was rebuilt here in Kellamare marking it as the capital of Elegit Terram. And that is the way things have been for the last three hundred years."

Darven gestured to the map spread out on the table. "Come, make yourselves familiar with the layout of the land and the names of the other great cities."

The three of us hunched over the large map and began examining it.

At the top of the map near the ocean was the city where we were now. It had the name *Kellamare* printed above it. To the east of Kellamare was the Portal surrounded by the White Forest. I began to closely inspect the other parts of the land on the map that I was unfamiliar with. Not too far southeast of Kellamare was a town called *Beckstead*, and south of that was *Calverstone*. The other two cities, *Gregorious* and *Ausidor*, were a lot further away and I assumed it would be a long trip to get to either of them. Those were the only named cities on the map, but it looked like there was smaller unnamed towns scattered all over. I pointed them out and asked, "What are those?"

"Good question," Darven replied. "You see, those little towns and settlements are not actually ruled by the Archduke or the Dukes. When Oran Kellamare established the new system, there were many people who were still convinced it wasn't a good idea. They were certain that it was going to end in more war and bloodshed. Because they had no desire to be a part of it, Oran gave them permission to start their own settlements and towns outside of the great cities. He said that if they chose to do so, they would be exempt from his laws and taxes, and instead they were to choose someone from among them to be their governor.

"The Governor has the authority to create any laws he wants inside his own settlement and neither the Archduke or the Dukes can meddle in their affairs, though there have been times in the past where we have chosen to interfere because of corrupt laws being established, like legalization of slavery and other ridiculous ideas. Some things we will not let stand. The reason none of the settlements and towns have names written above them is because they change so frequently. When a new governor is chosen, he will usually change the name of the town. We don't want to have to update our maps every few months, so we just leave them blank."

"Is this the whole Dream World?" I asked.

Darven laughed. "No this is just Elegit Terram. The entire Dream World seems to be as large as the whole Waking World. It's a big round earth just like the one in reality. Every now and then we get visitors from foreign lands, but that doesn't happen often."

"So, I guess this new system thing has been working out well?" Autumn asked.

"It was until recently. Things have become a little complicated with the Duke of Ausidor, which brings us to the topic we really need to discuss."

"Duke Brighton of Ausidor is a man who is greatly loved by his people," Grayson explained. "He has a kind heart and great wisdom. Many look to Brighton for counsel and guidance, as with his father before him, who was the previous Duke of Ausidor. Because of who he is and who his father was, people are quick to see his strengths but slow to see his flaws.

"You see, we have many spies throughout the land. They are in every city and every settlement. Because of these spies, as of a few months ago, we have discovered that Duke Brighton has secretly declared allegiance with the Quin Anulus. We had a spy observe him more than once meeting with Mors Somnia. And that isn't the only thing that leads us to believe he has sided with them. Ever since we heard about him meeting with the dark ones that night, he has started preaching to the people of Ausidor about neutrality, coexisting in peace with the Nightmares, and other ridiculousness.

"Over the past few months he has been brainwashing the people with small amounts of propaganda, convincing them that fighting the Nightmares is pointless and frivolous. Many people in Ausidor have taken a liking to the idea of neutrality, the idea of no more war. It is obviously foolish though. If we simply sit by and do nothing, then the people in the Waking World will suffer. I also highly doubt that it is possible to coexist in peace with those monsters. Their only purpose is to feed, and in order to feed, they need us to fear them. If they don't attack us, then we will stop fearing them. It would never work. You either fight for us, or you are against us."

We said nothing after he finished speaking, his final words echoing in the momentary silence surrounding us.

"I've heard you guys talk about the problem of this Duke from the moment I arrived here," Juliet said. "I still don't understand why the Archduke can't fire him or whatever."

"We wish things were that simple," Grayson said. "Going back to what I said earlier, Duke Brighton is greatly loved and respected by his people. If we were to simply remove him from office, there would be outrage. Yes, we could claim that he has sided with the Quin Anulus, but we have no proof. He hasn't committed treason or openly done anything wrong, therefore he could claim that he had been wronged by the Archduke. He would most likely challenge him for his office, and many would rally behind him. It would ultimately lead to civil war. At first, a war of words, but it wouldn't take long to escalate into something worse."

"I had no idea things were so bad," Juliet admitted. "Do we have a plan?"

"Not a good one," Darven said with a sigh. "We sent a Waker, Lord Brevan, to take up residence in the city, hoping that he can make a difference. We schooled him in politics and war strategies for almost a year and a half. He is a bright young man, and even though the people don't know him well yet, the fact that he's a Waker will immediately help him earn their respect and love. They will begin to look to him for guidance as much as Duke Brighton, and hopefully he will be able to convince them of how evil the idea is."

"Until we can come up with a better plan," Grayson added, "we wait, we learn, and we train."

"Well, let's train then," I said. I was tired of wasting time doing stuff that wasn't going to help me be a better warrior.

"If you would like, we can start today," Grayson said. "Or if you'd rather, I can take you on a tour of the city and introduce you to some other government leaders."

"I think I'd rather train," Autumn said as she glanced at the two of us. "I really want to be prepared for whatever happens."

Juliet and I both agreed.

"Great. Let's be off to the training grounds."

Chapter 14

I Have a Gift

Juliet, Autumn and I followed Master Grayson out of the castle. We were met by the usual paparazzi as soon as we stepped outside. Once we made our way through the guarded entrance in the hedge, we found the training grounds quiet and empty.

I was so excited to finally start my training that it was all I could think about. I imagined it was going to be something like *The Karate Kid,* where we did normal everyday stuff, like mop the floor or trim the trees, but in reality, we're actually mastering ancient fighting techniques.

Grayson stopped under a pergola near the edge of the training grounds. There were four wooden benches resting underneath. He stood in front of the benches and motioned for us to sit.

"You should each sit on a separate bench," Grayson said as I was about to sit on the same one as Autumn and Juliet. "I promise it will help."

Autumn and I both moved to different benches.

"When we train each day, the first thing we will always start with is the mind. The mind is at its peak in the morning. We are going to do some exercises to strengthen your focus and concentration, and that is exactly what it takes to see the future. You have to center all your focus on a single moment in time that hasn't happened yet. Let's say that moment in time is a minute from now; you're trying to see what I'm going to say before I say it. You have to concentrate so completely on that moment that you forget reality. You forget where you are now, and you actually believe you are in that moment.

"I am going to discipline you in daydreaming and swordplay separately until you have excelled at both, then we will practice them together. We will start with the basics. I know Juliet is a few days ahead of you two, but if it's okay with her, I would like to start you all on the same lesson."

"Go for it," Juliet replied. "I'm not very good at it anyway."

"That is as expected. Have either of you two had any glimpses of the future yet?"

"I've had a few visions," I replied.

"Tell me about them."

I briefly told him about the three visions I'd had so far, leaving out the one about my death because it probably wasn't real.

"Interesting," Grayson said, thoughtfully.

"Why is that?" I asked.

"Well, those were certainly visions you saw, but most

Dreamchasers–or Wakers for that matter–will only see one or two visions throughout their whole lifetime. You must have a gift for it."

"What do you mean?"

"Over time, we have found that some Wakers are gifted in certain aspects of reality-bending, whether it is visions, premonitions, foresight, or maybe even something else. Out of all the gifts that we have seen, visions are the rarest. The last Waker I know of to have that gift is our current Seer. Make sure you pay close attention to those visions, Chaz. Write them down. They will show you the choices that will greatly impact your life."

"Okay," I replied, not sure how to feel. Hopefully my 'gift' wouldn't make them even more suspicious of me.

"What about you, Autumn?" Grayson asked. "Any glimpses of the future?"

"Not exactly," she said shyly.

She began to explain what she told me during breakfast about how she can feel if something good or bad is about to happen. After she finished, she asked, "Isn't that how premonitions work?"

Grayson raised an eyebrow, questioningly. "That is also very interesting." He paused. "You are right, Autumn, that is how premonitions work. It seems we have another gifted Waker in our midst. The Archduke will be pleased to hear about this. Juliet, do you have any unique talents you need to reveal to us as well?"

"Besides my witty remarks?" she asked. "Nope."

Grayson chuckled. "Now that we understand where

everyone is at, let's get started with our training. The first thing we will do when you come here in the morning is meditate. You may wonder why we would waste our time with that, but I promise it will help increase your ability to concentrate."

Grayson began pacing back and forth in front of us as he spoke. "I want you all to get as comfortable as you can and try to relax. Close your eyes, breathe slow and deep. When you feel relaxed, I want you to think of someone or something that is very important to you. Think about that person, thing, or place until I tell you we are finished. Try hard not to let your mind wander."

I did my best to follow his instructions, but it was hard for me to relax sitting on such an uncomfortable bench. When he told me to think of someone or something that was important to me, my thoughts immediately turned to Presley. I thought about her all day every day, so it was nothing new. I felt bad that she got sprayed by the skunk, mostly because it ruined our plans for the night. I continued to think about the fun things we could do together until Master Grayson's voice interrupted my thoughts.

"It's time to come back," he said. "Meditation is now over. I'm sure you all likely found it very difficult to stay focused on the person or thing you started thinking about in the first place."

"My thoughts were all over the place," Autumn said.

"So were mine," Juliet added. "I've done this a few times now and it's still so hard to think about one thing for thirty minutes."

It wasn't hard at all, but I wasn't going to tell them that. If I did, they would probably ask me what I was thinking about.

"The more you practice the easier it will get," Grayson said. "This next exercise might seem a little ridiculous, or silly, but I assure you it will help you learn how to master the art of foresight." He put a hand behind his back so that none of us could see it. "I am holding a certain number of fingers up behind my back, after about thirty seconds or so I will reveal how many fingers I am holding up. What I want you to do is focus on putting yourself about thirty to forty seconds into the future when I reveal my hand. But before I reveal it to you, I will have you tell me the number of fingers you saw in the future. Now, let's try it. Imagine yourself in the future."

I almost laughed. It seemed like it might've been a prank to make us look stupid. After he went silent, I looked over to see Autumn and Juliet with their eyes shut. If they were going to go along with it, then I had better go along with it as well. I tried to imagine Grayson pulling his hand from behind his back and showing his fingers, but it didn't feel like I was there. I tried a couple times, but it didn't feel real.

"Time's up," Grayson said. "What did you see?"

I was certain I didn't see the future, but the last time I imagined it, he was holding up four so that would be my guess.

"Two," Juliet said.

"Four?" Autumn said, uncertainly.

"Four," I said.

Grayson pulled out his hand from behind his back, revealing five fingers standing up. "Let's try again."

He put his hand behind his back, and I tried to see the future again. I tried to imagine myself actually there, but I just wasn't feeling it. I imagined him holding up his hand a couple of times, but I was certain anything I came up with was just my head making it up.

"Time's up," He said.

"One."

"Three."

"Four."

"Well done, Autumn," he said, clapping his hands. "It was three."

"I just guessed," Autumn replied. "I don't think I actually saw it."

We continued to do the same thing over and over again. I don't think it was until maybe the fifth time that Juliet finally got it right.

"I felt like I was actually there," she said, excitedly. "I think I finally get it now."

"Prove it to me," Grayson said. "Again."

Juliet guessed it right again. And then again. While Autumn and I were getting frustrated, Juliet was getting more confident. After getting it right once, she was able to get it right every single time after. We probably played that ridiculous little game for a whole hour until Grayson told us it was enough.

"I didn't expect all three of you to figure it out today,"

he said. "Juliet has had a few days to practice and I expect it will take you that long as well."

I didn't want to practice *it* anymore. *It* was so stupid. Plus, I supposedly had a gift for seeing visions, so why wasn't I able to see something as simple as that? Maybe he had planned this whole thing with Juliet earlier so they could prank us.

"Now we will move on to swordplay. Follow me."

We followed him over to dirt sparring arena surrounded by the short wooden fence.

"Can I use two swords?" I asked, my excitement returning.

"Ask me again a year from now and we will consider it," he replied.

I was very disappointed by his answer.

There were a few barrels lined up against the wooden fence. Grayson walked over to one and pulled out three wooden swords. He handed one to each of us and then grabbed one for himself. I swung it around like a Jedi, making lightsaber noises as we followed him to the middle of the arena.

"We won't be doing any sparring for a week or two," Grayson said. "First we will be doing a series of exercises to help you learn proper footwork and basic techniques. I expect you to memorize each exercise so you can eventually practice them without my supervision." He turned so he was facing the same direction as we were. He held his wooden sword out in front of him with both hands and shifted his body into a position that made him look ready to attack. "Position your body like mine and get ready to follow my lead. The first few times I will go very slow so you can keep up."

I positioned my body like his and looked over at Autumn who looked as awkward as I assumed I looked. She caught my eye and gave me an embarrassed smile. I shifted my gaze to Juliet who looked just as natural as Grayson did. She'd probably already memorized it. When Grayson started, the three of us did our best to mirror him as he moved. The exercise consisted of steps forward and backward, sidesteps, lunges, pivots, and motions where we had to bring the sword in front of us as if blocking an opponent's attack.

I was very sloppy at the exercise because I had never done it before, but at the same time, it almost felt familiar. Throughout the exercise I frequently glanced at Juliet and Autumn to see if they were any better than I was. Of course, Juliet looked like she almost had it memorized, which made me just a little jealous, but after watching Autumn, I instantly felt better.

After maybe five times through the pattern, I began to feel more comfortable doing it, but I definitely wasn't even close to memorizing it. If Grayson wasn't there to lead me, I would get lost in the steps very quickly. It didn't take long until he started moving a little faster. It was harder to follow, but I managed to make it through.

By the time Grayson ended the exercise, us Wakers were all sweaty and exhausted. I sat down on the dusty ground and tried to catch my breath. Looking at Grayson,

I noticed that he wasn't sweaty or even breathing very hard.

"Go ahead and take a brief respite and then we will begin our next exercise," He said before walking away.

"You are such a pro, Juliet," Autumn praised as she sat down next to me. "Do you have the whole thing memorized?"

"Almost," Juliet said, her hands on her knees, her breathing heavy. "After a few days, you'll have it down pretty well."

"She probably taught it to her dance class." I joked. "That way, they could all look ridiculous together."

"Yeah, actually I did. And you know what's sad? My little four-year-olds can do it a lot better than you."

Autumn laughed.

Her comebacks were always too good. I had better stick with being the nice guy.

After a couple of minutes, Grayson came back with a water skin and handed it to Autumn. We all took turns drinking from it before Grayson told us our break was over. We immediately began the second exercise, which was similar to the first, but it was a lot more offensive, with a lot of jabs, lunges, and swings. We did it for almost the same amount of time as the first exercise, and after we finished, I felt like I was ready to go to bed and sleep for a year.

Juliet, Autumn and I all sat on the ground resting while Grayson put our wooden swords away and got us some more water. When he came back, another man was walking beside him. The stranger was wearing a gray robe and was a bit taller than Grayson. He looked older too, probably in his late 50s. He had short graying hair, a thick mustache, and bright green eyes. As the two approached, we stood up.

"We have a special guest," Grayson said. "He came here to meet you three."

"Good afternoon, Wakers." the man said in a familiar deep voice. "My name is Barry Farnsworth, High Seer of Elegit Terram. Most call me Seer Farnsworth."

I was pretty sure it was the man we heard talking to the Archduke in the castle. If it was him, he probably just wanted to see how much I looked like this guy they were talking about.

Autumn, Juliet, and I introduced ourselves to him.

"It's wonderful to meet you all," he said with a kind smile. "Thank you for choosing to join the Dreamchasers. I'm certain you will help change the Dream World for the better." He turned to Grayson. "Are you finished training for the day?"

"Yes, we are."

"Lord Chaz, would you walk with me for a few minutes?" the Seer asked. "I have some things I want to talk to you about."

"Um, yeah," I replied, startled. I assumed he was going to interrogate me. Hopefully I wouldn't get tortured. Who knew what kind of pain you could put someone in by bending reality?

I walked next to Farnsworth as he led me away from

my friends, heading toward what looked like an archery field. I saw a few targets in the distance.

"You're probably wondering why I would want to talk with you specifically when we don't even know each other," Farnsworth guessed. "Do you know what a seer is?"

"Not really. I know it has something to do with seeing the future."

"You are right. A seer is an individual who gazes into the future for the benefit of others. So, with that in mind, you wouldn't be wrong if you said that every person with the reality bending ability is a seer. While that is true, a High Seer is different. It is a special calling that is appointed to only one person at a time. The Archduke is the one who chooses the High Seer, and he will only choose someone who is known to be extremely visionary.

"As High Seer, it is my duty to receive visions for the whole country. You could almost call me a prophet. I prophesy of danger and I guide and protect the people. I see many visions daily. Sometimes a vision may concern everyone, but most often it concerns only an individual or two. Of course, there are also many things I don't see."

He paused as we continued to walk through the green field. I noticed a fox stealthily bouncing away, jumping low over the tall grass. "Do you understand now why I wanted to talk with you?"

"I think so," I replied. "Is it because I have a gift for seeing visions?"

"That's right. The reason I know that is because I have

already seen this moment."

"Really?" I asked. I kind of already knew that, but it would probably be a good idea to act surprised.

"Really. Just this morning I was directed in a vision to come and talk to you about your gift. There are things I need to tell you that will help you greatly in the near future. Listen carefully, I need you to remember my words."

We stopped walking and faced each other, the bright sun burning the back of my neck.

"The first thing I want to tell you is that your destiny is up to you," the Seer began. "You can be who you want to be and do whatever you want to do. Every dream is worth chasing, and every dream is possible to achieve. It doesn't matter what you see in the future, it is still un-written and uncertain. You can change it.

"The second thing you need to understand is that your visions are not subject to time. Many people without our gift believe that even the most powerful daydreamers can only see visions up to a few days in the future. Those who have written down their visions and studied them closely have come to find that is false. You can have a vision about something that happens ten years from now and it will come to pass, just not in the way you expected.

"Understand this, when you see more than a few days into the future, it's like looking through a cracked window, you can't quite make out what's happening on the other side, but you have a pretty good idea.

"Chaz, all of your visions will come to pass, just not

exactly as you see them. Write them down, study them and learn from them. Your visions will teach you that there is no reason to fear the future. Now, go and make the most out of your life and enjoy it."

"Is that everything you wanted to tell me?" I asked, wanting to hear more. I was hoping he would actually tell me something important that will happen in my future, like who I would marry or how I was going to save the world. I also couldn't help but think about the vision of me dying. According to him, that was going to come true in one way or another. I wanted to bring it up, but I didn't.

"That's everything, Chaz. I will walk you back to your company."

We started back toward the others and walked in silence for a few minutes.

"So, are you a… a Waker?" I asked.

"Yes, I am."

"Where are you from?"

"I will not share that information at the moment. You should also be careful about sharing your location as well. This war between good and evil is real, Chaz. And it doesn't just exist here. It's in the Waking World as well. The members of the Quin Anulus are also in both worlds, and if need be, they might decide that the best way to stop you here is to do something horrible to you in the Waking World. They have spies everywhere. If you give out your location freely, they will learn it."

"They would really harm me in real life?" I asked.

"They would get caught by the police and go to jail or

something."

"They would find a way to do it with no evidence that led back to them."

I had never considered the fact that the members of the Quin Anulus existed here *and* in reality. If Farnsworth was right, I had better be careful in both worlds.

A few minutes later, we found the others hanging out exactly where we had left them. We all said goodbye to Seer Farnsworth before he left. After he walked away, Grayson turned his attention to us. "What would you like to do for the rest of the day?"

"I think I'm ready to eat," I replied.

Juliet and Autumn agreed.

"I will escort you to the dining hall," Grayson said.

The four of us headed inside the castle. On our way to the dining hall, Master Grayson retrieved a decent sized knife for each of us along with a scabbard to strap to our waist.

"In case you need to defend yourselves," he explained. "These will have to do until you learn how to properly handle a sword."

Once we reached the dining hall, we thanked Grayson before parting ways. We entered the spacious room and I slowly gazed around at all the people eating, looking for familiar faces. We headed to the kitchen where we found Gina, and she sent us away with large plates full of biscuits and gravy and veggies.

I led Juliet and Autumn over to a table occupied by two Asian guys who looked to be a little bit older than us.

One had noticeably darker skin than the other, with a long black ponytail hanging down his back. The other guy had short, dark red hair that was obviously dyed.

"Can we sit with you guys?" I asked.

"Yes, you can," the one with the ponytail said with a slight oriental accent. We joined them at their table. "I'm Raiden," the ponytail guy continued, introducing himself. "And this is Jo."

"Hello!" Jo said enthusiastically without a hint of an accent.

"Raiden and Jo," I repeated, trying to commit their names to memory. "I'm Chaz. That's Autumn and Juliet."

"Hi," Autumn said. "It's nice to meet you both."

"You three must be the new Wakers everyone is talking about," Raiden said. "It is good to finally meet you as well. Where are you from?"

"Utah."

"Colorado."

"California."

"All from the USA, huh?" Raiden commented.

"I lived in California for a year," Jo said. "I liked it a lot."

"Are you two new Wakers as well?" Juliet asked. "I've never seen you before."

"No, we've been here for a while." Raiden answered. "We both live on the opposite side of the world from you. We come here at night because it is also night for us. We both went to bed really early tonight because we have a lot to do here."

"Where do you live?" I asked.

"I live in South Korea," Jo answered. "Raiden lives in Japan. We have both been Dreamchasers for almost three years."

"Really? What do you guys do when you come here at night?"

"The dirty work," Jo replied. "Nightmares mostly come out at night, so we patrol outside the city and prevent them from getting inside. It's dangerous work, and lately we have been losing a lot of men."

"Oh, no!" Autumn exclaimed. "That's awful! Why have you been losing so many lately?"

"There have been a lot more Nightmares attacking," Raiden said. "Every single night for the past few months. They don't stop coming."

"Are there any other Wakers who patrol the border with you?" Juliet asked.

"Nope," Jo replied. "It's just us and the Dreamers. There aren't enough Wakers to go around. They either get wiped out or join the wrong side. It's okay though, we'll be fine. Raiden is pretty much a samurai." He tugged on Raiden's ponytail before his hand got slapped away.

"You guys be careful," Autumn said, worry written all over her face. "Watch out for each other."

"You three as well," Jo said as he and Raiden stood up. "Things are probably only going to get worse. Catch you later."

We finished our food in silence. After we were done eating, we headed back to our rooms.

"Do you guys want to hang out for a little bit?" Autumn asked when we reached the Wakers' hall. "It's the weekend, so we don't have to be up early or anything."

"Okay," Juliet said. "Just for a little bit."

We followed Juliet into her room. I took a seat on the chair in the corner and they sat on the bed. I noticed a vase of flowers and what looked like a note on her dresser. Did she have a secret admirer? Gross.

"Let's talk about something positive," Autumn suggested.

"Something positive like, who sent Juliet flowers?" I said, half joking and half curious. What kind of weirdo would be into her?

"Or something positive like, how many girls Chaz has kissed?" Juliet said.

Autumn smiled at me apologetically. "I have a better idea. Chaz, how about you tell us what you and the Seer talked about."

I had completely forgotten about that. The depressing thoughts of people dying on border patrol had distracted me from *my other* depressing thoughts about how the Seer confirmed that I was going to die.

"We didn't talk about too much," I muttered. "We talked about what he does as a Seer and stuff like that. He gave me some good advice and told me that no matter what we see in the future, it is not set. We can still change it . . ." I trailed off.

"Anything else?" Autumn prodded, clearly sensing that there was something I wasn't telling her.

"He also told me about how visions work." I rehearsed to them what the Seer told me about visions and how they all happen in one way or another. I then reminded them about the vision I had about my death right outside the door.

"Oh, Chaz! Don't worry," Autumn said. "We're not going to let that happen. He said we can change the future."

"I don't think it's that easy."

"It is that easy," Juliet said. "I know you're scared because you know how you might possibly die, but you need to think. We know now what *not* to do so that doesn't happen. All you have to do is wake us up instead of being an idiot and trying to face those things on your own. We will start training extra hard to make sure we're even more ready for something like that. And I'm sure if we asked, we could get guards stationed outside of each of our doors. It's that easy, Chaz."

"I guess that could help," I said quietly. That girl really knew how to make me feel stupid. She was definitely right though.

"We won't let you die, Chaz. We just have to remember to rely on each other."

"You're right," I admitted. "I'm not a superhero, I can't run off and try to save the day alone. I need you two."

"I need you both as well," Autumn said, shifting her gaze between the two of us. "I know this might sound silly, but we should make a promise or something."

"What kind of promise?" Juliet asked, a confused grin

on her face.

"A promise that we'll always stick together and have each other's backs."

"Why?" I asked. It was a weird suggestion.

"Because promises mean a lot to me," Autumn replied. "And I want you to really mean it."

"If it makes you feel better," Juliet said with a light laugh. "I promise."

"I promise too," I said.

"Thanks, guys." Autumn smiled. "You two are the best."

Chapter 15

Do Visions Get Any Weirder Than That?

I woke up in my bed at home and tried to remember what day it was. After racking my brain for about a minute, I remembered it was Saturday. Again. Experiencing the same day twice was still unusual for me. It had me feeling all mixed up.

By the time I got out of bed and ready for the day, it was only 8:34. I wasn't one who slept in much, so getting up that early on a weekend was normal. After I ate breakfast, I went back to my room and decided it would be a good time to get ahead on my homework. I worked on it a couple of hours before I couldn't take anymore. So, I decided to spend some time on the homework Master Grayson had given me. I hoped I could impress everyone by mastering the finger trick before we started training again next week.

After my brother Garrett finally got up for the day, I told him I wanted to show him a cool trick. I explained to him that I had magical powers that would help me know the number of fingers he was about to hold up. I thought maybe if I tried hard enough, I would finally be able to do it. I was wrong though. I tried for ten minutes until Garrett got bored of it and walked away.

I didn't do much for the rest of the day My dad had to work until that night, so I didn't see much of him, and my mom was busy cleaning and shopping. I texted all of my close friends frequently throughout the day, Jake was still sick, and Isaac was at the zoo with his family. When I finally heard back from Presley, she said that she still smelled pretty bad and wouldn't be able to hang out today. I texted back and forth with Juliet and Autumn frequently throughout the day, so that made it a lot less boring.

Later that night, Autumn was the only one still texting me. Everyone else was busy with friends and family and who knows what.

Well since Juliet is too cool to talk anymore, you should call me. :)

After I read that text from her, I instantly felt nervous. I didn't talk to people on the phone often, and when I did, it was usually just Jake or Isaac. I had never talked to Presley or any other girl on the phone. Why in the world did she want me to call her? I was perfectly fine with texting.

I sent a reply.

Haha, seriously?

A few seconds later, I got her response.

Why not? We're both bored. :)

I thought about it for maybe a minute before I finally pressed the green phone icon under her name and braced myself for a very awkward few minutes. My heart banged against my chest like King Kong trying to break out of a cage. Talking to girls on the phone had to be one of my greatest fears.

"Hey, Chaz," Autumn greeted from the phone.

"Hey," I replied. "I don't ever really talk on the phone, so this will probably be awkward."

"I guess we'll have to practice more often then."

"Hah, I guess so."

As I talked to her, I slowly relaxed and felt less awkward. We talked about our families, hobbies and school. I got to know so much more about her, and we actually had a lot in common. We talked until I realized it was a few minutes passed ten. That was late for me.

"Hey, I just realized it's already ten," I said into the phone. "Let's go to bed and we can talk in person."

She laughed and said, "I still think it's so crazy that we go to this secret dream world every night and get to hang out."

"Me too. I guess I'll see you in a little bit."

"Can't wait."

I blushed and tried to wipe the grin off my face.

"Goodnight," I said.

"Goodnight, Chaz."

I plugged in my dying cell phone and wriggled under my covers. After a few minutes of being excited to go to the Dream World, I finally started to relax.

Suddenly, I was sitting on the chair in the corner of Juliet's room as she and Autumn sat on her bed. I instantly recognized the moment because it was still fresh in my memory. It just happened last night.

Autumn shifted her gaze to me. "I know this might sound silly, but we should make a promise or something."

"What kind of promise?" Juliet asked.

"A promise that we will always stick together and have each other's back."

Right after she said it, everything around me slowly dissolved until my world was black. A few seconds after that, everything lit up and slowly came into focus.

I was walking on a beach, the cold breeze helping to cool my body as my skin baked in the sun. I followed behind Juliet as she headed towards the shore, Autumn was walking beside me. Autumn and I talked and laughed as we enjoyed the beautiful day. Suddenly, I noticed a bad feeling in the pit of my stomach. Something was very wrong. I felt like I shouldn't be there.

My vision blurred, and when it came back into focus, I found myself in the familiar forest of white trees. Juliet and Autumn were there as well. Juliet had a blank stare on her face and Autumn looked like she was about to cry. I didn't know why, but I felt an urgency to run away, like I needed to get away from there. Autumn raised her hand to me, as if she wanted me to take it. I still had the same horrible feeling inside; it was telling me something was wrong. I turned away from her and took off running as fast as I could.

When I looked back, I was shocked by what I saw.

I saw my dad, and he was running after me. He was quickly gaining on me and I heard his voice calling out, telling me everything was going to be okay. I didn't believe him though, so I kept running without slowing at all. Once again, the scenery changed, and before I knew it, I was running through a trampled field covered in tall grass. Monstrous mountains loomed in front of me. They had to have only been a mile or so away.

I slowed to a stop and turned around to find that my dad stopped as well. Suddenly, I felt a strong anger flare up inside me. The anger was directed at my dad. This time, he started running away and I was chasing him. He ran so fast that he quickly moved out of sight and I had no idea where he was. I didn't stop running though. I knew I would eventually find him again.

I continued to run until I spotted him in the distance, and as I caught up to him, I found Autumn standing beside him. I felt scared, I didn't want him to do what I knew he was about to do. He gave me a smug grin before shoving her toward me and sprinting away. This time, the anger I felt was stronger than any emotion I had ever felt before. It made me feel sick and empty inside. I ran after him until I caught up to him again. I was about to tackle him when my vision quickly blurred, and I found myself standing on Presley's front porch. Presley stood in front of me trembling as tears fell from her eyes. She looked hurt and confused.

"Why?" she asked.

I quickly sat up in bed, my forehead covered in sweat. Fully awake now, I looked around as light spilled through the curtains into my castle bedroom. What a crazy dream! What in the world was that all about? If that was a vision, then I had no idea what it was supposed to mean.

Either way, it probably wouldn't be a good idea to ignore it. The whole dream seemed to revolve around Autumn. But why was my dad there? And why was Presley so sad? Just thinking about the way that she looked at me made my heart ache.

I sat in bed pondering the dream a while longer until I thought I might have understood what it meant. Maybe what I was supposed to learn from that vision was that if I spent too much time around Autumn, then I would fall in love and get my heart broken. And maybe my dad would be able to discern that there was something wrong and try to give me some advice–some terrible advice that would make me want to beat him up . . . and then I would end up breaking Presley's heart because she would be able to tell that I was in love with someone else.

Okay, that didn't make any sense at all. Well, whatever the case, spending too much time around Autumn was probably a bad idea. I had better keep my distance.

I hopped out of bed and got ready for the day. As I changed, I thought about how the Seer had told me to write my visions down. I checked the dresser drawers and found a pen and paper in one of them. I began to write down everything I remembered about the dream until I heard a knock on my door.

"Hey, Chaz," Autumn's muffled voice said. "Are you awake yet?"

As much as I wanted to answer, I felt it would be best if I didn't hang out with her until Juliet was around, so I just ignored her and kept writing. I finally heard her walk away and knock on another door.

The door opened. "Perfect timing," I heard Juliet say.

"I don't think Chaz is here yet," Autumn said.

"That's also perfect. Just kidding. We can go get breakfast and then check on him again."

Juliet's door shut and I heard the two walking away. I took a few more minutes to finish writing down my dream and then stuck the pen and paper back in the drawer. Giving my hair a quick check in the mirror, I headed to breakfast.

The dining hall was slamming busy when I arrived, and that was probably because it was already lunch time. I looked around the room until I spotted Juliet and Autumn sitting with a few knights, two of whom I recognized as Captain Fynn and Garriton. I grabbed a ham sandwich off a table topped with a small variety of food and joined my friends at their table.

"Good afternoon, sleepy head," Autumn said.

I sat down across from her, next to Juliet.

"It took me awhile to fall asleep last night," I said. It was kind of true.

"Good afternoon, Lord Chaz," Fynn said with his usual cheerfulness. "It's been a day or two since we last saw you. Glad to see you're still as young and healthy as ever."

"Maybe even healthier," Garriton commented with a grin. "He looks like he might have gained a pound or six." He winked at me.

"How could you not with this kind of cooking?" The other knight added. "I've gained almost twenty pounds since I became a knight."

He looked like a younger version of Garriton, the same red hair and all.

"Chaz, meet my brother, Charles," Garriton said.

"Only my mother calls me Charles, and that's when she's angry," he said with a loud laugh. "Call me Charley."

"Nice to meet you, Charley," I said.

"Me and Autumn were just asking what they think we should do today," Juliet explained. "We were thinking it would be fun to get out of the city and see something new. What do you think?"

"Sounds good to me. I would love to see more of this world."

"I know of a couple things you can do that will take up most of your day," Fynn said. "First you should go to the beach at the edge of the White Forest."

When I heard the word 'beach,' I froze. The weird dream had started at the beach. Maybe it was a warning.

"That beach is the most enjoyable out of all of them," Fynn continued. "It has perfect sand and the best ocean life. Last time Garriton and I were there, I had to rescue him from a giant sea turtle. You remember that?"

"I don't think 'rescue' is the right word," Garriton said, shaking his head. "It's a long story that we'll have to share another time, but I assure you, it was vicious."

"Anyway," Fynn said, "after the beach, I could take you on a beautiful hike with all the best views. It's about three hours round trip. It's not too difficult either."

"Those both sound like great ideas to me." Juliet replied.

"Well if you're going to the beach, you better leave now," Charley said. "You'll only have a few hours before it gets too cold and windy to enjoy."

I was about to suggest that we go another time, but Autumn cut me off. "I don't think that will work . . . I promised Gina I would help out in the kitchen this afternoon."

"Don't fret about it," Fynn said. "It's not your job, she will be fine. She has been working in the kitchen for many years and hasn't needed a bit of help."

"I know she doesn't need help. I just want to. And I said I would, so I have to."

"That is very nice of you, Lady Autumn," Garriton commented.

"I guess we could go to the beach another time," Juliet said thoughtfully. "We could help out in the kitchen as well and then go on a hike."

The more I thought about my dream, the more I was starting to convince myself that maybe it wasn't the beach that was a bad idea. Maybe it was spending a lot of time around Autumn. And if we stayed with Autumn and helped out in the kitchen, then I would still be spending time around her. Maybe going to the beach would be a good idea after all. I didn't want to be rude or anything, but I had to do what I thought was best.

"Um . . ." I began, unsure of how to say what I wanted to say. "I was actually really hoping to go to the beach today. I would love to stay and help in the kitchen, but I feel like I need to go today."

"You feel like you need to go?" Juliet asked, giving me a doubtful look. "Is that an excuse to get out of doing dishes?"

"No really. I had a vision last night about the beach. I'm pretty sure I'm supposed to go there today."

"If you had a vision about it, then that's not something to ignore," Fynn said.

"Well if you're going, then I guess I'm going too," Autumn said, hesitation in her voice.

"Autumn I don't think you should," I said. The hurt look she gave me made me feel awful. It reminded me of the look I saw on Presley's face in my dream. "In my vision you stayed behind to help out in the kitchen. I think you're needed here. I'm pretty sure something bad will happen if all three of us go."

"Was I at the beach with you in your vision?" Juliet asked.

"Yeah, it was just you and me."

"Think you'll win me over with a simple walk on the beach, huh?"

"No, no. That's just what I saw."

"Chaz, I don't feel good about you two going without me," Autumn said with a pleading look on her face.

"I feel good about it," I replied, feeling even more awful. "We'll go hiking with you when we get back."

"Fine," she said, clearly upset. "Fynn, will you send some of your knights to go with them to keep them safe?"

"Of course," Fynn said. "All Wakers who leave the city are to have an escort. Because the two of you are going, I will also come along to ensure your safety."

"See you two in a few hours," Autumn said, glancing at me worriedly. She got up, stacked a few plates, and took them to the kitchen.

Chapter 16

Sometimes the Beach Is Not a Good Idea

Juliet and I rode silently, side by side on two large horses. Captain Fynn rode in front, guiding us down a path through the White Forest. Two other knights rode behind us Taten and West were their names. Other than their names, I didn't know anything about them.

"I hope you know that you really hurt her," Juliet said.

I thought about her words as I studied my surroundings. When we first entered the forest, it brought back the memory of being chased by a Nightmare only a few days ago. As we rode through the thick woods, I was slowly able to relax a little bit. So far, there was no sight of the dark creatures.

"I didn't mean to hurt her," I said, honestly. "It just didn't feel right letting her come along."

"Well, what did you see in your vision?"

"I don't really know what I saw. It all happened so fast and it wasn't very clear. All this bad stuff happened when we were at the beach. I got this bad feeling inside, like maybe I shouldn't have brought her."

Juliet gave me a sideways glance. "Do you even know if it's a good idea for us to go?"

"Not exactly."

She sighed. "Chaz, you are such an idiot sometimes. Hopefully you don't get us killed. If Fynn wasn't here to protect us, then I probably wouldn't have come."

I looked ahead to Fynn and then back to her. "Why is that? There are plenty of other knights who could do a good job at protecting us."

"Never mind, it doesn't matter."

I grinned and asked quietly, "Do you have a thing for Captain Fynn?"

"Uh, gross. He's like thirty."

"So?"

"I am not having this conversation with you."

She nudged her horse and moved ahead of me. She probably didn't want to talk about it because it was true. Maybe he was the one who got her flowers.

We probably rode for thirty minutes before we broke through the forest and found ourselves staring at an endless expanse of water. Right past the forest clearing, the ground sloped downward and suddenly turned into a beach full of sand, as if the whole forest was cut out from a distant land and then plopped onto the beach. The gold sand stretched out for at least a hundred yards before it met the ocean.

"You two go enjoy the beach for as long as you like,"

Fynn said. "My men and I will guard the perimeter of the forest."

"Do you think we'll get attacked?" Juliet asked.

"Not on a day like this. But Nightmares tend to roam near the Portal, as Lord Chaz found out. It is better to be safe than sorry. You can leave your mounts here."

Juliet and I dismounted and started towards the ocean, sinking into the loose sand as we walked. The clothes I was wearing wouldn't normally be my first choice for a trip to the beach, but I didn't have many options. Did they even have bathing suits here? Or did they just swim in their underwear? I definitely had no plans to do anything like that.

As I walked next to Juliet, I realized that this was the moment I had seen in my dream. Only this time, it was Juliet walking next to me and Autumn was nowhere in sight. The thought of her getting left behind made me feel sad. I really did want her to be there.

"Be honest," Juliet said, breaking the silence. "Do you like her?"

"Who? Autumn?" I asked, surprised.

"Well, duh."

"No. I mean not really. I think she's a great friend and all, but I have someone I like back home."

"Presley?"

"How do you and Autumn figure out these things so easily?"

"It's pretty obvious by the way you talk about her," Juliet said. "It's also kind of obvious that you have a crush on Autumn as well."

"What? What do you mean? I barely know her."

"Quit trying to deny it. I know you're both crushing on each other."

"Not even. Maybe she likes me, but I don't like her like that."

We stopped just a few feet away from where the tide last spilled onto the shore.

"You live in two worlds, why not have a girlfriend in each one?" I gave her a dumbfounded look before I got punched on the arm. "You know I'm kidding. Don't you dare do anything like that."

"I would never," I said defensively.

"Is that why you didn't want her to come? Did you make it all up?"

"No way, that would be so mean." I paused. "I really thought that my vision was warning me that she shouldn't come."

"Hopefully, we did the right thing," Juliet said as she gazed out into the ocean. "I wish she was here."

"Me too," I admitted.

I stared out at the water and silently wished for a surfboard and a swimsuit. Mostly a surfboard though.

"So, did Fynn give you the flowers?" I asked.

"No, Chaz. Nothing is going on with me and Fynn. Besides, he's not even a Waker."

"He's . . . dead?"

"Yeah. He died when he was a–"

She paused and turned to me with a worried look on

her face. Only then did I realize the horrible feeling that I had in the pit of my stomach. It was the same feeling I had felt in my dream.

"Do you feel that too?" I asked.

She nodded and we both turned around at the same time. What I saw sent a wave of shock and horror through me like I had never before felt.

A black silhouette in the shape of a man was silently walking toward us. It was maybe fifty feet away. I recognized it instantly. I knew it was a Mors Somnia. Its face might have been familiar, but it was too far away to be sure. The sunlight just seemed to sink right into its dark fur, not illuminating it at all. It looked impossibly black in contrast to the light sand.

Behind the Mors was another scene that made me want to lose all the breakfast I had eaten. There were two Nightmares that were so large, they made the first one I ran into seem like it was a newborn. What was even worse was that one of them was struggling to chew on something shiny that looked like it might have been a knight's armor. They shuffled their feet and opened and closed their claws restlessly, like they were eager to feed on our fear. One let out a low growl that seemed to vibrate the very air around us.

Neither Fynn nor his men were in sight, and I desperately hoped they weren't all eaten or dead. The Mors continued towards us, in no hurry, like it was enjoying watching us quake in fear, which it probably was. I turned, meeting Juliet's eyes with my own hard stare. She pulled out her knife like she was intending to fight. "We need to run!" I screamed to Juliet. "We won't stand a chance against those things. Run!"

She took off in a sprint and I followed close behind her. We ran away from the monsters back toward the forest. It was hard to go fast because the loose sand. I looked back and saw the Mors Somnia running after us with the Nightmares slowly falling behind as they leapt. My legs were already starting to burn, and my clothes were quickly getting drenched in sweat, but the fear of seeing the inside of one of those Nightmares kept me going.

"Maybe we can lose it in the forest!" Juliet shouted. I looked up and noticed we were almost to the trees. "Try to have a vision or something! Maybe we can get out of this!"

Yeah right. I had never been able to use my gift on command before. I tried though. I imagined us losing the monsters in the forest and finding our way to safety, but none of it felt real. Fear and hopelessness started growing inside me.

We were only about twenty yards from the forest when another large Nightmare leapt out of the trees, blocking our path. It opened its mouth and licked the air with its black tongue, shivering in delight as it gazed at us with its black eyes. I was ready to change my direction, but Juliet continued straight toward it.

"Juliet!" I cried as I struggled to keep up with her. "We can't go that way!"

"I'd rather take my chances with this one than the thing chasing us!" she yelled back.

As we neared the gross creature, I struggled to pull out my knife. I managed to get it out of the sheath when we were only fifteen feet away. My heart leapt in fear as the Nightmare crouched like it was about to pounce. Before it could leave the ground, Taten burst out of the trees and hacked off one of the Nightmare's legs with his sword, making it bellow like an injured pig as it fell to the ground. It swiped at him with its enormous claws, but he managed to block the attack, and then quicker than I could follow, he cut off its hand.

"Don't stop!" Taten screamed at us as he ducked a swipe of the monster's other clawed hand. "Keep going! Head to the Portal!"

We gave him and the monster a wide berth as we passed, reaching the shaded forest and entering the cover of the trees. My legs and lungs were screaming for me to stop, but I was too scared to listen. I risked a quick glance backward and instantly regretted it. The Mors pulled a sword as black as itself out of nowhere and hacked down the preoccupied knight as he passed, not slowing in the slightest. I screamed inside and began stumbling through the foliage, barely preventing myself from falling. The Mors was probably only twenty feet behind and still gaining.

Juliet was a little bit faster than me, so I was starting to fall behind even more. I tried to pick up the pace and ended up stumbling for a couple of seconds until I tripped over a short bush. I fell forward and barely got my hands in front of me in time to catch myself. Juliet must have heard me fall, because she looked back and then stopped in her tracks when she saw me on the ground. I waved her forward before getting to my feet in a low crouch and slipping behind a nearby tree.

The tree had a wide enough girth that it could easily hide my whole body from view. I peered to my right and saw Juliet spring behind a tree as well. I couldn't see the Mors, but I could hear it run quietly through the undergrowth. The sound of it pursuing me continued until it came very near, and then all went quiet.

I didn't know if it could hear me, smell me, or sense me in some other way, but I held still as I listened for any kind of sound. I quickly realized that there were no birds chirping, insects buzzing, or any of the usual forest noises. Thanks to the dead forest, my breathing sounded obnoxiously loud. My heart hammered so fast and hard in my chest that it was painful. I gripped my knife tightly with my shaky hand and slowly peered around the left side of the tree. I didn't see anything. I peeked around the right side and didn't see anything there either. There was no Mors Somnia in sight.

Juliet peeked her head out the side of the tree she was behind. She looked around and then shook her head at me with a worried frown. Where did it go? There was no way it just disappeared. And it had to have seen me trip. It was probably waiting to stab me in the back when I least expected it.

I was going to have to make a run for it, whether it was around or not. I couldn't stay in one place. I looked around the left side of the tree again and saw nothing. I turned to my right and my heart jumped to my throat. The face staring at me was only a couple of inches away. And what my eyes beheld was completely shocking. I quickly shuffled backward as I stared in horror at the Mors.

He had my dad's face.

Chapter 17

What an Awful Surprise!

The Mors Somnia stalked towards me as I backed away. It wore the same familiar grin Dad often wore when he was excited. It was disturbing how much the face looked like his, it was just darker and evil looking. Even his pitch-black orbs for eyes somehow resembled Dad's.

The creatures body had the same build as his as well, only it was covered in black fur that slightly waved as it stalked toward me. He carried a gleaming black blade that looked like it didn't have a hilt or handle, it was just one long piece of steel.

"Chaz," the Mors said in a penetrating voice that was similar to Dad's, but it was darker and more sinister. The voice seemed to have multiple tones, and one sounded like it could shatter glass. "Everything will be okay."

I continued to back away as my fear grew stronger and stronger. The closer it got, the more I felt like lying down and giving up. My body was threatening to lock up, I had to fight to keep moving. I couldn't think straight, I couldn't feel any emotions besides fear and hopelessness. All I could do was back away.

"Let me help you," the Mors hissed. "I will teach you to embrace your fears, to become one with them. You will never need to be afraid again. Please, let me help you."

My body began to slow down, I felt like I could hardly move. I was so cold and hopeless inside. I didn't want to find out what he was going to do to me, but maybe it wouldn't be so bad if I never had to feel fear again.

"Chaz!" Juliet's voice screamed, shaking me out of my stupor. "Run!"

Blinking and struggling to shake off the hypnotic hold I seemed to be caught in, I chucked my knife at the Mors and rushed in the direction of Juliet's voice. The creature growled, then I heard the sound of pursuit behind me.

"Everything is going to be okay," he hissed. "I'm here for you, Chaz."

Against my will, I felt my body starting to slow again. I suddenly heard a *thunk*, and then a growl. I turned around to see the Mors was no longer chasing me. Instead, he was facing Juliet who was throwing rocks at him. Her aim was off and most of them missed. I slowed to a stop as the ugly creature began walking toward her. He let his arm hang so that the blade dragged against the ground beside him.

"You will suffer," The Mors said, swiping his sword at the next rock Juliet threw, cutting it clean in half.

"Juliet, run!" I yelled.

I charged after the Mors, but before I got close to it, a figure jumped out from behind a group of trees, his sword clanging hard against the blade of the Mors. It was Fynn. His face was caked with dirt and sweat, and his left forearm had a nasty-looking gash, but besides that, he looked ready for a fight.

He leaned forward as he pushed his sword against the Mors' blade. The Mors pushed back for a few seconds and then sprang backwards out of reach. Faster than any man can move, he rushed toward Fynn and began attacking with precise swings, each one meant to mortally injure him. Fynn must have been able to see each strike before it happened because he blocked every single one.

Fynn quickly took the offensive. He hacked at the creature with his sword like his life depended on it, which it did. Even though the Mors wasn't able to see the future, he was Fynn's equal match with his inhuman speed. Swords clashed loudly as they danced back in forth, both trying to gain the upper hand. Their struggle went on for a few more minutes until Fynn pulled back and they slowly began circling each other.

"Stop delaying your death," Fynn said. "It's only a matter of time before I see a future where I end you."

"I will kill you before that happens," The Mors promised.

"That is exactly what the last Mors Somnia told me before I cut him to pieces."

The Mors growled and rushed Fynn, but unlike before, it attacked with strength instead of speed. Their blades rang out even louder as they struck. Captain Fynn's arms shook with every blow he blocked. The Mors was determined to overpower him rather than outclass him. Once again, their swords met and held in place, each pushing with all their might.

In one swift motion, the Mors crouched and shoved the end of the blade he was holding at Fynn. Because both ends of the Mors' blade were sharp, he managed to drive it right into Fynn's left arm. Before the Mors could pull out his blade, Fynn cleaved off the creature's sword hand with a quick swing, then he quickly followed it with another swing, severing his other hand.

Both hands dissolved when they hit the ground. The Mors shook with anger as he backed away from Fynn. He turned his head towards me and glared at me in rage before he took off running into the trees.

"Fynn!" Juliet cried as she ran to him. "Are you okay?"

I ran over to him as well and stared numbly at the blade protruding right above his elbow.

"Don't worry about me," he said. "It looks a lot worse than it is. It barely cut my arm."

He used his gloved to grasp the blade and quickly yanked it out of his armor, then tossed it away. It dissolved when it hit the ground.

"What happened?" Juliet asked, looking like she might cry. "I thought you were all dead."

"I'm so sorry, Lady Juliet. I saw two Nightmares at the edge of the forest and thought I could dispose of them quickly. As soon as they saw me, they leaped away, and I chased them for a while. I thought it was strange that they didn't attack me, but until I found you two and the Mors Somnia, I didn't realize what was going on. It seems this attack was planned. Either they saw us on our way here or they knew we were coming."

"How would they know that? We didn't tell anyone."

"I'm not certain. The Quin Anulus have spies everywhere. Maybe they overheard us. I will have to investigate when we get back."

"Thanks for saving us," I said sincerely. "We would both be dead if it wasn't for you."

"It is my duty to keep you safe. Did either of you see what happened to Taten or West?"

"I think a Nightmare might have . . . eaten West. And Taten was killed by the Mors Somnia." I paused. "My dad's Mors Somnia."

I felt like I was on the verge of tears as I took in the magnitude of everything that had just happened. I didn't listen to Autumn and I hurt her feelings. Two men who probably had families of their own were both dead now because of me. My dad had a Mors Somnia and he would never start doing anything with his life until it was destroyed. Everything had dramatically changed for the worse after one quick trip to the beach.

"Your father's Mors Somnia?" Fynn asked. "Are you certain?"

"Yeah. There's no doubt. It looked and sounded just like him. It even acted like it knew me."

"Chaz," Juliet said softly. "That's so awful. I had no idea."

"This is all my fault," I said as a tear slid down my face. "Because of me, two people are dead now. I could have avoided this. And now Autumn probably hates me."

"You didn't know this would happen," Fynn said.

"I should have known. My vision made it pretty obvious. So did Autumn. She said she had a bad feeling about us going and I didn't listen. Her feelings are never wrong."

"You thought you were making the right decision," Juliet said. "That's all that matters. It's not your fault."

I shrugged off her words, wishing that this whole day was just a dream that I wouldn't have to come back to.

"We can talk about it later," Fynn said, scanning the forest. "It's not safe here. We need to head to the Portal. From there, we will get new mounts and head back to Kellamare. I will send some men back here to look for the bodies."

• • •

It took around forty-five minutes to reach the Portal, and thankfully we didn't run into anymore Nightmares or Mors on the way. Once we reached the Portal, Captain Fynn quickly grabbed a horse for each of us to ride and we set off towards Kellamare. We rode straight to the castle without any interruptions. On the way there, I couldn't stop thinking about the men who died. I also couldn't help thinking about how upset Autumn was going to be. I would understand if she didn't want to talk to me anymore.

When we reached the castle, we took our mounts

straight to the stable.

"You two should go look for Autumn so you can tell her what happened," Fynn said as we headed inside the castle. "I'm going to find the Archduke so I can fill him in. For now, don't leave the castle. I will return shortly."

After Fynn walked away, Juliet said, "Since we're over here, we should check her room first."

"Okay," I muttered, not wanting to face her.

We headed to Wakers' Hall and knocked on her door. To my surprise, she opened the door. She looked like she had been crying. The sadness in her eyes changed to concern when she saw us.

"Is everything okay?" she asked, inviting us in.

"Sort of," Juliet said. "For once, the beach wasn't a great idea."

"What happened?"

Thankfully, Juliet explained everything that happened when we were away, I wouldn't have been able to without breaking down and crying. She was also kind enough to explain how awful I felt about not listening to her and leaving her behind.

"Oh, Chaz," Autumn said. "I'm not mad at you." She held open her arms. I was a little reluctant, but I gave in to a quick hug. "None of this is your fault. If I'd had that confusing vision, I might have thought it meant the same thing. You're a good guy, Chaz."

Her words made me feel a lot better about myself than I did moments ago.

"Thanks, Autumn," I said.

"Remember the promise we made the other night? We promised to stick together. We need to stay true to that from now on."

"You're right," Juliet said. "I was thinking about that the whole way here. No more splitting up."

"I'm actually starting to think," I paused, gathering my thoughts. "Maybe that was what my vision was trying to tell me. We're supposed to stick together no matter what. Nothing good will come from splitting up."

"I'm glad you both understand now," Autumn said with a smile.

"So, how was helping out in the kitchen?" Juliet asked.

"It was actually kind of fun. The people there are so wonderful, and it was so interesting to hear about their lives before they died. Gina started her own restaurant. That's why she's such a good cook."

"That's really awesome."

"Yeah. And a lot of them have kids or grandkids that they worry about. I promised I would check on some of them."

"Be sure to let them know that their dead grandparents sent you," Juliet joked.

"Maybe I will," Autumn replied, mischievously.

It wasn't long before Captain Fynn came looking for us. We were just exiting Autumn's room when he approached the door.

"Would you three like to come over to my parents' house for dinner?" Fynn asked.

"Seriously?" I laughed. "Right now?"

"Yes, seriously. I forgot she told me to invite you earlier today. I can't cancel now after she has most likely already prepared everything."

"That's sweet of her," Autumn said. "We would love to."

"Well then, follow me." As we headed out of the castle, Fynn began rehearsing to us his conversation with the Archduke. "He wants to try to accelerate your training. It has been getting too dangerous for Wakers to be outside the city anymore. The sooner you know how to fight, the better. But until then, you are not to leave unless you are on official business assigned to you by the Archduke himself. And when you do leave the city, each one of you will be assigned four knights to be your escort.

"We can no longer afford to be careless. The Quin Anulus are on the move. Because you are all new, they will come after you. I wouldn't be surprised if sometime in the coming weeks, one of the members of the group comes to you directly and tries to recruit you. We know they have members in each city. They are cunning and discreet as they spy and recruit. Be on your guard."

Fynn's family lived in a large, red brick house in the nice part of the city. It looked similar to all the rest, but it was one of the biggest homes, which made sense once we met his family. He said he had eight siblings, and I have no idea if I even met all of them. There were so many names that the only ones I remembered were his parents, Albor and Cecilia, as well as his sister Gwen, who looked like a model.

The house was chaos. Fynn and Gwen were the oldest, and all the other kids were younger with insane amounts of energy. All they wanted to do was play and fake sword fight. When it was finally time to go, all the kids were sad to see us leave, but I wasn't. I was exhausted and tired of being their jungle gym.

Fynn insisted that he escort us back to the castle and I was okay with that, especially after what happened earlier. Autumn and I fell back a little behind him and Juliet as we talked.

"You know what would be fun?" Autumn asked as we walked through the twilight covered city.

"What?" I asked.

"If you, me, and Juliet got together in the real world sometime and hung out."

"Yeah, that would be fun. We should plan something like that."

"It's just going to be hard explaining to my parents how I know you two." Autumn laughed.

"Hey, Mom and Dad, I'm gonna go to Colorado and hang out with this girl I met in my dreams," I joked. "Don't worry, I know her pretty well. We fight monsters together all the time."

We both laughed, and for a few minutes, I forgot all about my dad's Mors Somnia.

Just for a few minutes.

Chapter 18

Things Are About to Get Real

For the next two weeks, the time I spent in the Dream World was pretty repetitive. Almost every day was the same schedule: meditation, daydream training, physical exercise, and then weapon's training. We trained with all kinds of different weapons, including swords, bows, spears, maces, and crossbows.

Master Grayson wanted us to spend some time getting familiar with each weapon and its fighting style so we could choose which one we liked best. Autumn and I also got as good at Juliet at Master Grayson's little 'future finger' game. It took maybe a week until I really mastered it, and now it only took me a couple of seconds to see which finger he was going to hold up.

Two days after the beach incident, a funeral service was held for Taten and West. Taten's body was recovered, but there was no sign of West, so we assumed the worst. I still felt a deep sense of guilt that lingered through the whole funeral, and I didn't pay much attention to any of the words spoken. The whole time, I just kept telling my-self that it was all my fault. And I felt even worse when I saw Taten's wife and two little girls–girls who were now fatherless. West didn't leave a wife and kids behind, but it was still sad to see his brothers and sisters mourn for him. After the service, I promised myself that I would never let anyone die for me again.

My life in the Waking World was pretty normal besides all the excitement of prom. Every time I hung out with Presley it was pretty much all she wanted to talk about. Sadly, I hadn't made any moves yet to show her that I liked her, but I was still working on it. I was just waiting for the right moment. It was so much easier to make choices when I already knew the outcome. Because I had no idea how she would react, I was too scared to go for it.

I did practice seeing the future in everyday situations at school. Every now and then, I was able to see what someone was going to say before they said it. I started having a lot of fun finishing people's sentences and pretending to be a psychic. I was feeling pretty confident in myself. But that confidence lasted up until the day we were supposed to finally choose our own weapon.

Master Grayson took us to the castle armory, which was a lot larger than any of the other weapon shops in the city. Every wall, nook, and cranny were lined with weapons, many of which I had never seen before. The floor of the large brick room was a maze of tables covered with even more weapons. Juliet, Autumn and I walked around the room admiring the vast selection as Grayson patiently waited at the door for us to choose.

"I already know I'm getting a sword," I said, gazing at the different styles of blades. "I just need to figure out which one."

"I would recommend a saber for you, Chaz," Grayson advised. "Those are the curved ones to your right."

I grabbed a curved sword that was sheathed in a green scabbard. I took it out of the sheath and weighed it in my hand. It felt pretty good.

"How does it feel?" he asked.

"It's not too heavy and not too light," I answered. "But I don't know. Isn't it supposed to feel like an extension of my arm or something?"

Grayson chuckled. "That's what they say in story books I suppose, but that's not really how it works. You have only practiced with wooden swords, so any sword made of steel is going to feel strange at first."

"Oh, well then." I held the sword up and decided I liked it. "I guess I'll go with this one."

"I think I'm going to choose a sword too," Juliet said as she examined swords next to the ones I had examined. "Why are there so many different kinds?"

"Because we have swords from many different eras and countries," Grayson explained. "We probably have the most diverse collection you will ever see."

"What would you recommend for me?"

"There are two that I think would suit you." Grayson made his way over and started showing her some different options. As he and Juliet were occupied, I strapped on my new sword and gazed at myself in a mirror leaning against the wall.

"Looking good Chaz!" Autumn called from across the room. Turning, I saw her in the bow section and headed in her direction, gazing longingly at the crossbows as I passed. Maybe Master Grayson would let me have one of those too. It would be nice to have a secret weapon.

"Are you planning on getting a bow?" I asked.

"I think so," she said, holding a short bow in her hand and examining it. "Do you think that's too wimpy?"

"What do you mean?"

"Do you think I'm being a wimp by choosing a bow? I mean, I know I kind of am, because I would rather fight from a safe distance." She paused and then added, "But that's not the only reason. I also thought it would be a good idea because you will both be close range fighters, so wouldn't it be smart to have someone covering you from a distance?"

"Yeah, it would be smart," I admitted. "As long as you don't accidentally shoot me in the back when you're covering me."

She slapped my arm. "I would never! I'll train super hard so I never miss."

"Sounds good to me. But you better ask Grayson what kind of bow he thinks you should have." I pointed at the bow in her hand. "That little thing probably can't shoot very far."

She laughed. "You're right. I wasn't really thinking

when I picked up this one."

It didn't take long for the three of us to head back to the training grounds with the weapons we had chosen. Juliet ended up choosing a two-handed sword called a claymore, and Autumn had a large longbow that I was sure she would have trouble using.

"Now that you have each chosen a weapon, it is time for the real training to begin," Grayson said as we arrived near the sparring area. "Autumn, because you will be using a bow, you will be training under a different instructor than Chaz and Juliet."

"Will you not be instructing us?" Juliet asked.

"Some of the time, yes. But I won't always be there. From now on you will be sparring."

"I'm sad I won't be training with you guys anymore," Autumn said.

"Me too," I agreed.

"You two wait here while I introduce Autumn to her instructor," Grayson said. He and Autumn walked away, heading to the archery field. Juliet and I watched others sparring as we waited.

"Hey, Juliet. Hey, Chaz."

We both turned to find our friend Devin strolling towards us, his blond hair bouncing with every step. I had met Devin probably a week ago. He was a really friendly guy who had just started training to become a knight. I guess Juliet already knew him pretty well. She told me that Grayson and the other trainers had high hopes for him because he had shown promising reality-bending abilities.

"Are either of you going to finally duel me today?" he asked with a grin, showing his perfectly white teeth.

"I don't know," I said. "It depends on what Master Grayson says."

"Have you started sparring yet?"

"Today is supposed to be our first day," Juliet replied.

Devin winced slightly. "The first few days are the worst. I have never been more sore or bruised in my life. Master Grayson does not take it easy on you."

"Good," Juliet said. "We don't have time for him to take it easy on us. I don't want to have to run away from another Nightmare."

"Yeah," I agreed. "The sooner we can take on some monsters, the better."

"It's still pretty impressive," Devin said. "The way you handled yourself at the beach. I would have panicked."

"Well, I kind of did panic," I admitted.

"You were just playing it smart."

We stood in awkward silence for maybe a minute until Devin asked, "So what's the Waking World like? I've never really talked to anyone about it."

"What do you mean?" I asked. "Were you never . . . alive?"

"I was told I died when I was a baby. I don't remember anything before this."

"I'm sorry,"

"No need to be sorry. I don't remember it happening, so it's no big deal."

"So . . . how does it all work?"

"How does *what* work?" Devin asked.

"Like . . ." I wasn't sure how to phrase my question. "Are people like, born again as babies here? And are their families the same families they have on earth? Do they age? I'm confused."

"Oh." He laughed. "When a Dreamer comes here, they come through the Portal just like Wakers. When they arrive, they are the same age as when the died. So, since I came as a baby, a random couple was assigned to raise me, which makes them my family. And I'm no longer a baby, so yes, people age."

"That makes a lot more sense," I replied.

"Good to know," Juliet added. "I've always wondered that too."

"But what about Garriton's brother?" I asked. "They look so much alike."

"Yeah," Devin said. "They were actually brothers when they were alive. They both passed on at the same time, I'm not sure how though."

"That's kind of sad."

"It is. Sooooo, back to my question. What's the Waking World like?"

"That's a very hard and very broad question," Juliet said. "It's a lot different than this. There's no sword fighting . . . at least not anymore. Kids our age go to school to learn, and adults go to work to make money."

"I already know about that stuff," Devin said. "I want to hear about stuff like aero-planes and television."

"Devin!" We turned our attention to a man who had just finished sparring. "No more distractions."

"Sorry!" Devin yelled back. He turned to us. "I'll talk to you two later. See ya Juliet." He headed in the direction of the man.

"I think he has a thing for you," I said.

"I could have told you that. He makes it very obvious when it's just the two of us."

I laughed as Grayson finally returned.

"It is time for us to get started," he said. He pointed to one of the barrels near the fence. "There's padding in there. Wear as much or as little as you would like."

Juliet and I walked over to the barrel and peered inside. It was half-full of various kinds of body padding.

"What are you gonna wear?" I asked, not wanting to look like a pansy by wearing more padding than her.

"I think I'll just keep my head and chest covered," she replied, picking up a green vest.

"I think I'll do that too." I picked up a blue one and then dug inside until I found a blue padded helmet. I put on the helmet and then tried pulling the vest on over it but ended up getting it stuck. I took everything off and tried putting on my vest first this time.

"Do you need help getting dressed?" Juliet teased as she tightened her green vest.

I just ignored her as I tightened my own vest.

Once we were both outfitted, we followed Grayson into the sparring area. He took two wooden swords from a barrel and handed one to each of us.

"Are we not practicing with our new swords?" I asked, feeling disappointed.

"Of course not," Grayson replied. "That would be very dangerous, and we would dull the weapons. Use your new sword when you practice your exercises. That will help you get used to the weight and feel of it. For now, you can set it aside. It will only get in the way."

Juliet and I unbuckled the swords and rested them against the fence. I couldn't help but gaze at it longingly as it lay there looking shiny and new.

"Howard," Grayson called out, looking over my shoulder. He waved someone over, and I turned around to see a short, stocky man wearing blue padding walking over. As he neared, he pulled off his helmet to reveal his sweaty, short brown hair matted against his head. His chubby face was red from exhaustion as he panted.

"I'm Howard. Nice to meet you," he said quickly as he shook my hand, then Juliet's. We both introduced ourselves to him.

"Howard, will you train with us for the rest of the week?" Grayson asked. "We could use your expertise."

"The only thing I'm an expert at is tiring myself out quickly," He said. "But yes, it would be my pleasure to help train these young Wakers."

"Thank you. Today, Chaz will train with me, Juliet will train with you."

I shared a look with Juliet before Grayson led me away from the other two.

"Today we will start with the basic fundamentals of

swordplay," Grayson explained as he positioned himself so that he was facing me. "All I want you to do is go through the defensive drill you know so well. As long as you don't miss a step or falter, this should go pretty smoothly. Also, it is very important to remember that you should not try to see the future. You're not nearly ready to be practicing two things at once. Understand?"

"Yeah," I replied, feeling a little nervous. Sure, it was all muscle memory now, but what if I messed up? Hopefully, he wouldn't hurt me too much.

"Ready stance."

I held my wooden sword out in front of me and adjusted my body so that I was ready to move.

"Fight."

I did exactly what I had done probably a hundred times before by taking three steps forward and then bringing my sword crosswise in front of me. As I lifted my sword like I was supposed to, I weakly blocked an attack by Grayson. I was so surprised that I had actually blocked his attack, I paused, but Grayson didn't pause, and he whacked me on my hip.

"Ouch!" I exclaimed, rubbing my hip.

"Did you forget the next step?" he asked.

"No, I was just . . ." I trailed off.

"Don't stop. Go through the entire drill and then we can talk. The first block was very weak, try to be more firm. Ready stance."

I got ready again, determined to impress him.

"Fight."

Once again, I performed the exercise that I knew like the back of my hand. I felt really cool as I blocked and dodged without even meaning to. I tried to be more firm, but it just made my arms jar even more whenever our swords would clash. As I went through the exercise, my confidence grew stronger, but my arms grew weaker. When we neared the end, my arms faltered, the sword was knocked out of my grasp, and I got smacked on the arm.

"Why do you have to hit so hard?" I complained as I retrieved my sword.

"You need to learn how to embrace the force of your enemy's attack," Grayson explained with patience. "Your foe will be striking a lot harder than that. We will slowly work up to it. Now, again."

We started the drill again and I actually made it the whole way through without getting whacked. The next time I made it about halfway through before my arms gave out and I got smacked on the thigh.

"Rest for a minute or two, then we will resume," Grayson said.

I stood there rubbing my arm as I glanced in the direction of Juliet and Howard. They were doing the same thing we were, only a lot faster. Juliet was moving through the motions with ease as she blocked Howard's attacks without flinching. Each time they finished going through the exercise, they would immediately start again, going even faster. I felt a warm wave of jealousy hit me as I watched. How was she so much better than me? I was supposed to be the gifted swordsman.

"Let's try again, Chaz" Grayson said, interrupting my thoughts. "We will keep going until you are too tired to continue."

We did our little fight dance once, and then twice before my sword was knocked out of my hand and I was knocked to the ground. I was no longer in a good mood, and watching Juliet was only making it worse.

"Chaz, I can clearly see the envy in your eyes when you glance at Juliet," Grayson said. "You should be happy Juliet has found her gift. You and Autumn found yours early on. You see many visions, Autumn has many premonitions, and Juliet is clearly a gifted swordsman. You should focus on being a better you rather than being better than Juliet. When you're ready, we will go again."

His words didn't help my mood at all. If anything, it made me more determined to be better than her. I felt I *had* to be better, but I didn't know why. I just had to.

We continued training and I made it through the whole drill about four more times before my arms couldn't take anymore and I let Grayson's sword smack me in the ribs.

"That was good, Chaz," he praised. "I do not know if you noticed, but we did speed up with each run through."

"I thought we did, but I wasn't sure," I replied.

"Now it is your turn to try the offensive. This time you will be using the second drill you memorized."

"Oh!" I said, realizing he was doing the offensive exercise the whole time. I had no idea they went together like that. It was really cool how it worked. "That's why your movements were so familiar when we first started."

"Correct. Those two exercises will help you master the basics. Once you master using those against an opponent, then we can move on to freestyle sparring."

Freestyle sparring. I liked the sound of that. I started imagining myself busting out some sweet breakdance moves as I blocked Grayson's sword, and did flips over him as I attacked. I *had* to be good at something with a cool name like that.

"Chaz, are you still with me?"

"Sorry," I apologized, getting in my ready stance. "Let's do it."

"Fight."

I effortlessly went through the offensive exercise I knew so well, and it felt so good being the one doing the attacking. It might have been because I didn't hit as hard as Grayson, so when our swords connected, it didn't hurt my arms as much. It also felt good because I was the one in control. I got to choose how fast we went and when we stopped.

We went through the exercise maybe five times when my arms started getting really tired, and I was starting to get annoyed by Grayson effortlessly blocking my attacks. Eventually, I decided I was going to surprise him by attacking in a way that wasn't part of the exercise. I was sure he wouldn't see it coming. I attempted a surprise hit to his calf, but he knocked the sword out of my hand and whacked me on the head. Hard. I saw stars for a second.

"I would advise you not to try that again, Chaz,"

Grayson said calmly. "For the last hour I want you to practice those exercises with your new sword. Practice alternating between the two. We will be doing that tomorrow. I will give Juliet the same instructions. See you tomorrow." He headed over to Juliet and Howard and talked with them for a minute before he and Howard walked away together. Juliet looked my way and headed over.

"How did it go?" she asked, sweat dripping down her forehead.

"Really good," I lied. "You?"

"It was good. Howard is a really good teacher."

"Well, let's get this last hour over with."

Juliet picked up her huge sword. "I don't think I can swing this thing around for an hour."

"Me either," I said before I picked up my smaller sword and began moving through the defensive drill. It was a lot more awkward and tiring doing it with a real sword. I was happy to see that Juliet was struggling a little bit too.

It was just about an hour later when Autumn met up with us. We decided it was a good time to be done with training for the day.

"How are your bow skills?" I asked as we left the training grounds.

"I think towards the end, I got pretty close to the target," Autumn replied with an embarrassed smile. "But I made improvement, so I guess that's good."

"You got this, girl," Juliet encouraged.

"Yeah, I hope so. I don't want to have to be afraid when I face a Nightmare for the first time."

"I don't know if I'll ever stop being afraid," I said honestly.

• • •

Later that evening, Autumn and I were hanging out right outside her bedroom door. Juliet had already gone to bed, but neither of us were tired. We sat on the floor with our legs folded, my left knee touching her right.

"Isn't prom this weekend?" Autumn asked.

"Yeah," I answered.

"Are you excited?"

"Yeah, I'm really excited. We've got some fun plans for the whole day."

"Are you excited to spend lots of time with Presley?" she asked, a curious tone in her voice.

"Yup, she's really cool. It's always fun to hang out with her."

"Do you still have a big crush on her?"

It was an awkward question coming from her and I didn't feel like talking about it.

"You could say that." I stood up. "It's late, our alarms will probably be going off anytime now."

"Okay," she said with a small smile as she stood up too. She wrapped her arms around me, and we quickly hugged. When I let her go, her right hand slid down my arm and caught hold of the bracelet I was wearing. It fell off and landed on the ground, and only then did I realize that I had been wearing it ever since Presley gave it to me. After a few days, I got so used to wearing it that I no longer noticed. I was also surprised that it came with me to the Dream World.

"Oh, I'm sorry!" Autumn apologized. She picked it up and handed it to me. I examined it closely, noticing how dirty and worn it now looked after only a few weeks. "I've been meaning to ask you where you got it from. It must be special since you wear it every day."

"Kind of," I said, pocketing it. "It was a birthday present from a friend. Goodnight, Autumn." I smiled at her before turning around and heading to my room.

"Goodnight, Chaz."

Chapter 19

I Was Hoping They Wouldn't Come Back

I arrived at school expecting it to be another normal day, but just a simple walk through the halls led me to believe otherwise. The whole school was buzzing with talk about Trevor, Jace and Ben coming back. I couldn't believe it had already been three weeks. I had been dreading this day ever since they first got suspended. Jace and Trevor were for sure going to do something stupid to get back at Ben.

"Hey, Chaz," Presley greeted as I joined her on the way to class.

"Hey, how are you?"

"I'm good. I'm way excited for this weekend."

"Me too. Can you believe Jace and Trevor are back? That went by fast."

"Way too fast. I kind of liked not having them around. I hope they don't try to do anything to Ben."

"Oh, I know they will." We entered the classroom and

headed to our seats. "We'll talk about it later."

She nodded in response.

Once class started, I couldn't stop wondering about what crazy thing Jace and Trevor might do to get back at Ben. Maybe they would just go old-school and give him a mega wedgie or a swirly. Wouldn't that be nice? My mind began to wander as I sorted through the possibilities.

I suddenly found myself standing in a random crowded hall of the high school. Students moved past me in all directions. Most dodged me, but some bumped into me. I looked around and found Jace and Trevor walking in my direction. I noticed the cast on Trevor's arm as he pulled a backpack off of his shoulder. Jace began unlocking a padlock on a locker that I assumed was his. They talked softly to each other as they hunched together. Once Jace unlocked the locker, they squeezed the backpack inside and locked it shut.

The scene quickly changed, and I was once again in the same hall facing the same locker, only this time there were no students around. The hall was empty, and I heard loud dance music coming from somewhere nearby. Once again, I saw Trevor and Jace heading in my direction, only this time, they were both wearing suit pants and button up shirts with colorful ties. It had to be prom night.

"Did you text Jason?" Trevor asked as they neared the locker.

"Yeah!" Jace squealed as he began working the lock again. "He texted me the combination." Once the locker was open, Trevor pulled out the same backpack I had just

seen them stuff in there.

"Let's do this quick," Trevor said as Jace shut the locker.

Trevor started jogging down the hall with Jace following. I jogged after them, curious about what they were up to.

"It's number 312," Jace said as they stopped in front of some more lockers. Once they found locker 312, Jace read numbers off of his phone before he started working the lock. It must have been the combination.

"That geek freak is going to get in trouble for sure," Trevor said, unzipping the backpack.

It took Jace two tries before he got the combination right. He opened the locker and both of them quickly looked down the hall in both directions. Once they saw that the coast was clear, Trevor pulled out what looked like an airsoft gun. I shook my head in disappointment as I realized what they were doing. They were trying to get Ben in trouble by putting a weapon in his locker. It was more of a toy, but he would still get in trouble for it. And it could actually shoot little bb's.

My vision blurred and I was suddenly back in class sitting at my desk. It sure was nice of my vision to show me exactly what they were going to do. Why didn't it show me something like that with the beach incident? What an annoying gift. Now that I knew what they were up to, I could stop them. But how? I could confront them about it. They would definitely be freaked out if they knew I found out. Or maybe it would be better to catch them in the act.

Isaac and I met up with Jake and Presley in the cafeteria. We all grabbed our food and found a table outside where it was less noisy.

"What's new with you guys?" Isaac asked after we sat down.

"I just got my new tux for prom," Jake replied. "I can't wait for you guys to see it. Got it tailored and everything."

"You actually bought a tux for prom?" Presley asked.

"Yeah. Why not? It'll be nice to have for the next formal event I attend."

"Like next year's prom and then your funeral?" Jake and Isaac both chuckled. Presley glanced at me, probably noticing how quiet I was. "You okay, Chaz? You look stressed."

"I need to talk to you guys about something," I said, pausing. "I overheard Jace and Trevor talking in the hall today about how they were going to get back at Ben."

"No way!" Isaac said. "What did they say?"

"On prom night, they're going to sneak an airsoft gun into his locker and tattle on him."

"Really? They're going to frame him?" Jake said, shaking his head. "Those guys are unbelievable."

"That's good that you overheard them," Presley said. "What should we do about it?"

"That's what I was going to ask you guys," I said. "We could confront them now or catch them in the act on prom."

"I want to dance that night, not babysit those two,"

Isaac complained.

"I feel like it would be better to catch them in the act so we have proof," I said. "Plus, I know they plan on doing it before the school gets too crowded. We just have to get there early and watch Ben's locker."

"We can do that," Presley said. "Chaz and I will watch them and you two can enjoy the dance."

"Sounds like a plan," Jake said.

For the rest of the school day, I kept my eyes peeled, but I didn't ever catch a glimpse of Ben. I wanted to talk to him and try to be his friend, but that would be impossible if I couldn't find him. Hopefully, he didn't drop out or move to a different school. On second thought, maybe that would actually be a good thing.

That evening after dinner, on my way to the bathroom, I stopped in my tracks when I heard my parents talking in the kitchen. It was hard to hear what they were saying, but I was pretty sure it wasn't a positive conversation. I crept towards the kitchen as silently as I could and stood right by the doorway, out of sight.

"I don't know what you want from me," Dad's voice whined. "I'm doing my best. I go to work every day for you and the kids. What else can I do?"

"Honey, I'm sorry," Mom said in her soft voice. "I don't mean to make you feel bad. I know you work very hard for us, but I also know there's better work than this. You used to have so many plans to do great things. You sure you really don't even want to try anymore? I will do everything I can to help you make it happen."

"It can't happen. It won't happen. I'm not the kind of person who can accomplish great things. I don't have what it takes."

I quickly crept back toward my room and shut the door behind me. My poor dad. He had no confidence in himself, and I knew why. I also knew how to help him, but I couldn't yet. I wasn't strong enough. I felt frustrated as I thought about that, and everything else that was going on. I really needed to talk to someone about it.

It took me a few minutes, but I eventually convinced myself to call Autumn.

Chapter 20

My First Mission

The next few days of training, I improved a little, but it wasn't much compared to Juliet. It was quickly becoming obvious that I would probably never be on her level–she really was a natural. I was still practicing the basics, but at least I was getting pretty good at it. I could go through the exercises for almost an hour straight without messing up. Master Grayson had said that in another week, we could start on freestyle sparring.

During a late breakfast on Friday afternoon, Grayson told us that Archduke Bradford wanted us to join him in an important meeting. We quickly finished our food and rushed over. When we entered the meeting room, everyone was already seated at the table. There was Archduke Bradford, Constable Darvin, Chancellor Kaden, Master Grayson, and Captain Fynn.

Bradford smiled and gestured for us to sit. "Go ahead and have a seat, we need to get things going." After we sat, he pointed to one of the five cities on the map. "What have you learned about the city of Calverstone over these past few weeks?"

"It's pretty much where everything happens," Juliet answered. "It's the most populated and eventful place in the country."

"Very good, Lady Juliet. You are correct. And in case you didn't know, one of the reasons Calverstone is so popular is because it's a trade city. And it's not just great for trading materials and supplies, but also for gossip and rumors. Knowledge is a valuable currency there. The nobles will pay a high price to learn things that no one else knows. Interesting enough, Calverstone also sets the trends for the rest of the country. Whatever people start doing or wearing in that city, the others will follow.

"Now, to explain the problem at hand, it seems the Quin Anulus have finally decided to take advantage of the influence Calverstone has over the rest of the country. I have been informed that they have been very active of late, spreading their propaganda about neutrality and co-existence all throughout the city. Mostly, it has been the work of their followers, but there have been reports of a few identified members of the Quin Anulus seen openly roaming the city during the day.

"You should know that it is very unlike them to reveal themselves during the day. It is even more unlike them to place so many members in one location. They must have figured out that if they can convince Calverston to agree with their plan, then they will have already convinced the rest of the country."

The Archduke paused. "Do you now understand the predicament we are in? We've waited too long to interfere with Ausidor, and now it might be too late. But if we act fast, we can prevent the same thing from happening in Calverstone."

"What about the Duke of Calverstone?" I asked. "Is he the kind of man who would listen to their crazy ideas?"

"Duke Alvered isn't much of a thinker," Chancellor Kaden answered, looking as annoyed as ever. "If a convincing man like Duke Brighton was to explain to Alvered how neutrality is the way to end the war and suffering, then he would probably be all for it. And it's not because he's an idiot. It's because he doesn't take time to think things through and look at both sides of the spectrum. He will do anything to keep his people safe, and because of that, they love him."

"Kaden is very good friends with Duke Alvered," Bradford explained. "Which is why he is leaving for the city today. I would like you three to join him."

"Us?" Juliet said, her tone incredulous. "What are we going to be able to do to help?"

"Quite a lot actually. We have told you many times that Wakers have always had a strong voice in politics. Well, this will be your chance to use that voice. Kaden will host a mandatory conference in the name of the Archduke. At this conference, which will be attended by hundreds of thousands, he will speak on behalf of the city of Kellamare and let them know where we stand when it comes to the idea of neutrality. I would like each of you to speak at the conference as well."

I glanced at Autumn and Juliet, noticing that they looked as horrified as I did. Having three inexperienced teens speak at an important conference with other government officials had to be a bad idea. I would probably start a war without meaning to.

"You are the newest Wakers in the land," Darven said. "You would represent hope. Because of who you are, they look to you for guidance. They will take you more seriously than someone like me, Grayson, or Captain Fynn. Sadly, I don't know if we will be able to persuade them without you. I know it sounds like a lot of responsibility, but that's what is expected of you as a Waker and a Dreamchaser."

I shared a look with Juliet and Autumn.

"I'll go," Juliet said.

"If she's going, then I'm going," I added.

"Me too," Autumn said. "I feel good about it."

"Wonderful!" Bradford said, clapping his hands together. "As always, we are grateful for all you do."

"But what happens if we can't convince Duke Alvered?" I asked. "Could you just fire him?"

"It's almost the same exact situation with Duke Brighton. I wish it was that simple, but it isn't. I cannot remove him from his office without fear of the people revolting, and possibly removing me from mine. It would be especially easy because they would have Ausidor on their side. I am as helpless as a puppet. The people rule this land."

"Which is exactly what Oran Kellamare wanted." Darven added.

"Yes, it is. Anyway, back to the topic of your trip."

Bradford looked to Fynn

"To ensure your safety, you will be escorted by fourteen knights," Fynn explained. "As soon as you are packed and ready to go, head to the southwest city entrance. There you will find your party and a horse for each of you. You will most likely be spending two nights in Calverstone, so plan accordingly. Stick together and don't travel at night. Stay on the main road and you shouldn't have any trouble. But if you do end up running into trouble on the way, let the knights handle it. They will keep you safe. Any questions?"

We all shook our heads.

"Our meeting is now adjourned," the Archduke said, standing up.

● ● ●

"All ready to go?" I asked Autumn as she walked out of her room. Juliet and I had been standing outside her door waiting for her to finish packing.

"Yup," she answered, shouldering her pack. She had a quiver full of arrows on her back and her bow in her hand. I looked over at Juliet and saw her sheathed sword strapped to her back. I adjusted my sword on my hip and slung my pack over my shoulder.

"How are you two feeling about this?" I asked.

"I'm excited to finally get out of here," Juliet replied. "Hopefully there's more to do in Calverstone."

"I'm actually kind of scared," Autumn said.

"Why are you scared?" I asked.

"Because there's a good chance we'll run into trouble on the way. I've never even seen a Nightmare yet, unlike you two."

"We'll be okay," Juliet assured her. "The knights will keep us safe."

"Yeah I know. I need to stop worrying."

"Let's get going," I said impatiently.

We left the castle and followed the main road straight to the entrance of the city. People cheered and thanked us as we passed. For once, I didn't like it. It made me feel like a soldier about to go to war. Who knew if we would make it back? What a scary thought.

Once we stepped outside the gates of the city, we found our party waiting, just like Fynn had said. Kaden sat astride a beautiful brown horse, dressed in light armor with short sword hanging on his side and a cool war hammer strapped to his back. He looked pretty intimidating. Most of the knights sat astride their own horses as well, patiently waiting to go. A few wore helmets, so I wasn't sure who they were, but when I noticed Garriton and Charley among the men, I grinned excitedly. This was going to be a fun ride.

When Kaden noticed us approach, he whistled, and two knights walked three saddled horses over to us.

"Pick your horse and mount up," Kaden commanded.

"We need to get on the road quickly and pray that we don't get stuck in the storm."

I examined the weather as Juliet and Autumn chose their mounts. The sky was covered in dark clouds to the south, which was the direction we were heading. Where we were standing, there was a good amount of clouds that veiled the sun every few minutes, but it wasn't nearly as bad as what we were heading into. The day was pretty warm besides the sporadic chilly wind that would blow past every now and then.

Juliet and Autumn both chose the two black horses which left me with the larger brown one. It had been a couple weeks since I'd last ridden a horse and I still found it a struggle mounting them. Once I got myself situated in the saddle, Kaden turned to face everyone.

"If we keep a steady pace, it should take around five hours to reach Calverstone. No matter what happens, stay with the group. If you see any Nightmares, don't worry about it unless they are following us, or we are headed straight toward them. My guess is, we won't run into any trouble unless we get caught in the storm. Any questions?" When no one spoke he nodded and said, "Good. No one do anything stupid and we'll be fine."

"Actually, I have a question," Charley spoke up. "Can you define *stupid* so I can make sure that I don't do it?" Garriton punched his brother in the arm before they both grinned.

Kaden didn't respond. He took the lead of the company and we set off on the road toward the south. The wind chilled my exposed skin as the horses trotted at a steady pace. I tried to get comfortable in my saddle, but it was no use. It was going to be a long and uncomfortable trip. I was hoping the sun would come out from behind the clouds and warm me up, but the longer we rode, the more doubtful I was that it would happen.

I rode next to Autumn and tried to talk with her, but she seemed distant, and worry lines constantly creased her brow.

"You doing okay?" I asked. "You look worried."

"I don't know what it is," she said, finally looking at me. "Before we left, I had a good feeling about this trip, but ever since we started riding, I feel a lot different."

"Different how?"

"Uneasy. On edge. Like maybe this isn't a good idea after all."

"Is it because there's a good chance we might run into Nightmares?"

"I don't know. Maybe. It's all I can think about."

"Well, let me know if the feeling gets worse. If it does, I'll tell Kaden."

"Okay." She turned her attention back to the road ahead.

Since I couldn't have a conversation with her, I tried to enjoy the scenery, but there wasn't much to look at. We were surrounded by miles and miles of tall green grass in every direction. The large fields were definitely beautiful, but it got boring pretty quickly. You would think that a place called the Dream World would be a lot less generic.

So far, there was nothing dreamy about the place.

We rode for probably an hour before we could make out the approaching city of Beckstead. From what I understood, there was a road through the city and a road around, and we were taking the one around because it was faster. As we got closer to Beckstead, the scenery slowly changed from beautiful grassy fields to ugly marshy land covered in weeds and bushes. We took a quick break, letting the horses drink and rest for a few minutes before we resumed our trip.

As we got closer to the city, the trees grew wider and most were covered with moss. Eventually, we came to a fork in the road; the left led straight to the gates of the city which was still maybe a mile away while the right went around. We took the right and continued on our way.

We went for maybe another mile before we reached a wooden bridge that stretched across a massive river. Kaden decided it would be as good a spot as any to take a break. I took advantage of the break and quickly lowered myself off of my horse to stretch. It felt so good to be on my own two feet. I walked over to check on Autumn and Juliet as they dismounted.

"You two doing alright?" I asked, stretching my arms.

"I should be asking you that question," Juliet said. "I'm surprised you haven't fallen off yet."

"I'm not *that* bad at horseback riding." I looked to Autumn. "What about you? You doing okay?"

"I guess so," she said. "The feeling hasn't gotten any worse, so that's probably a good sign. I still feel like we're in danger though."

"We should let Kaden know," Juliet said. "I'll go tell him."

As Juliet walked away, Garriton and Charley came over.

"I hope you two brought something warmer than what you're wearing," Garriton said. "It's about to get even colder. I would suggest you put on another layer while you still have the chance."

"Good idea," I agreed.

"I didn't bring anything warm," Autumn said.

"You can use my coat, Lady Autumn," Garriton replied.

"Oh no, I don't want to take yours."

"Don't worry about him," Charley said. "His hot head is all he needs to stay warm."

"He might be right," Garriton chuckled. "I don't get cold easy. I'll be right back."

After Garriton walked away, Autumn said, "He's so kind."

"That he is," Charley agreed, nodding. "He would do anything for anyone."

I took the opportunity to go put on something warmer too. I walked away and pulled a thick coat out of one of the saddlebags hanging on my horse. I had purposely picked out the thickest one I could find, just to be safe. I put it on and instantly felt warmer. It would probably get a little too toasty inside, but I didn't care. I would rather be hot than cold.

"Someone's prepared for the ice age," A hoarse voice said behind me.

I turned around to find an older man staring at me as he leaned against his mount. He had long black hair and a thick mustache.

"The name is Guy," he said. He walked over with his hand outstretched.

"I'm Chaz." As I shook his hand, I noticed a few scars on his face and tried not to stare.

"What is your age, Lord Chaz?" he asked.

"Sixteen. Why?"

"You are one brave sixteen-year-old."

"Why do you say that?"

"Well, first of all, you joined the Dreamchasers. That, in and of itself, is a very brave act." He nodded to me respectfully. "And second, you're planning on speaking in front of thousands of people on a subject you probably know little about. I would rather face ten Nightmares unarmed than public speaking."

"Seriously?" I asked, doubtful.

"Seriously."

"It's about time to get moving," Kaden's voice spoke. I turned to see him approaching the group. "We've made good time, but it looks like we're about to get hit with the storm. We haven't even glimpsed a Nightmare, but that doesn't mean they're not out there. Watch the trees. If you see anything, let me know. They're more likely to attack in the storm."

Everyone began climbing onto their horses, so I did

the same. When I was ready to go, Guy trotted over on his own horse and pulled up beside me.

"I'll watch out for you and your friends," he said.

"Oh, thanks," I said, surprised. "But, why?"

"You're all Wakers. I owe it to you. And for some reason, I just feel like I should."

He gave me another nod before turning away.

Once everyone was mounted and ready to go, Kaden led the way across the bridge. The old wooden bridge was barely wide enough for two horses to ride side by side. As I crossed, I stared at the rushing water below while the bridge creaked and groaned underfoot. The white rapids moved so quickly that I knew if fell in, there would be no way to get out.

We continued on the road for another mile or so when the trees began to thin out. And of course, once the trees thinned out, it started raining. It was light at first, but the darker clouds quickly moved above us and let go of every ounce of water they had. Lightning flashed across the sky every now and then, followed by the boom of thunder. It didn't take long until all of us were completely soaked. I felt a little on edge because Kaden had said that the Nightmares would most likely attack in the storm.

Not until the light fog descended upon us did I really begin to worry. I could see maybe twenty feet in every direction. Who knew what was beyond that? There could easily have been Nightmares creeping up on us as we went. Thankfully, even though the weather was bad, we didn't slow too much. We went for probably another hour before stopping to rest the horses. By then, my worries had mostly faded. We hadn't been attacked yet and no one had even glimpsed a Nightmare.

I dismounted and fed my horse an apple from one of my saddlebags.

"That's a good boy," I said as I stroked his neck. "I forgot to find out what your name is."

Right after I said it, my horse, as well as the others whinnied in fright. Some reared up on their hind legs while most stamped around restlessly. And just like that, the scene turned into chaos. Many of the knights shouted in confusion as most of the horses bolted. I tried to soothe my own horse from a safe distance as he stamped around wildly, but after a minute, he decided to bolt with the rest.

"Don't fret about the horses!" Kaden yelled above the noise. "We all know what this means."

Those who were wrestling with the horses stopped their struggle, letting the few that remained take off as well. Everything quickly became quiet, besides the sounds of the storm. Every head turned their attention to Kaden. The worry on his face was obvious.

"The Nightmares are coming."

Chapter 21

It's Raining Black Frogs of Death

To me!" Kaden commanded. "Form a defensive circle around the kids!"

As the knights pulled out their weapons and formed a circle around us, I was somewhat insulted that Kaden referred to us as kids. I was sixteen years old! And I wasn't helpless. I could probably take out a Nightmare or two. I mean, how hard could it be?

The knights stood ready with their weapons drawn as they stared out into the fog. I turned to Autumn and the scared look on her face sent waves of courage through me. I suddenly felt a strong desire to protect her. As I contemplated pulling out my sword, Juliet unsheathed her own. Motivated by Juliet's determination, I unsheathed mine as well and stood ready. Probably not wanting to be the odd one out, Autumn pulled her bow off her back. Her hands shook as she nocked an arrow.

"There's no need for you to use those," Kaden said, noticing our drawn weapons. "Let us handle this. You'll only get in the way."

His words only made me more determined to use my sword. I was going to prove him so wrong. There was no way I was just going to stand there while others put their lives on the line for me. I was going to do everything I could to make sure my friends didn't get hurt. I gripped my sword tightly with both hands as I readied myself. If I came face to face with a Nightmare, I wouldn't hesitate, I would slay it.

The lightning and thunder had stopped, but the rain continued to pour upon us, limiting our visibility along with the fog. We waited impatiently for a few minutes, but still there were no other sights or sounds that stood out above the rest. I gazed around for a few minutes before they were suddenly there.

In every direction, round silhouettes started appearing as they leapt towards us. There had to be at least two dozen of them. The fear slowly crept up my throat as my hands shakily held my sword in front of me. It didn't take long for the sounds of their grunting and leaping to rise above the noise of the rain. It made a pretty good soundtrack to the horror movie I was living in.

I stared into the black empty eyes of one of the closest Nightmares to our group. It was as big as me, and it had claws that were at least a foot long raking the air as it leapt. The closer it got, the more restless it became. Its black tongue flicked around wildly, like it tasted something really good in the air.

"Don't break formation!" Kaden commanded above

all the clamor. "We can win if we watch each other's backs!"

As the first wave of Nightmares neared, Garriton shouted, "For Kellamare!" He swung his sword at an airborne Nightmare, cutting it clean in half before it could reach him with its claws. When the two halves of the Nightmare hit the ground, they slowly dissolved.

"For Kellamare!" all the other knights shouted in unison as the first wave of monsters hit us.

All I could do was watch in awe as the knights kept their tight formation while the creatures came at them from every direction. A knight in front of me hacked off a Nightmare's arm when it tried to scratch him with its claws. Before the creature could retaliate with its other claws, the knight hacked that arm off as well.

To my surprise, the armless Nightmare shot out its black tongue, which was a lot longer than it seemed, and wrapped it around the knight's body, pinning his arms in place. As the Nightmare crouched to spring at him, a knight next to him severed its tongue with a quick flash of his blade. The Nightmare screeched right before it was impaled with a sword, making it dissolve into dust.

I was pretty impressed as I watched Kaden mow down Nightmare after Nightmare with his mad hammer skills. He smashed one flat, making it pop before he quickly spun around and smacked another one, sending it flying into the trees. Another small Nightmare shot its tongue out and wrapped it around his ankle. Kaden used his other foot to kick the Nightmare up into the air and then swung his hammer like a baseball bat and sent it flying further than the last one.

As I glanced around the circle, I noticed some of the men were not faring as well. I watched in fear as Charley tried to fend off two Nightmares at once. While he was preoccupied with one, the other jumped at him and sunk its teeth into his leg. He screamed in pain and dropped his sword. Weaponless he began punching at the Nightmare munching on his leg, but it was no use. It wouldn't let go.

Before the other Nightmare he was fending off could get to him as well, Garriton threw a tomahawk at it. The weapon sunk deep into the Nightmares face before the creature dissolved. He quickly used his sword to dispose of the one munching on Charley's leg.

The men were doing pretty well considering how out-numbered they were, but there were many of them who were injured, most of whom I doubted would be standing much longer. I wanted to help, but I wasn't sure how.

"We need to do something!" Juliet said, voicing my thoughts.

"Like what?" I asked.

I turned my attention to her as she scanned the battle-field. Before I could ask if she had any ideas, she sprinted away. I watched in surprise as she ran straight into the battle and thrust her sword through a Nightmare that had a knight pinned to the ground as it chewed on his helmet. She made it look so easy. After the creature turned to dust, the knight sat up and threw off his disfigured helmet, re-vealing blond haired Devin.

"Thanks," he said, standing up and wiping a trickle of blood from his eye. Compared to the damage his helmet received, he looked to be in pretty good condition.

"Don't mention it," Juliet said before she moved on to help a knight fending off two Nightmares.

I wasn't sure what Devin was doing there, but I didn't worry about it for long. Invigorated by Juliet's courage, I turned to Autumn. "I'm going to help too."

She looked at me sadly and replied, "I want to help, I just . . . I'm not as brave as you two."

"You are brave, Autumn. You're brave for coming with us. You can do this. You've been training so hard."

"But– but what if I miss? What if I hit one of the knights or something?"

Even though it was raining, I could see tears spilling from her eyes.

"Only take the easy shots. You got this."

I turned from her and scanned the battlegrounds. There was a knight tugging at the tongue of a Nightmare. It was wrapped around his sword arm. He could definitely use some help. I held my sword in front of me and charged. When I came near, the Nightmare rushed at me, causing me to panic and close my eyes as I pointed my sword toward it. I felt the Nightmare impale itself on my sword, and I opened my eyes just as it dissolved.

"Nice one," the knight said.

I actually killed one. I mean, it was an accident, but still. Maybe I wasn't useless after all. And I was a Waker. I had superpowers that could help me slay these things. It was probably time I started using it. I took a deep breath and tried to focus. Instead of searching the battlefield for the next knight that needed help, I searched the future for the next Nightmare I would slay. Surprisingly, it only took a few seconds before I saw it happen, then I knew exactly what to do.

A Nightmare hopped right over one of the knights nearest to me and lashed at me with its tongue. Just like I had seen in my vision, I let the tongue wrap around my leg before I severed it with my sword. Then I quickly brought my sword down and cut the monster right in half. I was surprised at how natural the ability to do exactly what I saw myself do in the future was.

Another Nightmare jumped up high, heading straight toward my head. I sidestepped it and cut it in half as it sailed past. I turned to my right just in time to see another Nightmare leaping at me. As it landed about two feet away, an arrow lodged itself into one of its eyes, making it flail around before dissolving into dust. I searched for where the arrow came from and found Autumn gazing at me as she pulled another one from behind her back.

"You have an amazing aim!" I praised.

"I'm just taking the easy shots," she said before she fired another arrow at an approaching Nightmare, hitting it under the mouth.

Chaaaaaazzz.

The voice penetrated the noise of the battlefield and I was convinced it was in my head. I looked around, search- ing for someone who might have called my name, but the only person I saw looking at me was Autumn.

"Did you hear that?" I asked.

"I did." She nocked another arrow and held it ready.

Chaaaazzz. It's time.

The hair on the back of my neck stood up when I finally recognized the voice. I searched the fog beyond the battle until I saw a silhouette of a man, only I knew it wasn't a man. It was my dad's Mors Somnia. It had to be. He was back for me.

"Don't do it," Autumn's voice pleaded from behind. "It's too dangerous."

Chaz, you're the only one who can stop me. It's your destiny. Do it now or I will hurt everyone you love, starting with Autumn. Come to me.

"Chaz, it's a trap," Autumn said. "Please don't do it."

"No one else is going to get hurt protecting me," I said. Before I let her say anything else, I charged towards the Mors as fast as I could. After killing a few Nightmares, I was a little more confident in myself, but I was still a little worried that I was running to my death.

"Chaz!" Autumn screamed desperately.

"Chaz, no!" Another voice yelled.

I knew I should have listened, but I didn't. I kept running. I dodged knights and Nightmares, maneuvering past all of the fighting. I continued running until I was about ten feet away from the Mors. I was just close enough to see the dark version of my dad's face smiling at me. Somehow, he had both of his hands back, and he was holding the same black blade as before.

"You know what to do, Chaz," The Mors said. "Show them you're not helpless. Show them you're not weak. Use your power and end me. Do it for your father."

I tried to summon the anger I had felt for the creature before, but it wasn't there. Instead, I felt fear and doubt, just like I did the last time I was in its presence. I couldn't let it overcome me this time. I needed to fight. Sure, I wasn't very good with a sword yet, but I could see the future. It helped me kill a couple Nightmares, and now it was going to help me kill him.

I began searching the future for a way to hurt or destroy my father's Mors, but all I could see was it hurting me. It started walking toward me with his evil fatherly grin, and I began to search more frantically for any possible way that I might win. My fear began to grow as I saw that each outcome ended with me on the ground crying in pain as I clutched a wound to my stomach, or a wound to my thigh. There was even one where I lost my hand.

I began to back away as I realized that there was no way for me to win. I was a little surprised that I saw no outcome where the Mors killed me. Maybe he wanted me to suffer, or maybe I just simply couldn't see what happened because I was dead. Either way, I was going to get hurt.

As the negative emotions started to overwhelm me, I remembered something the Seer had told me. *It doesn't matter what you see in the future, it is still unwritten and uncertain, you can change it.*

It was a nice thought, but I had no idea how I was going to change this moment so that I didn't lose. There was no way I could best him in a sword fight. But maybe I could talk my way out of it, or at least stall him.

"How do you know so much about me?" I asked.

"I know what Robert knows," the Mors answered, still moving closer to me. Hearing him say my dad's name was a little funny, even in such a scary situation.

"But how do you always know where I'm going to be? How do you know who I care about?"

"Me." the Mors hissed. I was about to ask him what that was supposed to mean, but then he continued. "The Mors Somnia. The Somnum Exterreri. The Quin Anulus. Others."

"The somnum ex-what?"

"The Nightmares."

I was out of ideas and just about out of time, he was close enough that I was sure he would attack at any moment. My only option left was to stand my ground and fight. My body began to tense up with fear as the Mors raised its blade, ready to strike me down.

As quick as lightning, an arrow streaked right past my head and the Mors blocked it with the flat of his blade with a flick of his wrist. I turned to find Autumn advancing towards us, her hands still shaking as she nocked another arrow. She released another one straight towards the Mors, but this time he didn't even have to block it, it missed him by at least a foot.

It was nice of her to come save me, but I wished that

she didn't. Now we would both die.

"It's okay, Autumn," I said. "I can handle this. Please go back."

I raised my sword, ready to attack, but hesitated as the Mors stared at Autumn with an evil grin that I hoped to never see on Dad's face again.

"Autumn, run!" I screamed, taking a step toward the creature.

She didn't listen. She continued to shoot arrows at him, missing most, while the others got blocked.

"I won't leave you, Chaz," she said as she released her last arrow.

Not too far in the distance, I could see the silhouette of a man behind Autumn running toward us. Whoever it was, they probably wouldn't get here in time to save us. I turned my attention back to the Mors, who still had the evil grin on his face. He looked at me and winked as he raised his blade like he was about to throw it in Autumn's direction.

"No!" I shouted, rushing towards him right as he chucked the blade.

Everything seemed to happen in slow motion as I watched the black blade sail end over end right at Autumn. The figure running to us was close enough that I recognized it was Guy, but he wasn't nearly close enough to save Autumn. Then, quicker than I could blink, Guy was suddenly there, diving at her. I have no idea how, but he managed to push Autumn out of the way as the sword lodged itself deep into his calf.

Grunting, he staggered to his feet and pulled out a short sword. What happened next was like something I would only expect to see in a super cool action movie; he grabbed the sword's handle with both hands and yanked it apart, revealing that it was two swords disguised as one. My heart leaped with excitement and thrill at the sight.

"Stay back!" Guy commanded.

Before I could back away, the Mors slapped the sword out of my hand and kicked me hard in the stomach, sending me summer-salting backward. I landed hard on my back, panicking as I struggled to breathe. Autumn ran to me as I slowly and painfully sat up. It didn't feel like anything was broken, just badly bruised. Once she reached me, she knelt down next to me, threw her arms around me, and closed her eyes.

I watched as the Mors, now with my sword in hand, quickly closed the distance between himself and Guy. He struck downward, aiming a blow at Guy's chest. Guy blocked the swing with the sword in his right hand, while swinging at the Mors' midsection with the left. The Mors dodged the swing deftly by jumping back a few feet. Then he streaked toward Guy in a blur of movement.

Because of his leg wound, Guy struggled to stay on two feet as the Mors relentlessly attacked him. Somehow the Mors was able to block and dodge two swords at the same time while slipping in a couple attacks of his own. He was too fast.

The relentless clinking of sword against sword went on for an intense few minutes. The Mors hopped around like a ninja as it continued to dodge and search for openings in Guy's defense. Guy shuffled his feet a lot, but he mostly stayed in one spot as he rained blows down upon his opponent.

Though Guy was doing well against a foe with inhuman speed, I was worried. I could tell that he couldn't see all of the attacks before they happened like Fynn could when he fought this same Mors. He was at a disadvantage and he was barely able to keep up. His leg was bleeding profusely, and he wore a constant expression of pain on his face. He was definitely slowing. If he didn't finish the Mors off soon, he would lose.

They continued to dance back and forth until Guy's injured leg gave out and he fell to one knee. Before he could regain his composure or get up, the Mors jabbed his sword at Guy, piercing his abdomen. I cried inside as the Mors pulled out the sword and Guy fell forward onto his hands, gasping for breath. I held Autumn tightly and stared numbly at the creature as he turned to us and smiled.

He took one step in our direction before Guy, still on his knees, swung his sword in a flash and severed the Mors' leg above the knee. The Mors howled and fell to the ground, before he quickly rose up on its hands and one leg.

"You!" the Mors screeched, baring its teeth at Guy.

"They're over here!" a voice called in the distance.

The fog was a lot thinner now, I could see a small group in the distance heading in our direction.

The Mors, still on his hands and one good leg, turned to look at me and growled, "More death will come." Then quicker than I thought possible, the maimed creature bear-crawled away like some kind of freak in a horror movie.

As the group neared, Autumn and I ran to Guy and fell to the ground next to him. His eyes were closed, his breathing shallow. We sat next to him in silence as the others arrived.

There were a few knights, along with Juliet, Devin and Kaden. All the faces gazed at us sadly. I stared into Autumn's sad eyes, unsure of what to do at that point. I felt a hand on my arm and looked down to see Guy staring at me.

"Don't ever…" he began weakly. "Don't wallow in sorrow from what happened here. It will do you no good. In–instead . . . learn from this experience and try to . . . do better." He paused and took a couple of short breaths. "I–" He coughed hard a couple times before he was able to continue. "I give you my swords. May they someday protect you . . . on the field of battle." He closed his eyes, his voice growing softer. "I'm certain there are other ways . . . to defeat . . . the Mors . . . outside of the dream . . . "

He became still, and I finally let the tears fall.

Chapter 22

I'm Sorry, Ben

Three men. Three men had died for me. They died because I was just a helpless kid who didn't know how to use a sword. I wouldn't let it happen again. I would train harder than ever so that the next time I ran into the Mors Somnia, I would destroy him. Or I would die trying. I was a Waker. I was supposed to be the one saving people, not the other way around.

I sat cross-legged on the muddy ground with Guy's twin swords resting in my lap. Autumn sat next to me, being the good friend that she was. She didn't say anything, she just sat there silently. Everyone one else was just getting back from searching for the horses, and surprisingly, they had managed to round up most of them. They hadn't traveled far off and only three were missing.

"Do you blame yourself for what happened?"

I turned to find Charley standing next to me. I hadn't heard him approach.

"Of course, I do" I said as I stared at the ground.

Charley sat down on the ground next to me. "I know how you feel," he said. "For the longest time, I felt like it was my fault that Garriton is . . . is here."

I looked up at him. "What do you mean?"

It took him a whole minute to respond. "Well . . . when we were kids, Garriton and I did a lot of stupid stuff. We lived on a farm and we were able to get away with anything. One day, I was out practicing archery near our barn, I had gotten pretty good and I never missed. When I was in the middle of practicing, Garriton poked his head out the window at the top of the loft. He yelled out from up in the window and dared me to light an arrow on fire. Well I did, and for once, I missed the target. It went straight into the hay bales that sat against the barn, and the whole thing quickly went up in flames."

He took in a deep breath. "Well, after the barn caught fire, I was convinced that Garriton wouldn't be able to get out, so I tried to be a hero and ran in after him. It was so smoky that I couldn't find him anywhere. Eventually, I made my way up to the loft where he had been, and I couldn't find him up there either. I looked out the window and saw him already outside, looking up at me. I quickly realized I was now the one trapped in a burning barn. The fire had spread everywhere, and I couldn't find a way out.

"When Garriton realized I was trapped, he yelled up at me and told me he was going to get me out right before he raced back into the barn. We both died in that fire. For a while, I blamed myself for his death. Eventually, he convinced me to stop it. He told me he knew that if he went back into the barn, he probably wouldn't make it out alive. But he still went. He thought if there was a chance, then it was a chance worth taking."

Charley smiled sadly. "I bet Guy probably thought the same thing. He was as good a person as Garriton. Even if he'd known from the beginning that he'd had no chance against that Mors, he still would have tried. Don't blame yourself, Chaz."

I thought deeply about Charley's words as he stood up and walked away. I looked at Autumn and saw her crying. She probably blamed herself as well.

"Charley's right," I said, my voice shaking a little. "We can't blame ourselves for what happened. I don't think Guy would want us to."

Autumn wiped her eyes but didn't respond.

"Let's get this show on the road," Kaden said, interrupting the moment.

I slowly stood up and Autumn steadied me as I wobbled slightly from my leg falling asleep. We gathered around Kaden with the others.

"This trip has quickly strayed from our plans so far, but we shouldn't let that slow us more than we have to. We lost a great warrior, and an even greater man today. I knew Guy well and I'm certain he wouldn't want us to waste time weeping over him. He sacrificed his life for these young Wakers for a reason. That reason is because he believed their voice would make a difference at the conference in Calverstone."

He paused, gazing around at the faces in our group. "I

will bear his body on my horse the rest of the way. Many of you may not know it, but Guy was actually a native to Calverstone. He would be very grateful to be buried in his homeland. We will make sure he has an honorable funeral."

Kaden paused again and shifted his attention in my direction. "Chaz, Juliet, Autumn and Devin, since you four are the lightest and smallest, and we're short on horses, we will pair you in twos to ride the rest of the way." He narrowed his eyes at Devin. "And we will deal with your insubordination later."

Everyone began mounting up as Juliet came over and smacked me on the shoulder.

"So, I'm riding with either you or Autumn," Juliet said.

"Why?" I asked. "Afraid you'll fall in love with Devin on the way?"

"Never. I just don't want him hitting on me the whole way there."

"You seriously think he will?"

"He's the one who gave me the flowers," she said, making a disgusted face. "I know he will."

"Okay. You can ride with Autumn."

"Thanks." She was about to turn away but paused. "I know I haven't been very nice to you, but I'm always just joking. You're one of my closest friends now, so like, if you need anything, then I'm here for you."

I smiled at her. "Weird hearing that come from you. Thanks, Juliet."

She smiled back. "That still doesn't mean I'm *always* going to be nice to you."

•••

It didn't take long for us to put a good distance between us and the foggy forest of bad memories. Once we cleared the forest, the fog had cleared as well. The sky was cloudy, but a lot brighter and a little warmer. The land was pretty flat and grassy from here on out and we could see the city of Calverstone in the distance.

"So, what did you do to get in trouble?" I asked Devin, who was sitting behind me on the same horse.

"I came along when he specifically told me not to," Devin answered casually.

"Why would you want to come?"

"To prove everyone wrong. Kaden and Grayson and many others think I'm not ready for a mission like this, but I know I am. I came along so I could show them what I can really do."

"I don't mean to be rude . . ." I spoke slowly. "But Juliet had to save you."

"And I had to save Kaden," he replied. Though I couldn't see his face, I imagined him grinning smugly.

"What? When?"

"It wasn't too long after Juliet saved me. Once I took my helmet off, he noticed I was there. He started scolding me in the middle of the battle. Well, while he was busy throwing a tantrum, a Nightmare was sneaking up behind him. Right as it jumped at him, I threw my knife at it, hitting it right between the eyes. It was really cool." He paused, stifling a laugh. "You should have seen his face when he realized what I did. It was honestly priceless. I will treasure that memory for the rest of my life."

I chuckled. "I would pay money to see that. What's that guy's problem anyway? Why does he always act like . . ."? I paused, trying to think of the right way to phrase it. "Like he's the greatest person that's ever walked the earth?"

"I asked Master Grayson that same question. What I understand is that in the Waking World, he comes from a very wealthy family, and he's been spoiled his whole life. Then he finds out he has a special power and gets sent to this world every night where everyone treats him like a celebrity. And then to make his head even bigger, he's given the position of chancellor over the whole land. I think if you got all that attention and power, you would be a prideful dirtbag too."

"Yeah, that makes a lot of sense," I answered honestly. "What does a chancellor do anyway?"

"I don't know. I don't think anyone really knows anymore. None of the titles mean what they used to. All I know is that he gets to order people around and they have to listen. Now don't get me wrong, I'm not saying he doesn't deserve the title. I know that he has proven himself a capable leader many times. And he's unstoppable with a sword."

"Really? I only saw him use his hammer."

"Yup, he's one of the best. He even beat captain Fynn in a duel."

"No way! I had a front row seat to watch Fynn fight a Mors Somnia. You're saying Kaden is better than that?"

"I mean, they only dueled once. But yes, Kaden won. And ever since then, Kaden has claimed he's the best swordsman in Kellamare. But I'm pretty sure everyone knows that's Master Grayson."

"Yeah, I haven't even seen Master Grayson duel anyone and I'm already convinced he's the best."

Devin didn't respond for almost a minute. "There's only one person who might be better."

"Who?" I asked, super curious.

"Seer Farnsworth," Devin replied, then quickly added. "It's only a rumor though. I asked Constable Darven, but he wouldn't confirm or deny it."

"That'd be crazy cool! He'd be like Yoda."

"Yo-da?" Devin questioned.

"Never mind," I said, remembering that he didn't know anything about the Waking World. I felt sorry for him. He would never get to go to the movies with friends or play video games, or any of the fun stuff I enjoyed every day. I really was lucky to be alive.

We reached Calverstone without any other delays. As we got closer, we passed by many travelers heading to and from the city. Only when we arrived was I able to fully appreciate the size of the buildings that towered above the brick wall. Just from the outside, it looked like the whole city was a bunch of castles squished together. They were all built of beautiful white bricks that seemed to sparkle in the sunlight.

The wall that surrounded the city had to be at least twenty feet tall with many watch towers rising above it. There were many knights patrolling the walls above, each holding a crossbow. Six knights stood guard at the entrance. They saluted Kaden the same way I'd seen others salute Captain Fynn.

Until I stepped foot in Calverstone, I had thought that Kellamare was busy. The streets were so full of people that it was difficult for our party to go anywhere on horseback. The area was obnoxiously loud with conversation, laughing, and singing all blending together in one.

The streets were made from red bricks that stretched in multiple directions. There were many shops and inns that lined the streets, giving the city a strong tourist vibe. There were countless booths and carts with people selling various items. The city had a much more modern feel than Kellamare.

The people of the city showed great interest in us as we passed by. Many waved and cheered like I was used to, but some just stared and eagerly whispered to each other. Maybe a party of knights with a few teenagers tagging along wasn't something you saw here every day in Calverstone. Either way, all the interest was quickly getting uncomfortable.

Kaden led us to a large wooden dome-shaped building that looked a little out of place in the city. When we got close, I noticed it kind of smelled like a barn, so I thought it must be the stables. Everyone in our group started dismounting, so Devin and I did as well. Kaden rang a bell hanging near the door and after a couple seconds, a few people wearing dirty aprons came out. They began escorting all of our horses besides Kaden's into the barn. Guy's covered body laid on the back of his horse.

"It's a lot easier to get around the city on foot," Kaden explained. He turned his attention to a knight with brown hair pulled up in a manbun. "Frederick, take the rest of the group to Lazy Joe's Inn and secure rooms for us all. I will deliver Guy's body to his daughter and visit with them for a bit before I head to the capitol."

He turned to address the whole group. "After you're all settled at the Inn, the rest of the evening is yours to do whatever you would like. If you decide to explore, make sure you travel in pairs, and don't make a scene of any kind or get yourselves lost." He looked at me when he said the last part.

I couldn't wait for the day when I would get to make him look like an idiot.

"We will meet at noon tomorrow to discuss plans for the rest of our stay."

Kaden pulled the horse behind him as he walked away.

"Right then," Frederick said in what sounded like a German accent. "This train is heading to the Lazy Joe's Inn." He had very expressive eyebrows that moved when he talked, and I couldn't help but chuckle.

As group followed Frederick, I caught up to Juliet and

Autumn and walked next to them.

"How was the ride with Devin?" Juliet asked, looking around to make sure he wasn't within earshot. "Please tell me he didn't talk about me."

"He might've said something about you two being destined to be together," I replied casually.

"No, he didn't."

"No." I laughed. "We were too busy talking about other things."

"How are you doing, Chaz?" Autumn checked.

"As okay as I can be right now. I'll just feel a lot better once this whole trip is over. Something about being here is giving me a bad feeling inside." And I meant it. I had just barely noticed the feeling of unease growing inside the pit of my stomach.

As we made our way through the noisy streets, more than once, a person manning a booth would try to lure me over to look at their interesting stuff. It was tempting. I saw some really cool gauntlets that would be nice to own, but I didn't have any money. Why hadn't I thought of asking Master Grayson for some before we left? They had to have a reserved stash of money for the Wakers.

It was almost a ten-minute walk from the stables until we reached Lazy Joe's Inn. I felt very hungry and tired, so I was eager to get inside. The inn was a large, dark gray building with a sign that was a painting of a ridiculously fat man eating a ridiculously large sandwich. People frequently entered and exited the building. Delicious smells that made me even hungrier wafted through the doorway.

"You smell that?" Frederick asked with a grin. "That is the wonderous smell of where we will all be sleeping tonight."

"I heard their food is the best in Calverstone," one of the knights commented.

When we entered the building, I was immediately greeted by a wave of warm air, cheerful singing and more delicious smells. The spacious room was very bright with many candles lighting every inch of the place. The tan, wooden floor was topped with dozens of tables, all of them full of people enjoying large quantities of food. There was a fireplace in the corner, and off to the side of it were three men with instruments playing and singing a jolly tune. It was the liveliest place I had been to during my entire time in the Dream World. It was exactly what I imagined a medieval tavern or inn would be like.

"Sit tight while I secure rooms for us," Frederick said to the group. He headed over to talk to the lady behind the counter. The rest of the knights in the group turned their attention to the musical trio, bobbing their heads to the music.

"This is a fun place," Autumn said.

"Yeah," I agreed. "I can't wait to try their food."

"It looks really greasy." Juliet commented in disgust.

"That's the way I like it," Garriton said, standing next to his brother.

"Aye! The greasier, the better," Charley added.

"That's so gross!" Juliet said.

Frederick returned with a few keys and handed the

first one to Juliet.

"One room for the ladies. It's room number 29."

He handed one to me.

"One for you and the troublemaker." He gestured to Devin, who smiled back guiltily. "Room 28."

"And the rest for the men." He divided three more keys randomly among the knights. "Rooms 21,22 and 24." He then pulled out a small purple pouch and handed it to me. It felt like it was full of coins.

"For your dinner, and whatever else you might need. Remember to not stray very far, and not to do anything stupid." He winked at me and then turned away.

"What's the plan?" Devin asked, rubbing his hands together.

"I say we eat first," I suggested.

"I'm pretty hungry too," Autumn agreed.

"Okay, fine," Juliet said. "But they better have salads or something healthy."

We went up to the counter and inspected the menu for almost ten minutes before everyone decided what they wanted. I ended up ordering roast duck with baked beans and corn on the cob. We all sat down at an empty table in the corner and waited for our food. When the waitress finally arrived with our food, I was excited by the large portion I received. I already knew I wouldn't be able to eat it all.

"So, do you want to do any exploring after we eat?" Devin asked, between bites of food.

"I don't know," Juliet answered. "It's almost time for

us to go to bed."

"Oh right," Devin said. "I forgot you guys have a super early bedtime."

"It's not that early," I insisted, then added, "Okay, maybe it is."

"I heard someone say that the roof has a really cool view," Autumn said. "Maybe we could check it out after?"

"I like that idea," Devin said.

After we all finished eating, most of us still had a lot of food left on our plates. It really was some of the best stuff I had eaten in a while. I wasn't sure how much to tip, so I left a couple of silver coins on the table. That had to be a good tip. We asked the lady behind the counter how to get to the roof, and she pointed to the stairs on her right. Before we went up, we walked past the table Garriton and Charley were sitting at.

"We're gonna go hang out on the roof," I said to them. "You guys want to come?"

"Not this time," Garriton answered. "I think our future wives are about to perform."

I noticed all of the men in the room had their attention on the two beautiful women who replaced the band that had been jamming out only moments earlier.

"Suit yourself." I laughed.

We hiked up the creaky wooden stairs and I counted five levels before we reached the door to the roof. Beyond the door was a spacious, flat area surrounded by brick walls that came up to my chest. There were a couple of benches and tables sitting against the walls. They were occupied by people eating and playing card games. Many others also rested against the west wall as they stared out at the orange sky.

The four of us made our way to an empty spot against the wall and took in the beautiful scene before us. The building sat near the west side of the city, so there were no other tall buildings obstructing our view of the valley beyond. The yellow-green grassy field went on for miles until it reached the orange sun that was just barely touching down. It had to be one of the most perfect sunsets I had ever seen.

"That's beautiful," Autumn breathed, resting her arms on top of the wall next to mine.

We watched in silence as the sun continued to slowly sink below the horizon. No one spoke until it was gone.

"That was nice," Juliet said after the sun had completely sunk below the horizon. "I'm ready for bed. You coming, Autumn?"

"Yeah," she replied before turning to me. "You ready for bed too?"

"I will be soon." I felt like I should stay out just a little longer. "I'm going to hang out for a few more minutes."

"I'll hang out with you," Devin offered.

"Goodnight, you two," Autumn said, following Juliet to the stairs.

"Goodnight," I said back.

Devin stood next to me as I continued to stare off into the distance, letting my thoughts drift. I began thinking about Presley, and then Autumn, and then back to Presley again. Maybe I did like both of them.

"I don't know about you, but I'm ready to head in," Devin said, interrupting my thoughts.

I considered going inside, but still, the feeling persisted that I should stay outside a little longer. It was strange, but it just felt like it was the right thing to do.

"I need some more time to think," I said. "I'll catch up to you."

"Don't get lost on the dark roof," he joked before walking away.

With the sun now gone, the night was fast approaching. I could still see beyond the walls, but pretty soon I wouldn't be able to. I continued to stand there, silently wondering why I felt like I needed to stay.

"You'd better get to bed before you fall asleep where you're standing," a soft voice said behind me.

I turned around and was greatly surprised by the person I saw standing in front of me.

It was Ben, the kid I went to high school with. I hadn't seen him in weeks. He was dressed like a native to the Dream World with his boots, leather pants and cloak. The only thing that made him stand out was his pitch-black clothing, I didn't see a speck of color on him. His face was the same though, still pale and sad looking.

"Ben? What are you doing here? How are you here? You're a Waker?"

Ben was silent as he moved next to me and leaned against the wall. He stared out into the dark valley.

After a minute he said, "I've been coming to the

Dream World longer than you have. It's probably been almost two years, and I have learned quite a bit since being here. You want to know something that I know for sure?"

It was an awkward question. "Sure."

"You're on the wrong side."

"What? I'm on the same side as the Archduke and the Dreamchasers, how can that be the wrong side?"

"I can tell you without a doubt that the Dreamchasers are not the good guys here. They're going about the war against the Nightmares the wrong way. The Quin Anulus actually know how to end all war and suffering."

"Don't tell me you let them brainwash you. When did you start talking to them? They're insane people!"

"I am one of them." Ben said, glaring at me. "I am a member of the Quin Anulus."

"Why?" I asked, dumbfounded. "Why would you want to join them?"

"It all started when I first came here. At that time, there were a lot of newcomers from the Waking World. Just like he did with everyone else, the Archduke pressured me into joining the Dreamchasers. I didn't feel like I had any other choice, so I said I would join. Well, after a couple of weeks of me not showing much potential with weapons or reality bending, I quickly became a nobody, just like at school. No one cared and no one noticed me anymore. That's when I met Victor."

"You actually met Victor?" I interrupted.

"Yes, I did. Unlike the Archduke, Victor didn't even know me, but I was still somebody to him. He was interested in my life and my story. He took the time to get to know me. After we became friends, he started training me, not just to fight and to daydream, but also to control my anger."

He must have noticed the doubtful look on my face. He nodded and said, "Yeah, if it wasn't for his training, I would have lost my temper way before I did with Jace and Trevor. He has been helping me to achieve my full potential, and it's because he cares. And he doesn't only care about me, he cares about everyone. That's why he's trying to get all the cities to declare neutrality."

"He's trying to get the cities to declare neutrality so it's easier for him to rule the world," I insisted, starting to feel irritated.

"Really? So, he can rule the world? That's what they teach you now? That's pretty funny."

Heat rushed to my face as I tried to think of how to respond. "Ben, he's obviously the bad guy here. He wants to team up with the Nightmares! Those creatures are pure evil. All they do his hurt people."

"Chaz, you don't know what the Quin Anulus know," he said calmly. "Joining the Nightmares is the only way to get them to stop hurting people. It's the only way to stop fearing them. If we don't fear them, they won't hurt us."

"That's the stupidest thing I've ever heard. There's no way to get everyone in the world to stop fearing them, not after all they've done."

"Oh, there's a way, trust me. Like I said before, the Quin Anulus know things. They also have powers you wouldn't believe. And it's all because they teamed up with the Nightmares."

"Ben, what about the people in the Waking World? You know what will happen to them if we just let the Nightmares and Mors Somnia run free. These monsters are affecting them in so many negative ways." I thought about my dad and how his stupid Mors Somnia was ruining his life. "This is real Ben. I've seen the way people's lives turn out when influenced by those things."

"Do you think I care what they do to the people in the Waking World?" Ben spat angrily. I was surprised by the way he was suddenly acting. "Do you think I care about the kids at school who ignore me unless they're bullying me? Or the ones who are supposed to be my friends who talk bad about me behind my back? Or my own family who have never said a nice word to me . . ." He was a lot quieter when he said the last part. "Those people have never done anything for me, so I will never do anything for them. All I care about is helping the Quin Anulus, my real family."

I had no idea how to respond. There wasn't really anything I could say it fix the past. So many people had failed him, and I was one of them. I never even tried to reach out to him, now it was probably too late.

"I'm sorry, Ben," I said, sincerely. "I'm sorry I was only there for you when you were bullied. I promise I really did want to be your friend. I just wasn't sure how to go about it."

"It doesn't matter anymore," Ben said, turning away

from me. "I have friends now. I will support the Quin Anulus in whatever they do." He paused, then turned back to me. "They want you to join them."

"What? Are you serious?"

Ben didn't respond, instead he turned around and walked away. He seemed to fade into the night, after a few seconds I couldn't see him anymore.

"Yes," his voice echoed softly in the darkness. "Think it over. Tomorrow, Victor will visit you."

Chapter 23

At Least He's Trying

The next day at school, I literally found it impossible to focus on anything else besides what Ben had said. Did he really not care about anyone here in the Waking World? Was it too late to be his friend? I didn't want to give up on him, but I had no idea how to help him.

And then there was Victor. I was terrified at the thought of meeting the man in charge of the Quin Anulus. He was like the ultimate bad guy of my story at the moment. That was pretty intimidating. I didn't even know anything about him. I didn't know what kind of personality he had, what he looked like, or what kind of powers he had. What if he could shoot lightning out of his fingertips and shocked me to death?

Thoughts like those swam through my head the whole day at school. Not even the fact that prom was the very next day could get me to think about anything else. I was pretty sure my friends could tell I was distracted too, because at lunch they kept asking if I was okay.

"You with us, Chaz?" Presley asked as we claimed a table in the cafeteria.

"Yeah, seriously bro," Isaac said. "Everything okay? You've been checked out all morning."

"Sorry guys," I apologized. "I've just been stressed. Midterms are coming up, and then we have Trevor and Jace causing problems on top of that."

"Um, don't you mean finals?" Jake asked.

"Broooo," Isaac said. "You've been out of it for so long, you don't even know what time of the year it is."

"I meant finals," I responded. "My mind is just all over the place."

"Don't let Trevor and Jace stress you out," Presley said. "We can handle them tomorrow. And if you're stressed about finals, I can help you study."

"Okay."

"Anything else stressing you out?" Jake asked. "We're your friends, we're here for you, ya know."

I contemplated just letting it all out and telling them everything I had to deal with since my sixteenth birthday. I quickly decided against it, they probably wouldn't believe me. And even if they did, what could they possibly do to help?

"No, that's everything," I said.

After school, it quickly became pointless even trying to do my homework. I couldn't focus. I asked Presley if she wanted to come over and study with me, but she said that she was busy getting ready for prom. I wanted to ask her why in the world she was already getting ready for prom a day early, but I decided against it. She was a girl. No one knew why they did the things they did. After about two hours of trying to do homework, I took a break and headed to the kitchen for a snack. The house would've been silent, if it wasn't for the television show Dad was watching. Mom and Garrett were out grocery shopping. I grabbed a string cheese and stepped into the family room where Dad was. I noticed he was still in his Taco Bell uniform.

"Do you have to go back to work?" I asked.

"Oh hey, Chaz," he said, just noticing me. "Yeah, they're short staffed so I'm going to go help them out."

I noticed he hadn't shaved in a while and his eyes had dark bags under them. He looked exhausted. It made sense though; he worked a lot. As I stood there thinking about it, the realization hit me for the first time. He really did work *a lot*. Who was I to complain that he wasn't doing enough for our family? Or to accuse him of being lazy? At least he was working, and he was actually working hard. Even with a Mors Somnia draining all the motivation and life out of him.

I started to think about all the pain and suffering his Mors Somnia had caused in the Dream World. It had taken the lives of three men, and most likely others. It was constantly taunting me and making me feel awful. If it was doing all those things to me, who knew what it was doing to my dad. Yet he still hadn't given up. My heart immediately swelled with warmth and gratitude as I realized how much Dad loved our family. He really was a great dad. But did he know that? Probably not, because all I ever did was focus on the negative and tell him he needed to do better. I couldn't believe how awful I had been to him. Not once had I thanked him for anything.

I swallowed, feeling the guilt grow inside me. It was time for a change.

"Hey, Dad?" I said.

"What's up, Chaz?" he asked, looking at me.

"Thanks for working so hard and providing for the family."

He looked taken aback at my words and his mouth opened, but nothing came out.

"You're an awesome dad." I added before heading out of the room.

"Thanks, Chaz." I heard him say quietly.

• • •

Later that night, I called Autumn and told her a little about Ben and my conversation with him. I purposely left out the part about Victor planning on meeting with me the next day. I didn't want her to worry or insist on coming with me. If I really was going to meet with this guy, I would do it alone. I didn't want to take the chance of anyone else getting hurt.

"Did you see Ben at school today?" Autumn asked over the phone.

"No. There was no sign of him. I don't know what I would do even if I did see him."

"Well, you can at least say hi every time you see him. Sometimes all people want is to be acknowledged."

"That's a good idea. But what about when that gets old?"

"I don't know, Chaz. You're good with people and you make friends easily. Just be yourself around him and I'm sure he'll come around."

"We can only hope," I sighed.

"I wish I lived closer so I could try to be his friend too," Autumn said. "He just needs someone to love him. It doesn't sound like his family even does that."

"You're right. It's sad. Well, I'm gonna go to bed now."

"I'll see you in a little bit."

Chapter 24

A Lovely Talk with The Lord of Darkness

It took a minute for me to remember who or where I was when I woke up. When I saw the bear skin rug on the floor and Devin sitting on the bed next to mine, it all came back to me. I immediately wished I could go back to sleep and skip the day. Today was the day I had to speak in front of thousands of people. It could also be the day that I would have a lovely talk with the Lord of Darkness himself.

I sat up on my bed and pushed the wooly gray blanket off me. I gazed around the plain room with its tan walls until my eyes rested on Devin, who was lacing up his boots and staring at me with wide eyes.

"What?" I asked.

"I thought you had already gotten up because I didn't see you in your bed," he said. "I started changing my clothes and suddenly you were there."

"Really?"

"Yeah. I mean, I've heard that you Wakers disappear when you go back to your world and then reappear when you come back, but it's really weird seeing it happen. Next time, don't do it while I'm changing."

I laughed. "I had no idea. Sorry, dude."

"Well, you'd better hurry up and get ready." Devin stood up. "It's about time to meet up with everyone else."

Devin left the room and I quickly got dressed. After I finished, I headed out the door and down to the main floor. Since it was already noon, the tables were almost as filled as they were last night. But even with all the people, it was definitely not as lively as before. That was probably because there was no band playing in the corner. I spotted my large group crowded around a couple of tables in the corner and made my way over. I found Juliet and Autumn already sitting at the table with Devin standing next to them.

"Good, we're all here," Kaden said, standing up. "You may have already heard whispers about it, but just so you know, the conference is scheduled for this afternoon around 4 PM. I had a long discussion with Duke Alvered about the Archduke's position on neutrality and coexistence, and he thinks it would be a good idea to hold a conference about it. Sadly, he has already talked with Duke Brighton, who has tried to sway him in the other direction. While Alvered is leaning more towards our side of the argument, he thinks that both sides are worth hearing."

Kaden paused and shook his head. "He said that if we

are going to speak against this idea, then it's only fair we have someone speak for it. He invited members of the Quin Anulus to give their spiel at the conference as well."

All at once, many of the knights in our company protested in outrage when Kaden finished speaking.

"That's ridiculous!"

"They can't let them do that!"

"Who cares about fair!"

Kaden held up a hand to silence them. "I know, I know." He shook his head. "I don't like it either. But he said if we want to speak, then they get to speak as well. There's no way around it. I will make sure I hit all the major points on why the Quin Anulus idea is idiotic and evil." Kaden turned, looking in my direction. "You three will also be speaking for a few minutes. All you have to do is let them know your personal feelings about why you think it's an awful idea. Can you do that?"

"Of course, we can," Juliet snapped. She must have noticed the condescending tone in his voice as well.

"Yeah, we've got this," I added.

"Great. Now, on to the subject of Guy," Kaden began. "I visited his family last night and told them what happened. Of course, they were sad, but they took it well. They were glad that he was able to die a hero. They want to hold his funeral immediately following the conference. Chaz, they want you to rehearse the story of how he died at the funeral."

"Me?" I asked, feeling uneasy.

"Yes, you. You will be able to rehearse the story

better than anyone."

"I guess if that's what they really want."

"Good." Kaden turned his attention back to the whole group. "Do whatever you want for the next few hours, just make sure you get to the conference early. It will be held on the castle grounds. If you don't know how to get there, I'm sure you could ask just about anyone."

After Kaden dismissed us, Juliet, Autumn, Devin and I all ate lunch together as we tried to figure out what to do for the next while. Garriton and Charley eventually joined us.

"What if we check out some of the cool shops?" Devin suggested. He jingled the coin pouch Frederick had given us. "We have money."

"That'd be fun," I replied.

"I saw an armor shop that looked kind of cool," Juliet said.

"Nothing wrong with looking fresh when you ride into battle," I said with a grin.

"I wish I could get souvenirs for my family," Autumn said. "But I wouldn't be able to take them to the Waking World."

"Well, we can get some souvenirs for ourselves," I said. "Who knows when we'll come here again?" I turned my attention to the two brothers. "You two can join us as well."

"We might have to take you up on that offer," Charley replied. Garriton cleared his throat and then Charley added, "After I buy my brother a new tomahawk, of course."

"We'll probably catch up to you later," Garriton said. "Just make sure you don't do anything stupid." He winked at me as he and Charley shared a laugh.

We finished eating our food and immediately headed out the door, wanting to see as much of the city as possible before the conference. Once we left Lazy Joe's, we wandered around busy Main Street for a little bit, checking out all the random booths and carts.

"Yoohoo!" a man at a booth called in a high falsetto voice. We looked in his direction and he waved at us. "Yes, you four. I think I have something that will interest you."

We made our way over to his little cart. The man was very tan with little eyes. When we got close enough to see, he gestured towards the items on his cart. They were all slick, black sticks varying in size. Most were around the size of my pointer finger, and all of them looked really sharp.

"How would you like to buy a genuine Nightmare claw?" The man asked.

"A Nightmare claw?" Juliet asked, skeptically.

"Yes, yes!" The man said, bobbing his head. "I assure you that they are as genuine and real as they come. I travel far and wide with a large group, so we often run into Nightmares on the road. After we slay them, I use a special technique to extract their claws myself just to make a little money."

"Seriously?" Devin asked.

"Seriously." The man smiled.

"Nice try, pal. We're not stupid. Nightmares dissolve when you kill them, there's no way these things are real."

The man's face flashed with anger for a second, but he quickly recovered. "How would silly kids like you know that?" he asked, his smile stuck in place. "You shouldn't believe everything you're told. Thank you and have a good day." He waved us away.

"That's sad that there are con artists in this world too," I said after we walked away.

"I wonder how many people fall for that?" Autumn asked, shaking her head.

"Not many," Devin replied. "It's pretty common knowledge that Nightmares are big masses of nothing. If you could harvest their parts, scientists would study those things like crazy."

We continued down main street until we found the armor shop Juliet had mentioned. Inside, we found a wide variety of armor. I had no idea what most of it was for. To my surprise, they even had horse armor. We spent awhile there before we headed out to search for another shop that caught our interest. Devin spotted a candy shop down the road and we all excitedly ran over.

The candy shop was enormous and had the biggest selection of candy I had ever seen. Most of the candy looked like stuff I was used to, only there were no brand names or fancy wrappers on them. There was also a lot of unfamiliar candy too. We ended up buying a couple small bags full before we left.

As we moved deeper into the city, it became more

crowded. There were a handful of street performers doing magic tricks, balancing acts and displaying all kinds of unique talents. We stopped to watch a man juggling two swords and an ax while he balanced a long spear on his chin. It was very impressive.

Autumn spotted a formal clothing store that she wanted to check out, so we headed in that direction. As we made our way over, I saw a booth that displayed a variety of dual-wielding swords. They even had a set that looked just like the ones Guy had given me. I thought it would be a good idea to talk to the merchant to see if he could tell me more about them.

"I'm gonna check out this booth real quick," I said to the others, stopping near it. "I'll catch up to you in a minute."

"You don't want to look at ball gowns?" Juliet asked, smirking. "Suit yourself."

"I'm only going to look at their hats," Devin insisted.

"It's okay," I said. "I'll be there in a minute."

"See you soon," Autumn said.

They continued inside the store as I made my way over to the booth. The only one around at the moment was a small Asian man. I assumed he was the merchant in charge of the booth. He was holding a pair of long daggers as he moved through an offensive drill that was a lot more intricate than the ones I often practiced. Once I got close, he stopped what he was doing and sheathed the daggers. He placed them on the booth and approached me.

"How are you, young man?" the guy asked. He was

wearing a black and red kimono-type thing.

"Good. My name is Chaz."

"Nice to meet you, Chaz," the man said, shaking my hand. "My name is Ken. How can I be of service?"

"I wanted to know what you could tell me about these swords," I said, gesturing to the blades that looked so similar to Guy's.

"Ah, the butterfly swords," he said with a smile.

"Butterfly swords?" I questioned. It was a disappointing name, but I didn't let him know that. "A friend recently gave me his before . . . before his passing. But I know nothing about them or how to use them."

"I probably wouldn't be able to teach you how to use them, unless you plan on staying in Calverstone for a few years?" Ken looked at me curiously, his statement more a question.

"No, I'm leaving tomorrow."

"Then all I can do is tell you a little bit about them. Hopefully, you'll find somebody in Kellamare who can teach you how to wield them."

"How did you know-"

Before I finish my question–how he knew I was from Kellamare–he started speaking again. "The butterfly sword is a single-handed, single-edged sword that originated in southern China. They are usually wielded in pairs and are excellent in close-quarter fighting. They are carried side by side in the same sheath, so it gives the appearance of a single weapon, which makes it a great way to surprise your enemy. The swords are not mass produced, and every set is unique. Any questions?"

"How did you know I'm from Kellamare?" I finally asked, suspicious.

"I was told that someone of your description would most likely stop by. He was right. It's also uncanny how much you two look alike."

"Like who?"

"Like me," said a smooth, deep voice.

I turned around to find a tall man in a blue, silky button-up shirt that didn't really look like it belonged in the Dream World. He looked like he was ready for a business meeting with his black pants and brown dress shoes. He had curly brown hair and looked so much like me that I stumbled backwards.

What the heck? Who in the world was this guy and why did he look like he could be my older brother? He had the same brown eyes, and the smile on his face looked like it belonged on mine. The only thing that was different about him was his thin eyebrows, deep slithery voice, and the scar in front of his left ear.

"You're right Ken," the man said. "It really is uncanny."

"Who . . . are you?" I asked slowly. Was this the guy that the Archduke was talking about when I overheard him in the castle?

"I'm Victor. It's nice to meet you." He held out his hand for me to shake it, but I didn't.

"There's no need to be scared, I'm just here to talk."

"I'm not scared of you," I insisted.

"Just wary," Victor guessed. "I understand. I'm a stranger and you've only heard bad things about me."

Victor walked over to a small stone bench that rested against a brick building and sat down. He gestured for me to sit as well. I hesitantly walked over and sat on the bench, leaving as much space between us as I could.

"I can tell you a little about myself if it would make you more comfortable," he said, crossing his legs and clasping his hands together on his knee.

"Sure."

"I grew up in Omaha, Nebraska with my parents and six siblings. I played baseball while growing up and even in college. My favorite movies are Star Wars and Lord of The Rings and . . . probably Newsies. I also enjoy long hikes, rodeos and swimming."

"And killing people," I added, angrily. Was this guy for real? Those were all of my favorite movies. It made sense that he was a fan of Star Wars and Lord of The Rings, but Newsies as well? He was probably trying to mess with my mind or something.

"There's no need to be rude." His tone was chastening. "How would you like it if I started making up negative things about you too?"

"Why do you hurt and kill people?"

"It's most definitely not because I enjoy it. I just do what's necessary to bring about the greater good. Plus, most of the time, it isn't me, it's the dark ones."

"Why do you let them?" I asked, my temper rising along with me as I rose up from the bench. "Why in the world would you side with something so evil?"

"It's not my choice anymore," he said, shaking his head. "Sit down and I'll explain what I mean."

I grudgingly sat down as I glared at him.

"When I first came to this world, I was just like you, young, naïve, and curious. I had good intentions and a desire to help the people here, so I joined the Dreamchasers. I fought alongside them for years, destroying Nightmare after Nightmare. Sadly, it never ended, and it never slowed. After getting tired of all the fighting and people getting hurt, I started looking for other ways to stop the Nightmares. There is always more than one way to do things.

"Now, as I think back on this story, I realize we are similar people in more than just our looks. You see, I also have the Gift of Visions, Chaz. Back when I was your age, I saw visions weekly. One of those visions that I saw was about myself. In the vision, I took the lead in a massive battle against the Nightmares, and in the end, I was the one who saved the day and stopped the war. I didn't know what it meant at first, but as I started looking for ways to end our struggle with the Nightmares. I realized that that was exactly what my vision was about.

"I became obsessed with finding a way to end the war. It's all I thought about for months. One evening while patrolling the border of the city, I ran into a Mors Somnia. Instead of slaying her, I decided to talk to her. I asked her if there was a way for us to live together in peace, or if there was a way to end the war. She told me there was, but that it would be hard to get everyone to go along with. Wanting to be the hero who ended the fighting for good, I told her that I would do whatever needed to be done.

"The Mors Somnia had me make promises and oaths to her. They were so small and simple I didn't think much of it. She had me do little tasks, and in return, granted me powers that were unheard of. Excited by the growth in my reality-bending powers and the possibility of peace, I continued to make oaths and do what the Mors asked. This continued for a few months, and by the time I realized that making oaths with dark creatures was a bad idea, it was too late. By making promises and doing what she asked of me, I was slowly binding myself to her."

He paused, so I took the opportunity to ask a question. "What do you mean you were binding yourself?"

"I became subject to the creature's will," he explained. "I could no longer truly act for myself. To a certain extent, I had to do whatever she wanted. Of course, If I had stopped when I realized what was happening, I might have eventually been able to untangle myself from all the oaths and promises I had made. But my heart had already become corrupt. All I cared about was power, so I continued to trade my freedom for it."

"Was it worth it?" I asked, hoping he'd learned his lesson.

"Actually, it was" Victor replied, running his hands through his hair. "Because of everything I went through I gained a great amount of knowledge about the Somnum Exterreri and Mors Somnia. I now know what it's going to take to live in peace with them."

"And what exactly is it going to take? All of the kingdoms declaring neutrality so you can rule over them while your monster friends feed off of their fears for the rest of their lives?"

"Not quite. It actually involves me helping everyone rid themselves of their fears. If no one fears, then there's no need for the Nightmares to bother them anymore. We could coexist in peace."

"That's a bunch of garbage. There's no way to completely rid the world of fear."

"There is a way," Victor said with certainty. "And I know that way."

"Why are you even telling me this?"

"Because I want you to join us, Chaz. I'm starting to think that you have an essential part to play."

"I would never join the Quin Anulus. Even if you *think* you have good intentions, what you do is evil."

"What we do is the only way to end all the pain and suffering caused by the Nightmares. Do you really want to continue to oppose us? If you somehow stopped us, which you can't, then the blood of the innocent would be on your hands whenever the Nightmares kill someone. Surely you don't want that on your conscience?"

Seriously? He was going to try to make me take the blame for all of the people that he and his friends hurt? He was probably just trying to use some sort of reverse psychology on me so that I would do what he wanted.

"I don't care what you say," I replied. "I'll never join

you."

"We'll see if you still feel the same later on," Victor said with a smile. "For now, I will continue to move forward with my plans."

"It won't work," I insisted. "Even if you convince all of the other cities to join you, Kellamare won't."

"Yes, you are right," he said thoughtfully. "And that's why Kellamare has to fall."

"What?"

"It's simple. The city and the Archduke need to be crushed. Or he needs to be removed from his office. Either one will work. But unless one of those scenarios happen, there will forever be a thorn in my side."

"Are you saying that you're going to go to war against Kellamare?"

"If I can't get rid of the Archduke, then yes."

"The other cities won't fight for you."

"I don't need them to," he replied with a wave of his hand. "It will be quite simple convincing them to stand by while I eradicate the one city that stands in the way of peace for the country. And you'd be very surprised at how many Nightmares I can gather. Come a year from now, Kellamare won't exist."

Victor stood up and patted his clothes, smoothing out the creases. "Tell Bradford to be ready. Whether that's ready to fight or ready to surrender, it doesn't matter to me."

He turned on his heel and walked away, disappearing into the crowd of people in the street.

Chapter 25

Things Get Creepy Real Fast

There you are," Autumn said as she and the others made their way over. I was still sitting on the same bench I sat on with Victor. As they got closer, she frowned. "You doing okay? You look kind of pale."

"I'm pretty sure I ate too much candy," I lied. I would tell them the truth later.

"I'm sorry. You going to be able to walk? It's time to head to the castle."

"Yeah, I should be fine," I said, standing up. "Did you find anything good?"

"Just ugly old-fashioned dresses that look like night-gowns," Juliet said.

"I thought some of them were cute," Autumn added

"Let's get going then," I said.

We started back the way we came, and eventually we asked for directions from a friendly-looking couple passing by. They explained that Main Street led straight to the castle and pointed in the direction we were supposed to go.

We thanked them and continued on our way. We followed the flow of traffic, as most of the people were heading in the same direction.

As we walked, Autumn kept glancing at me, like she noticed something was off.

"You seem kind of out of it, Chaz."

"I just have a lot to think about. I have no idea what I'm going to say at the conference."

She nodded. "I try not to plan out what I'm going to say. That way it will all come from my heart. And thinking about it makes me more nervous."

"That's a good point. I guess I shouldn't think about it too much either."

It didn't take long for the tall, white castle to come into view. It looked similar to the one in Kellamare, only bigger, whiter, and more majestic. I didn't know too much about castles, but I thought it looked new, like it was just built a few years ago. I was surprised to see it had flags with the same picture on it that I saw in Kellamare, the one with the sun peeking through the clouds.

"Devin, do you know what that symbol means?" I asked, pointing to a flag. "The one that is on all the flags and knight's armor."

"It's the insignia of Elegit Terram. It signifies the country as a whole, and it's also a symbol for hope. It's a reminder that no matter how dark the night or stormy the day, the sun will always return with light and warmth."

"Awe, I like that," Autumn beamed.

"Sounds cheesy," Juliet commented.

Devin just shrugged.

I thought about the symbol as we neared the castle walls. The intersection before the walls was a spacious cobblestone area covered in many large fountains spraying water overhead. Some even sprayed water into each other. Children ran around the fountains attempting to dodge the water, but it was obvious by their soaked clothes that they weren't very good at it. The whole area was surrounded by many trees dressed in pink cherry blossoms.

We passed the gates and entered the courtyard of the castle. The courtyard was filled to the brim with people, and it was hard to move around. Everyone was chattering excitedly as they gazed toward the castle. Children that were too short to see sat on their parents' shoulders or climbed many of the small trees in the area. Most of the trees looked like they were going to snap under the weight.

We pushed through the crowd until we reached the steps that led up to the doors of the castle. There were many knights guarding the bottom of the steps. At the top of the steps before the castle doors was a large landing where many familiar faces stood. I saw Kaden, Frederick, Ben, and even Victor standing on the landing, along with other faces I didn't recognize.

We tried to make our way up the steps, but the guard held out a hand to stop us.

"Names?" he inquired beneath his helmet.

"Chaz, Autumn, Juliet, and Devin," I answered

"I was told to admit all of you except Devin," he said. "You'll have to watch from down here, young man."

"No big deal," Devin said. "Do a good job."

"Thanks," I replied. "We'll see you soon."

As we headed up the steps, I felt the eyes of thousands of people boring into the back of my head. Were we seriously going to be addressing the people from these steps? I was expecting a large conference room or something with good acoustics. Out here, I doubted that most of the people would even be able to hear us. I didn't want to have to scream my whole speech.

"Perfect timing," Kaden said when we arrived at the top. "Come introduce yourselves to Duke Alvered."

He gestured to the tall blond-haired man next to him. Duke Alvered was a very pale man with a sad face. He also looked fairly young, maybe in his 30s.

"Duke Alvered," the man said in a nasally voice. He shook each of our hands in turn.

"Chaz."

"Juliet."

"Autumn."

"Good to meet you." He turned to Kaden. "This is everyone, isn't it?"

"Yes, it is." Kaden nodded. "Though, I haven't yet been introduced to your *other* guests."

"Right. Victor, will you introduce yourself and your friends to the Chancellor?"

"It would be my pleasure," Victor said smoothly. He walked over, followed by Ben and a black-haired woman with fierce eyes. He shook Kaden's hand. "I am Victor, leader of the Quin Anulus." I heard a gasp behind me, and

I thought it might've been Autumn. "I have heard many stories of your noble feats. It's wonderful to finally meet you."

"I wish I could say the same for you," Kaden said, giving him a hard stare while he gripped his hand tightly. After a few seconds of their stare down, Kaden let go of his hand.

"These other two are my friends and fellow members of the Quin Anulus. This is Victoria." The lady stepped forward. Her eyes looked so sharp and angry it was un-comfortable looking at her. She wore a simple blue and white dress that looked like it came straight from Beauty and the Beast. "And this is Ben." The small and pale boy I knew from school stepped forward. He looked very uncomfortable being there. Maybe it was because he was about to speak too?

Victor turned his attention to me. "I have already met Chaz," he said casually, shifting his gaze to Autumn and Juliet. "But I haven't had the pleasure of meeting you two yet."

"What do you mean, *you've already met*?" Kaden asked fiercely.

Why did I have to be in this situation right now? I would rather have gotten thrown into a den with a hundred Nightmares.

"Chaz will have to fill you in later," Victor said with a wave of his hand.

While Autumn and Juliet hesitantly introduced them-selves to Victor, Kaden glared at me as if I had just been revealed as a traitor.

"I'm sure it's time to start," Duke Alvered said. "I will address the audience and then Kaden and his group will speak first since they arranged this conference."

Alvered walked to the edge of the steps and waved to the gathering of people. As he did, they began to cheer and clap enthusiastically. After he stopped waving, the noise slowly died down until it was impressively silent.

"Good afternoon, friends and family," he called out, almost yelling. "I'm sure you all know why we are here. Chancellor Kaden of Kellamare has called this conference on behalf of Archduke Bradford. We will hear from him and his friends, as well as other special guests. The topic they will be discussing today is the subject of neutrality and coexisting in peace with the Nightmares."

There was a mixed response from the audience. It sounded like half the audience broke out into boos while the other half cheered.

"As you know, Calverstone has not declared an official stance on the matter yet, and we probably won't for some time. But it is good for us to be knowledgeable and informed on the subject. We will be hearing many different views on the idea, so keep your mind open to new possibilities and new ways of thinking. First, we will hear from Chancellor Kaden. Please show him your respect by remaining silent as he speaks."

The Duke stepped back and the crowd went wild as Kaden walked forward. They cheered even more for him than they did for the Duke. Did they even know him? If I was in the crowd, I would probably boo at him.

As Kaden addressed the crowd, I found it hard to pay attention. Partly because I didn't like him that much, and partly because I couldn't help but watch the members of the Quin Anulus that stood so near me. I closely observed their every move, feeling a little paranoid. Mostly because Victor was there, and every time he looked at me, I felt like he was staring into my soul.

The parts of Kaden's speech that I actually heard were great. He hit on all the major points, like how neutrality would lure us into a false sense of security, and how any idea to side with evil creatures had to be a bad idea.

He spoke for maybe twenty minutes and suddenly he was done.

"Next we will hear from one of our extremely gifted Dreamchasers," Alvered said to the audience. "Chaz of the Waking World."

I snapped out of my thoughts as soon as he said my name. My hands were sweaty. My throat felt dry. I looked around and saw Autumn and Juliet giving me encouraging looks. I shifted my gaze and found Victor giving me a smug smile, as if he knew something that I didn't. I was a little puzzled and disturbed, but I tried to ignore it. I had no idea what I was going to say. I wasn't ready for this.

I walked forward and stood where Kaden was just a minute ago. I slowly gazed around at the mass of people who seemed so far away. All their eyes were boring into mine and I felt very awkward being the center of attention.

"Hello," I said loudly, surprised at how well my voice

carried. "My name is Chaz. I'm new here. I came from the Waking World." My voice wasn't shaking too badly, so I started feeling a little more confident. I still wasn't sure what I was going to say, but I just kept talking.

"I'm sixteen years old. I was living a normal and boring life before I wound up in this place. It was pretty crazy at first, especially because as soon as I showed up at the Portal, I got chased by an ugly monster with big claws. Can you imagine, just out of nowhere getting pulled from the life that you know, and then all of the sudden you're expected to be someone else? And you're expected to do things you've never done before? In my world, there are no such things as Nightmares, or Mors Somnia, or anything like it. But I come here and all of the sudden, I'm supposed to fight these things.

"At first I didn't want to do it. I was scared. But now, after seeing those monsters hurt people, after seeing them kill people, I know now that it's not about me. It doesn't matter if I'm scared. I get to go to bed every night and then the dream is over. I'm back in my world where I don't have to touch a sword. But that's not how it is for you. The nightmare never ends for you. You don't get a break from the monsters like I do."

I paused, not really sure where I was going with the speech.

"Well, I'm not going to lie to you," I continued. "I don't know if there is a way to give you a break from the monsters. But what I do know is that declaring neutrality and siding with the Quin Anulus will not give you a break.

I think it will make the monster problem worse. All these creatures want to do is to feed off of your fear and doubt. There's nothing else that will . . ." I trailed off, suddenly feeling extremely drowsy. "There's nothing else . . ."

I tried to keep talking, but I was too tired to gather my thoughts. It felt like I had taken a double dose of drowsy allergy medicine and it had just finally hit me. I was so tired. It was a struggle to stand up. I just needed to go to sleep, then I would feel better.

I felt myself falling over as I closed my eyes, but I don't think I ever hit the ground.

• • •

I felt a hand shaking my shoulder, but I was so tired I just tried to ignore it and go back to sleep. The shaking stopped and I heard someone walk away. Suddenly, light began to shine through my closed eyelids and I felt greatly irritated.

"Chaz, wake up." It sounded like my brother Garrett.

I opened my eyes to find him sitting next to me on my bed, still in his pajamas. I was so tired that I was sure it couldn't possibly be morning yet. He stared at me as I rubbed my eyes and looked at the time on my phone. It was only 2:47 AM. Why in the world had he awakened me so early?

"Garrett, what are you doing?" I asked, sounding very annoyed. "Do you know how early it is?"

"I had a really creepy dream and I was too scared to be alone," he said quickly.

All I could do was stare at him. This was the first time he ever done something like this. He was never scared of being alone in his room.

"It was about you and Dad," Garrett explained. "At least, I think it was you. It looked like an older version of you, and a black monster that looked like Dad."

"What?" I gasped, alarmed. It couldn't be . . .

"Yeah, you and Dad chased me around a forest saying the same thing over and over again. Except Monster Dad was missing a leg and he crawled after me while you chased me. It was really creepy."

This was getting really weird. I had to be dreaming or something. How did Garrett have a dream about our Dad's Mors Somnia and Victor when he had never even seen or heard about them before?

"What were they saying?" I asked.

"*Victor says hello.*"

Chapter 26

Ready or Not, Here Comes Prom

After hearing about Garrett's dream, I was disturbed on so many levels. He said he wasn't scared anymore, so he went back to bed, then I quickly became the scared one. Was it just a coincidence, or did Victor have power over people's dreams?

If the latter was true, then that would mean he also had power over the dreams of people he didn't even know. He had never met Garrett before, and yet somehow, he forced himself and a Mors Somnia into his dream. How was that even possible?

After lying in bed for a few minutes worrying about Victors powers, I remembered my speech in the Dream World. I had fallen asleep in the middle of it. It must have been because Garrett woke me up. It was such a crazy feeling, getting super drowsy all of the sudden.

I was still tired, and I tried to go back to sleep, but I was so stressed out that it wasn't working too well. I laid in bed for who knows how long until I finally succumbed to sleep. When I woke up, I was expecting to be back in the Dream World but was surprised when I found myself still in my bedroom at home. I looked at my clock and it read 3:20. I had definitely fallen asleep for at least fifteen minutes, but for some reason, I didn't go to the Dream World. Maybe it wasn't long enough. Or could I not go back twice in the same night? My worries continued to add up as I tried to sleep.

By the time my alarm went off at 6:30, I felt just as tired as I did when Garrett woke me up. I groggily got out of bed, jumped in the shower and got ready for the day. As I got dressed, only then did I remember that it was the day of prom. We had big plans for the whole day, and I was supposed to pick Presley up at 11:00. Why did I need so much time to get ready? I decided I would get some more rest, so I set my alarm for 10:00 and tried to go back to sleep.

I slept for maybe two hours when I woke up to my phone buzzing on my nightstand. I picked it up and saw that I had a call from Autumn.

"Hey," I said into the phone.

"Chaz!" Autumn's voice screamed into my ear. "Is everything okay? You just fell asleep in the middle of your speech and disappeared."

"Yeah. My brother Garrett had a nightmare and he just wanted some company, so he woke me up." I contemplated telling her what his nightmare was about, but then decided to keep it to myself.

"I'm so glad you're okay. Juliet was worried about

you too. Neither of us knew what happened until Kaden explained that Wakers disappear when they fall asleep. Weird huh?"

"That is weird. What happened after I disappeared?"

"A lot. But isn't prom today? It would probably be better if I told you when I see you tomorrow."

"That's probably a good idea. I have enough to think about."

"Okay. Well, I'm so glad that you're okay. Go enjoy your day."

"Thanks, Autumn. I'll see you tomorrow."

"See you tomorrow, Chaz."

I put my phone in my pocket and headed to the closest mirror to fix my bedhead.

At about 10:45, Jake showed up at my house and we headed to pick up our dates. We picked up Jake's date, Lindsey first, and then headed over to Presley's. As we drove to her house, I silently promised myself I wouldn't let whatever was going on in the Dream World distract me from my date, because it wouldn't be fair to her. Once we arrived, I hopped out of the car and knocked on the front door.

"Hello, Chaz," Presley's mom greeted as she opened the door. "I'll let her know you're here."

Her mom hurried away, and less than a minute later Presley stepped out onto the porch.

"Hey," I said as a big smile forced its way onto my face.

"Hey, Chaz." She smiled back.

"You ready?"

"I'm so ready."

We got in the car and headed to an outdoor mini golf park where we met up with the rest of our group, which included Isaac, Danny, Quinn and others I didn't really know. We mini golfed until we were hungry, then we headed to Taco Bell for lunch. Yeah, Taco Bell was a lame place to take our prom dates, but my dad hooked us up with free food. After lunch, we went ice skating. Presley was so bad at it that she held onto my hand the whole time, which is what every guy hopes will happen.

After we were tired of skating, everybody went home so they could get ready for the dance. It took me about ten minutes to get ready, but I knew it would be another two hours or so for the girls to be ready. I had no idea why they took so long. I mostly just sat around doing nothing for those two long hours. When the time finally came and Jake picked me up, I started feeling a little nervous. I had been daydreaming about this night for the past few months.

After we arrived at her house, once again, I knocked on the door and her mom answered.

"Presley's almost ready," she said. "Come on in."

I sat on the couch in their living room for what seemed like an eternity until she finally walked in the room. I was speechless as I stared at her in her dark green dress with her curled hair. She looked *so* good.

"You look amazing." I said quietly, barely getting it out.

"Thanks, Chaz." She smiled. "You look great in a

suit."

"Thanks."

Her mom snapped a picture of us before we headed out the door and joined the others in the car. For dinner, we went to a really nice Italian restaurant where we had pizza and other things that were too fancy to remember the names. Thankfully, I was able to forget all about the stressful things going on at the time and just enjoy the night. After dinner we headed straight to the school dance. When we arrived, I grabbed Presley's hand on the way into the school.

She looked at me and smiled.

"Just making sure you don't slip and fall," I said. Smooth Chaz is at it again.

Once we were inside, we scoped out the loud dance floor in the gymnasium, which was decorated with lights and streamers, but we didn't see Jace or Trevor anywhere. The dance had just barely started, so there were only about a dozen people there.

"I don't think they're here yet," Jake said. "You guys should go wait near the locker just in case they head straight there."

"Good idea," I agreed.

Presley and I walked down the empty halls of the school until we found Ben's locker.

"How did you know which one it is?" Presley asked.

"I heard them talking about it," I said. Which was kind of true. "Let's hide somewhere."

We were close to where the hall branched left, so we

hid just around the corner from the locker. We both sat down on the ground, unsure of how long it would take. We sat in silence for a few minutes, the only sound was the distant thumping of music coming from the gym.

"Sorry we didn't get to hang out much these past few weeks," Presley said.

"It's no big deal," I replied, trying to be cool about it. "We were both pretty busy."

"Well, school is almost over so we'll be able to hang out more."

"Yeah. That'll be awesome."

"What should we do this summer?"

"Watch all the extended versions of Lord of The Rings in one day," I said, seriously. "Maybe have a Star Wars marathon. Oh, and learn to longboard."

"Seriously, Chaz?" She laughed. "You want to spend most of the summer watching movies?"

I was about to reply, but then I heard footsteps from down the hall. We both stood up and listened closely.

"It's number 312," I heard Jace say before the footsteps stopped. I slowly peeked around the corner to see Jace working on the combination as Trevor watched.

"That geek freak is going to get in trouble for sure," Trevor said, unzipping the backpack.

I turned to look at Presley and then nodded. We both walked around the corner toward the two troublemakers. As soon as we started our approach, they quickly turned around, guilty looks on their faces.

"What are you two doing here?" Trevor asked,

quickly wiping the surprise from his face. "Kissing in the halls I bet."

"I know you two are trying to frame Ben," I said. "I'm not going to let you do it."

"What are you talking about?" Trevor asked, pretending to be confused. "We're just putting some of our stuff in Jace's locker."

"I heard you two talking about it. I know your plan. If you go through with it, I'll make sure they know it was you."

Trevor and Jace shared an annoyed look.

"Thanks for ruining the fun, Chavez," Jace snapped.

We all went silent when we heard footsteps coming down the hall. I turned around to see Ben walk around the corner, obviously not dressed for prom. He was wearing his usual black jeans with a crazy looking anime shirt. I froze in surprise with Trevor and Jace as he walked towards us. I definitely didn't see this coming.

"What's going on here?" he asked, his voice louder than it normally was.

I wasn't sure what to do. I didn't want to tell Ben what Trevor and Jace were trying to do. Then I would make things worse between them. But if I lied, there was no telling what Ben would think.

"I won't lie," Trevor said, stepping closer to Ben. "Me and Jace were planning to get you suspended again. But thanks to your friends here, that didn't happen."

"They're not my friends," Ben said coldly. "I already knew what you guys were going to do. That's why I'm here."

"How does everyone know about this?" Trevor asked Jace. "I'll bet anything that Jason couldn't keep his mouth shut."

"Seriously," Jace agreed.

"I'm sorry, Ben," I apologized. "We were just trying to help you."

"I don't need anyone's help," he said. "I just need you all to leave me alone."

"I might have left you alone if it wasn't for this," Trevor said, pointing to his cast. "Maybe after its off, I'll *consider* leaving you alone."

"Trevor, you're awful." Presley said. "Stop being a bully."

"Not until high school is over," Trevor promised as he began walking away with Jace. "For now, all three of you are on my list of enemies. See you later, Ben."

I turned to Ben. "Can we just try to be friends or something?"

"You're on the wrong side, Chaz," Ben said, walking away. "Until you figure that out, you're on my enemy list as well."

He vanished around the corner and Presley looked at me, confused. "What does he mean by that?"

"I'm not sure," I lied.

After our encounter with Ben we went back into the gym and danced the night away with our group. It was fun being able to goof around with my friends. I didn't know how to breakdance, but my moves were still cool enough to attract attention. It was pretty awesome slow dancing with Presley as well. I really impressed her when I threw in a spin and a dip. I probably racked up a lot of smooth points that night.

Later that night, Jake pulled up to Presley's house. We hopped out of the car and slowly walked together up to the front door. As I stared up at the bright moon above and listened to our footsteps, I felt an odd sense of Deja vu. I got that so often these days that it wasn't a surprise. My palms got a little sweaty as I remembered how many times I had dreamed of this moment. It was time to either cash in those smooth points or throw them away. There was no point in saving them.

As we walked up the porch steps, I contemplated if I should go for it or not. If I did, it would for sure mean we were no longer 'just friends.' If I didn't, I would probably seal my fate in the friend zone forever. But if I did it and she didn't like me I would be in the 'extra friend zone.' It was a scary thought.

We stopped at the top of the steps and timidly faced each other.

"I had such an amazing time with you," she said, gazing at me shyly.

"Me too," I replied, my nervousness making it hard to speak.

"So far, the whole day has been perfect."

She said, *so far*. That was probably a hint. If I didn't kiss her, I would ruin her night. Or maybe she meant, if I try it, then her night will be ruined. Girls were too hard to understand. I stepped closer to her, making my heart beat so hard I felt like I was going to have a heart attack. I noticed a bad feeling creeping into my gut, but I thought it was probably just me being nervous.

"How can I . . ." I paused, realizing it was a stupid thing to ask. Embarrassed, I quickly leaned forward and kissed her on the lips. I stepped back, surprised that I actually did it. I grinned as I noticed the surprised smile on her face as well. She probably didn't think I was going to do it.

"Have a good night, Presley," I said giving her a quick hug.

After I pulled away, she said, "You too, Chaz."

I giddily turned away and skipped down the steps as I heard the front door shut behind me. I did it! I actually did it! I couldn't help but continue to grin as I skipped back to the car. No more friend zone for me! Though I was excited like I had never been before, I still had a bad feeling inside.

When I got in the car, Jake and Lindsey both looked back at me and smiled.

"Someone sure looks happy," Lindsey commented.

"Atta boy!" Jake praised.

"Thanks," I said, still grinning from ear to ear.

After Jake dropped me off, I headed straight to my room. I quickly threw off my suit and didn't even hang it up. I felt so carefree, but also really tired. I just wanted to get into bed and think about Presley as I fell asleep. Which is exactly what I did.

I found myself sitting in an open field. The grass was

very yellow and tall. I was hot and sweaty, like I had just run a few miles. My neck felt like it had been squished. It burned, and it was very hard to breathe. I looked up and saw Victor standing in front of me with a cruel smile on his face.

"I told you that I have powers beyond your imagination," he said. "What I did to your brother's dream is only a small glimpse of what I can do from afar." His smile somehow grew even bigger and uglier. "If you continue to oppose me, I just might have to corrupt the dreams of others you love. Maybe a special someone by the name of Presley? You see, dreams have a very powerful effect on the mind. It won't be hard to make her life miserable and wish that she had never met you." He chuckled evilly.

I sat up on my bed, my forehead covered in sweat, the vision I'd just had still fresh in my mind. *Please, no.* I pleaded inwardly. Why me? It was pretty obvious what the vision meant, and now it was also obvious why I had such a bad feeling inside before I kissed her. There was only one thing that I could possibly do right now to fix it, but it was the last thing I wanted to do. Literally, the last thing I wanted to do. The fact that I shared a kiss with her hadn't even really sunk in yet, and now it never would. There was no possible way for my life to get any worse.

I laid back down on my pillow and cried myself to sleep.

Chapter 27

A Surprise in Beckstead

My bed felt a lot harder and more uncomfortable than usual. I tried to ignore it and go back to sleep, but everything seemed so bright. As I slowly awoke, I realized that I wasn't even lying on a bed. It felt like concrete. I opened my eyes and found myself lying just above the steps to the castle. A girl who I assumed was Autumn, sat at the top of the steps turned away from me. The sun shone brightly overhead, warming my skin like a blanket. I sat up and Autumn turned around.

"You're finally back!" She smiled.

"Yeah," I said. The vision I had last night quickly moved to the forefront of my mind, bringing a wave of depression with it. Life was too cruel.

"You okay?" Autumn asked.

"I'm fine." I really wasn't, but I didn't want her to know that. "How long have you been here?"

"Umm, maybe an hour. I just didn't want you to be alone up here when you woke up."

I moved over and sat next to her on the steps. It was so odd seeing the courtyard so empty when it had only a day ago been full of thousands of people. Now, all I saw were a few kids climbing trees.

"So, what happened yesterday?" I asked as I watched the kids taking turns jumping out of a tree.

"Well, you collapsed in the middle of your speech," Autumn began. "Everyone kind of freaked out, especially when your body started to disappear. Then Kaden quickly explained that you fell asleep because someone was trying to wake you up on the other side. Then Juliet spoke. She did a great job. And then I spoke, and I did awful."

"I bet you didn't do as bad as you think you did."

"Well, no one could really hear me, so it doesn't matter. But after I was done, that Victor guy spoke and made fun of you for falling asleep during your speech."

"He did?"

"Yes, he did silly little impressions of you fainting while in battle and stuff." Autumn folded her arms angrily. "It was so rude. I wanted to smack him. Also, it's really weird how much he looks like you."

"Trust me, I know."

"Anyway, he gave his little speech about how he was going to protect everyone from the Nightmares and stuff. What's so ridiculous is that a lot of the people seemed to be buying it. I don't know which side the majority is leaning to now."

"That's so stupid. How could they believe that stuff?"

"I don't know, Chaz." Autumn shook her head sadly.

"After the conference, we went to the funeral. Because you weren't there, they made me tell the story of Guy's death."

"I'm sorry, Autumn," I apologized, feeling awful. "I should have been the one to do that."

"It's okay. I mean, I cried a lot, but I was eventually able to get the whole story out. It was a good service. After the funeral, we didn't really do anything. Today we've just been packing up and waiting for you so we can leave."

"Well, let's get going," I said, standing up. "I honestly won't miss this place."

"Me either," Autumn agreed, standing up as well.

Together we walked down the steps and headed in the direction of Lazy Joe's Inn.

"How was prom?" Autumn asked casually.

"It was good."

"That's good. What did you do during the day?"

"We played mini golf and stuff."

After a minute of silence, she asked, "You okay, Chaz? You seem kind of sad."

I hated how well she was able to read me. "I'm okay, Autumn."

"Okay." She clearly didn't believe me.

We walked the rest of the way to Lazy Joe's in silence. Once we got there, we found everyone else hanging out while they listened to a lady sing. Without them noticing, I headed straight upstairs to pack up my things. I didn't have much, so it was quick. When I came down, Autumn had already informed them I was back. Everyone quickly gathered their things and our company was ready to go.

As we headed to the stables to get our horses, Kaden approached me.

"You want to tell me about your secret meeting with the leader of the Quin Anulus?" He asked, not bothering to sound polite.

I was not in a good mood and I had no patience for him right now. "He found me on the way to the conference," I replied. "If you want to know any more than that, you'll have to wait until I talk to the Archduke."

He gave me an irritated look but didn't press me. After a minute, he moved to the front of the group.

When we arrived at the stables, we secured a horse for everyone and immediately made our way out of the city. I heard a lot of the knights talking about their wives and kids, so I knew they were just as eager, if not more so than me to get back. Thankfully, we had nice weather and there was no sign of a storm as we traveled the same path in the opposite direction. The first half of the trip was pretty uneventful compared to last time. We took a few breaks and quickly reached the split in the road where we could either travel through Beckstead or go around again. We took another break to decide which road to take.

"I know a trip through the city might take a little bit longer," Kaden said to the group. "But I'd rather not travel that forest again for a long time."

Many of the knights murmured their agreement.

"I don't feel good about it," Autumn whispered to me.

"About going through the city?" I whispered back, confused.

"Yeah. It doesn't feel like a good idea."

"How is the other option any better?"

"I don't know . . . I'm not sure what we should do."

"Well, I'm not going through that forest of death ever again." I said firmly.

"Okay . . ." Autumn replied, hesitantly.

"That settles it then," Kaden said after everyone shared their opinion. "We'll take the scenic route. As long as the streets aren't too busy, it shouldn't take much longer."

We took the road to Beckstead and we quickly found ourselves before the walls of the city. Inside, it looked very similar to Kellamare, just a little smaller. It seemed a lot dirtier too. There were lots of hobos lying in the streets with their blankets and small number of belongings. The buildings were made of a faded red brick and a light-colored wood. The city gave me the feeling that I was in a farmer's market. There were many people in the streets selling fresh baked goods and produce. I saw a lot more food for sale than anything else.

We hadn't made it far into the city when we heard numerous screams and other chaotic sounds in the direction we were headed. People began to run in the opposite direction we were going, while most went inside their houses and locked the doors. With so many people running around and screaming, it was hard to tell what was going on, but it didn't take long to figure it out. Up ahead,

I glimpsed black shadows zooming around in a blur as they threw people all over the place, smashed booths and carts, ripped front doors off of houses, and broke windows.

I didn't realize what they were until I glimpsed a Mors Somnia climbing a building like Spiderman. As it went, it smashed every window it passed and seemed to relish in the fear of those inside, excitedly biting at the air like it was thick taffy. There was a good number of knights trying to fight them off, but most of them quickly got hit with a flying door or thrown into a building.

"No, no, no!" Kaden cried, staring at the chaos as he climbed off his horse. "This can't be happening! This isn't normal. They don't just do stuff like this! Especially not in the daylight." He carefully unsheathed his sword as people rushed past him, running for their lives.

Everyone else in the company began dismounting and arming themselves. I did likewise as I stared numbly at the scene of horror before me. I counted four Mors, but I was pretty sure there were more that I couldn't see. How are we supposed to fight off so many? I knew I would prob-ably get in the way. Maybe I would just focus on keeping Autumn and Juliet safe instead.

"Something is definitely wrong here," Kaden said to the group, his face suddenly unreadable. "But whatever the case, we can't just stand by and let innocent people get hurt. Let's aid our brothers and send these monsters back to Dolorem Terra!"

The knights roared loudly as they raised their wea-pons in the air, and without another word, Kaden and everyone else charged into battle. I looked from Autumn, to Juliet, and then to Devin. All of them looked as unsure as I was.

"What do we do?" Autumn panicked. "There's so many of them!"

"I'm going to fight," Devin said. Before I could convince him otherwise, he was sprinting toward the battle.

"Devin!" I called after him. He didn't look back. "We have to do something."

"We can help get people to safety," Juliet suggested.

"Good idea" I replied.

Most of the people had already gotten themselves inside, but there were a few people still out in the open because they were too injured to get away. I saw a boy who looked like he might've been just a little younger than me. As I ran to help him, I glanced at the battle and saw a Mors lifting a stone bench off the ground and smash a knight with it. I also saw Kaden and Devin tag-teaming another one as it effortlessly dodged their swords and tripped Devin.

I reached the boy as he desperately tried to hobble away on one foot, dragging the other behind him. I put his arm around my neck and mostly dragged him to the nearest door. I banged on it hard and screamed for someone to open it. It only took a few seconds for a woman to open the door and invite us inside.

"Thank you," The boy said as I headed back out the door.

I scanned the area and saw Autumn and a little boy

dragging an unconscious man. I didn't see Juliet anywhere and I hoped that she was safe. As I searched the area, I glimpsed a Mors pick up Devin and throw him against the side of a building. I cringed as he crumpled to the ground. Kaden charged the monster and fiercely attacked it with impressive speed, but it managed to block every single one of his attacks.

Amazingly, it didn't take long for Devin to get back up on his feet and limp towards the Mors as Kaden attacked it with a hammer in one hand and a sword in the other. I don't know if the Mors just didn't know Devin was behind it or what, but Devin was able to easily plunge his sword through it from behind. It fell to the ground and turned into dust. Without any hesitation, both Kaden and Devin went to engage another Mors in battle.

I looked away and saw Juliet and Autumn back in the streets still helping people find shelter. I froze when I saw a little girl run into an alleyway between buildings as a Mors stood on the roof watching her with interest. There was no way I would let that thing hurt her. As I raced over to the alleyway, I glanced back up at the roof and no longer saw the Mors. I knew it was never safe to go into an alleyway in a big city, but I had to do something.

The further I ran down the alley, the closer together the buildings sat, eventually making it just barely wide enough for me to fit through. The alley ended with a fork that went left and right. I quickly scanned both ways before I saw the little girl to the right. She was knocking on a random door as she sobbed and begged for someone to let her in.

"It's okay." I said, crouching next to her. "Everything will be okay."

She fell to the ground, leaning against the door as she sobbed. "I want my mom and dad!"

"We'll find them," I replied.

I looked up just as a short Mors Somnia walked around the corner I had come from. It stopped when it saw me, a smile slowly creeping onto its face. I had only seen one Mors up close and it had my dad's face, so it was weird seeing one that I didn't recognize. This one had a woman's face. Her hair was pinned behind her head in a bun.

"Hello, there," she said in a high, piercing voice.

I slowly stood up and stepped in front of the girl as I unsheathed my sword. "Stay away," I commanded, my voice shaking a little.

The Mors smiled even wider and a black spear seeped out of the creature's arm, sliding right into her hand. She took a step towards me, when an arrow suddenly lodged itself in the side of her head. The Mors staggered and then turned to dust along with the spear. The arrow clattered to the ground as I stood there listening to the approaching footsteps.

I was so grateful when Autumn came around the corner with her bow in hand. She even wore a smile on her face.

"It was just standing there," Autumn said. "It made it an easy shot."

I lunged at her and gave her a hug. "Thanks," I said. "We need to get this girl to safety."

Autumn grabbed the girl's hand and tugged her along behind us as we headed out of the alley and back toward the main street. Right before we exited the alleyway, we ran into Juliet, who was heading into the alley.

"I saw both of you run in here," Juliet explained as she tried to catch her breath. "You guys okay?"

"Yeah, we're fine," I answered. We all exited the alley and took the girl to the nearest door. I knocked until they opened up and I quickly pushed the girl inside.

As I surveyed the street, I was amazed at the large amount of men who were obviously normal civilians battling alongside the knights. Most of them were using shovels, pitchforks and rakes as weapons. Sadly, the battle was not going well. Many people had fallen, and there seemed to be no end to the number of Mors. The sight made me feel awful.

"We have to help them," Juliet said.

"I agree," I replied.

"Enough!" A strong voice commanded, piercing the noise of battle. Everyone, including the Mors, immediately stopped and looked in our direction. I turned around to see Victor just a few feet away, walking toward the scene. He looked angry, and maybe upset? It was hard to tell. He definitely didn't look happy.

He continued approaching the skirmish of men and Mors Somnia, and still, no one moved.

"That is enough," He said again.

"What are you doing here?" a large Mors with an impossibly deep voice asked, stepping forward.

"What are *you* doing here?" Victor shot back angrily. "I thought we made a deal. If I show you peace, you would show me and my friends' peace."

"I didn't know these people were your *friends*," The Mors said with disgust.

"Everyone in Elegit Terram who no longer wish to fight are my friends. Those who choose peace and neutrality have my protection. The only reason they fight now is because you forced their hand."

Victor waved his hand as if dismissing them. "Now begone. Leave!"

The group of Mors quickly dispersed. Some disappeared into alleys, while others scaled buildings and disappeared over the roofs.

After they were all gone, I caught Victor give Kaden a smug look before his expression quickly switched back to one of disappointment.

"I've been trying to tell you that there is a way to have peace with these creatures," he said loudly, addressing everyone in earshot. "I can protect you. I can promise that there will be no more need for these knights to risk their lives for nothing. And now you've seen firsthand what making deals with the Mors Somnia can do. They listen to me, and they keep their promises. We can coexist in peace with them. Who here are my friends?"

Almost all of the men in the street began cheering.

• • •

Kaden was not happy. It was very obvious. After we finally left Beckstead, his ranting began. He went on and on about how Victor had staged the whole thing just so he could convince everyone to join his side. If I hadn't been there and seen what had happened, I might not have believed it. But because I was there, I knew it was probably true. Victor was a smart guy. I wouldn't be surprised if he had just won over the whole city. Of course, Duke Akoni would probably never go along with it, but he was currently in Ausidor on an important mission. Who knows how he will react when he returns?

Everyone stayed on their guard the rest of the way to Kellamare. We had so much trouble so far that there was sure to be more over the horizon. Thankfully, we made it the rest of the way there without any sign of Nightmares or Mors Somnia. When we finally got back, Kaden, Juliet, Autumn and I all went straight to meet with the Archduke. Devin wanted to come too, but Kaden refused. We found the Archduke, Captain Fynn and Constable Darven all pacing the room. Apparently, they had been eagerly waiting for us to return.

We sat down with them and Kaden told them about every single thing that happened, from the time we left, to when we got back. After he finished reviewing the mission, he told them that I had something to say as well. I briefly explained to them how Victor found me and why he wanted to talk to me. I made sure to include his plans about coming to war with us in a year or so, or at least removing the Archduke from his office.

"So, the Quin Anulus plan on waging war against us," Bradford said thoughtfully. "Let them come then. We will be ready. Maybe we'll finally be able to eliminate their silly group once and for all."

Chapter 28

My First Breakup

I woke up the next morning wishing that I didn't exist. I didn't want to face the day. I didn't want to do what I knew I needed to do. Life was already hard, but it was about to be unbearable. I took my time getting ready for the day. There was no need to rush. As I sat at my kitchen table eating cereal, Dad came in and joined me. He sat down on the chair across from me and poured himself a bowl of cereal.

"You doing okay, Chaz?" he asked.

I looked up to find him staring at me. "Yeah."

"You look a little down. Anything you want to talk about?"

I was surprised that he had even noticed. I was extra surprised that he wanted to talk about it. It seemed like it had been awhile since he really showed any interest in my life.

"That's okay. Thanks, Dad."

After breakfast, I sat on my bed holding my phone in

my hands. It was still the weekend so there was no school. I would have to go out of my way to meet up with her. It was still pretty early in the day, but the sooner I got it over with, the better. For once, I didn't want to text her. I sat contemplating it for a while before I finally did.

Hey. Can I come over real quick and talk to you?

I lay on my bed for an agonizing eight minutes before she texted back.

Of course! I would love that. :)

No, she really wouldn't.

Okay, see you in 20 minutes.

I headed outside and hopped on my red mountain bike with bad breaks. The chilly air rushed past my face as I pedaled down the street. The bright sun was directly in the east, just barely beginning to dry the morning dew on the tall, golden wheat that lined both sides of the road. The closer I got to her house, the more anxious and scared I felt. It was getting so bad that my arms started shaking a little and I felt like I was going to throw up. I wanted to turn around so bad, but I didn't. The only thing that kept me going was knowing that I was actually protecting her. It would hurt, but it was for the best

When I finally reached Presley's house, my legs burned. I hadn't ridden a bike since last summer. I stopped in front of the steps that led up to her porch and sent her a text, telling her to come outside. I was dying inside. I had never felt so awful in my life. Was there another way? Could I just tell her the truth? She probably wouldn't believe me, and if she did, Victor would still come after her.

The front door opened, and Presley stepped out, looking as amazing as she always did. She walked down the steps and gave me a long hug. It made me feel even more awful for what I was about to do. She pulled away and smiled at me. "I'm glad I get to see you today."

I didn't respond, I just swallowed and tried to not avoid eye contact too much.

"What's wrong?" she asked, suddenly concerned. She grabbed my hands. "Your hands are shaking, and you look pale. Are you sick?"

"No," I quietly replied. "I'm just scared."

"Why are you scared?"

I didn't respond for almost a minute. "I don't know how to explain this . . . but we can't be together." Before she could respond I continued. "There's a lot of things going on in my life right now . . . and it would be dangerous for you to be a part of it. I know it sounds stupid, and I wish it wasn't true, but it is."

She gave me that hurt and confused look I had seen in one of my visions. It made my heart feel like it was literally being torn in two.

"I'm so glad that I got to spend prom with you last night," I said as tears started spilling from her eyes. "I'm so glad I got to finally kiss you. I had dreamed of doing that ever since I first started having a crush on you. But even though I want to be in a relationship with you, I can't. I care about you too much to put you in danger. Maybe someday, I'll be able to explain everything, but right now I can't." I couldn't bear to look at her anymore. I looked at the ground and said, "I hope that we can still be friends. If not now, then someday. I'm so sorry, Presley."

I continued to stare at the ground as I wondered why in the world I wasn't crying. I felt like I should have been, but tears wouldn't come. I wished they would so she could know how awful I felt.

Finally, she walked away and shut the door, leaving me alone in her front yard. I got on my bike and pedaled slowly home. That's when the tears finally started falling from my own eyes. It hurt so much, I felt like I would have given anything to make it go away. Tears started blurring my vision and I hit a curb in front of one of her neighbor's houses. I fell onto the grass and laid there crying, wishing I was someone else.

<h1 style="text-align:center">Chapter 29</h1>

<h1 style="text-align:center">It's All a Distraction</h1>

After all the excitement of prom was over, life really turned on the turbo boosters and didn't stop. Finals came and went. Surprisingly, I only failed one class, which was math of course. I had to make up for it by taking a summer class, which wasn't too bad because it was the only one that I had to retake.

Things with Presley and me made very little improvement. She didn't talk to me during those next few weeks of school. She just pretended I didn't exist. It hurt at first, but it made sense after what I did to her. And in a way, I was glad she didn't talk to me because it would make Victor less likely to use her as leverage against me. Thankfully, during the last few days of school, she had actually started saying hi to me.

Once school got out, Jake tricked us both into hanging out as a group again. I think he was trying to help repair our friendship, but it was just awkward. She didn't try to talk to me, and I didn't try to talk to her. Even months later, it still hurt just thinking about how she pretty much got ripped out of my life like that. I had a secret hope that someday, after Victor was no longer a threat, we would get back together and maybe get married or something. I didn't think the odds were in my favor.

My dad seemed to be doing a little bit better. He paid more attention to us. That was really all of his improvement though. He still spent most of his time watching television and still had no hope of improving his work life or chasing old dreams. I continued to do my best to let him know that I cared, and I was thankful for all he did.

In the Dream World, though we were getting ready for war, things were going pretty well. Juliet, Autumn and I continued to train hard throughout the summer. We all got a little better with our weapons and even better at daydreaming.

I got pretty good at hand to hand combat, but I still could rarely ever best Juliet in a duel. But that was okay. Everyone knew she was ridiculously good with a sword. It also became very obvious how much stronger my body was in the Dream World than in the Waking World. I had to start working out in the Waking World as well to match my muscular dream body.

While we mostly trained for combat, we also got sent on a few missions around Kellamare. Mostly traveling to areas where there had been reports of frequent encounters with Nightmares, which we would hunt down and exterminate. I got pretty good at slaying Nightmares, but since Beckstead, we hadn't run into any Mors. I was thankful for that, but I also wondered if I was ready to face one in combat.

Things stayed pretty much the same until the end of summer.

"That was better, Chaz," Master Grayson complimented after a long sparring session. "But every now and then you still let yourself get hit. Knowing where your opponent's is going to strike should be used to your advantage. Instead of bracing yourself to get struck, at least attempt to block, dodge or parry it."

I felt a little annoyed as I rested with my hands on my knees. He made it sound so easy.

"Sorry, Master Grayson," I frowned. "I'll try harder."

"You're going to have to try harder later," he said, glancing at the sky. "I think it is about time to meet with the Archduke." He turned his attention to the two sparring a few yards away. "Juliet, it's time to wrap it up!" he yelled to them.

Catching Devin off guard, Juliet knocked the wooden sword out of his hand, pushed him to the ground and held her sword at his neck.

"You win, again. What a surprise," Devin said, sarcastically.

Juliet lowered the sword and helped him up with her free hand as I made my way over.

"You're getting a lot better," she said, putting away her sparring gear.

"Well, at least I can beat Chaz," he commented with a grin.

"Hey, we've only sparred once!" I replied, punching him on the arm.

"Right, but it's still 1 to 0."

"I'll change that when we get back from our meeting," I promised.

"That's right, then it will be 2 to 0," Devin joked.

"Keep talking, Devin."

We found Autumn at the archery range. She had an arrow nocked with the string pulled back, ready to fire. She released it and hit the bullseye. Autumn certainly was not the best in her age group at archery, but she was still amazing. She rarely missed, and she could pull that heavy bowstring back for hours without getting tired.

Whenever we happened to run into a few Nightmares, she would always take them all out before Juliet and I even reached them. She had changed a lot over the past months. She didn't lose her nerve like she used to. And she didn't often get scared anymore.

The four of us left the training grounds and headed inside the castle to the boardroom. I flashed a smile at Grace as we passed and entered the board room without knocking. We were there so often that I got used to just walking in without announcing myself.

Seated at the table was Archduke Bradford, Duke Akoni of Beckstead, Constable Darven, Captain Fynn and surprisingly, Seer Farnsworth. We joined them all at the table. I took a seat next to Duke Akoni. I still didn't know him very well, but he was super friendly, and I liked being around him. He gave me a big smile and a fist bump after

I sat down.

"Perfect timing," Bradford said. "Thank you, every-one for being here. And thank you, Seer Farnsworth for gracing us with your presence. A lot has happened since we last met, and most of it isn't good. We will start with the worst of the news. Captain Fynn, would you please give us your latest update on Ausidor?"

"Certainly," he answered, standing up. "Lord Brevan has gone missing. He hasn't been seen for almost a week now. No one seems to have a clue of his whereabouts or what has happened."

"No doubt it is Duke Brighton's doing," Akoni said, sounding as Jamaican as ever.

"Most likely," Fynn agreed. "But we have no evi-dence, and we don't have any type of lead to go on. He's gone without a trace. I am planning on personally going out there with a team of men to investigate his disappear-ance. An offence against a Waker is an offence against the Archduke, which is treason of the highest degree. We will do everything we can to find Lord Brevan."

"Is there anything we can do in the Waking World?" Juliet asked. "Could we find him there and ask him what happened?"

"Already working on that," Darven answered with a smile. "He's from Greenland. I've been searching the in-ternet for any information about him that I can find. I haven't found much, but when I get a better lead, I will fly out there and find him."

"Now, back to the topic of Ausidor," Fynn said. "The

second piece of bad news is that Duke Brighton has proposed that Archduke Bradford be challenged for his office because, and I quote, *"he won't even consider the possible peace that neutrality will bring."* The city of Ausidor took a vote and the majority was in favor of this proposal."

"So, does that mean he's going to try to become the Archduke?" I asked, not quite understanding their unique politics.

"Not exactly," Bradford answered. "It means that he wants me out of my position, and he wants someone who is in favor of neutrality to replace me. That could be anyone, including himself, or even Victor. It's completely up to the people. But of course, before I can even be challenged, at least three of the five cities have to be in favor of the proposal."

"And even if the proposal was accepted by all of the other cities," Darven began, "it would be months before they could even start the vote. There's so much to do to get ready for the challenge. Anyone who want to be considered have to publicly declare themselves a challenger."

Hearing him talk about challenges and challengers made me think of a wrestling match or a fight. I began to imagine Bradford dominating Victor in an intense boxing match.

"Beckstead will never be in favor of this challenge," Akoni stated. "I will make sure of that."

"It's all a distraction," the Seer spoke up and everyone turned to look at him.

"What exactly do you mean?" Bradford asked.

"For the past two years I have had the same recurring vision," Farnsworth explained. "At first, I couldn't make much sense of what I was seeing, but as time went on, it has slowly become clearer. The time isn't far off when the Quin Anulus and the Nightmares will be at our doorstep ready for war. The vision always begins with Lord Brevan disappearance and Duke Brighton proposing a challenge. Victor is simply diverting our attention so he can strike while we're preoccupied."

"How much time do we have before he attacks?" Bradford asked, unsettled.

"That has never been very clear to me in my vision. It could be a few days, weeks, a month or two. I just know it's soon."

"Why didn't you tell us this sooner?" The Archduke asked, concern in his voice.

"I have been seeing this vision for years, I have been slowly memorizing exactly how it will play out. I have been planning and preparing. If I had told you, I would have inevitably changed the future and in turn, changed the outcome of the battle. I know how we will win, and I will continue to do whatever it takes to make sure that happens."

"Is there anything else you can tell us?" Master Grayson asked. "Any war strategies or hints?"

"Just watch and be ready," The Seer answered. "And increase the number of men patrolling the outskirts."

"It will be done," Grayson assured him.

• • •

I felt unsettled after what the seer had told us. We could be at war any day now. Was I ready for war? I didn't feel like I was. Sure, I was a lot better with a sword and I could see the future, but would that really matter when I would be surrounded by an entire army? There would be too many people attacking, I wouldn't be able to see it all coming.

Those were the thoughts I was having as I strapped on my sparring pads. I tried to focus on my strategy against Devin, instead of the looming war. I needed to stay focused on the now. I couldn't lose to Devin again. I was a Waker. And I had seen all kinds of epic lightsaber battles from Star Wars. That had to count for something. I put on my helmet and grabbed a wooden sparring sword out of one of the barrels.

"You ready?" Devin asked, standing in the center of the sparring arena.

"Yeah, I'm ready," I said, striding over to him.

When I was about five feet away, we both got in our ready stances.

"Fight!" Juliet called from the bench she sat on.

We both held our swords in front of us as we circled each other, searching the future for an opening. In each scenario that I saw play out in the future, I wasn't able to land a hit, so I continued to search. After a couple more seconds I finally saw it, if I attacked him slower than he expected, it wouldn't take long for him to let his guard down, which I would then take advantage of and surprise him with a quick strike to the shoulder.

I attempted the moves I saw in the future, but he must've seen it as well because he blocked the strike to his shoulder. We began circling each other again. That was the thing with fighting another person with foresight, unless one of you saw further into the future than the other, the battle would go nowhere, you would just keep blocking each other's attacks until one of you gave up.

"Chaz, if you lose again, we're no longer friends," Juliet said.

As we circled each other, I saw him land a jab to my stomach. As soon as I saw it, he attacked. He performed the moves exactly as I had already seen him do in the future, because of that, I was able to block each one until he stopped. This pattern of attacking with little pauses in between went on for a few minutes, and neither of us was able to gain the upper hand.

I changed tactics, and instead of searching for the first attack I landed, I pushed further and further until he moved first. He attacked and we danced back and forth until I landed my third attempt to hit him.

"Nice one, Chaz!" Juliet cheered.

I continued to do the same thing as the battle went on, and I found that the further I pushed into the future, the easier it was to land my attacks. By the time Devin finally yielded, I had managed to hit him eight times, and he hit me once.

"Well, you beat me," Devin said, wiping sweat from

his forehead before a smile stretched across his face. "For now, we'll say we're an even match."

I laughed. "Whatever you say." I turned to Juliet. "I'm ready to call it for the day. I'll beat you tomorrow."

Now it was her turn to laugh. "Sounds good to me. Let's go find Autumn and get some dinner. You coming, Devin?"

"Yeah."

Once again, we found Autumn at the archery range and together the four of us headed to the dining hall. It was a little busier than usual, but there were still plenty of empty tables. We grabbed some food from the kitchen and went to sit with Raiden and Jo, who neither of us had seen in a while.

"Hey!" Raiden greeted enthusiastically when we sat down with them. "How are you guys?"

"We're doing good," I said. "What about you two?"

"I'm good. Jo's a little sick, so you should probably stay away from him."

"It's just a cold," Jo responded. "Nothing serious."

"Well, I hope you get better soon," Autumn said.

"You guys trying to get an early start today?" Juliet asked.

"Yes, I don't really know why though," Raiden answered. "It was Jo's idea."

"I just felt like we needed to be here," Jo said, running his hand through his red hair. "I don't know why either."

"Never ignore your feelings," I said, giving Autumn a smile.

"Yeah, Raiden," Devin said in a teasing voice. "Never ignore your *feelings*."

Jo busted out laughing and Raiden shook his head.

"Please don't bring up *that* story," Raiden said.

"What story?" I asked.

"Oh, nothing." Jo smirked. "It just involves Raiden peeing his pants during Devin's first day on border patrol."

"I'll never forget that," Devin said with a smile.

We joked around while we ate dinner for a whole hour before Jo and Raiden had to go. After we finished eating, the four of us hung out in Juliet's room until it was time for us to get ready for bed. Autumn lingered with me in the hall after we said goodnight to Devin and Juliet.

"What's up?" I asked her.

"Nothing really," she answered, smiling coyly. "It's just been a while since I've gotten to talk to you alone."

"Yeah, it has. We've been so busy lately."

"Yeah . . ." she trailed off. "It's been a while since I've asked how things are going between you and Presley."

It made sense that she was asking, I hadn't ever talked about her since prom. "We're just friends, if that's what you're wondering."

There was an awkward silence before she said anything. "Well, I think you're really great, Chaz."

"Thanks, Autumn." I said.

I knew what she was really trying to say, but I wasn't going to let it go there. "I think I'm ready for bed."

Looking a little disappointed, she moved forward and gave me a hug. "Have a good night."

"You too, Autumn."

I entered my room, shutting the door behind me. I sat down on my bed and contemplated getting ready to go to sleep but decided against it. I felt uneasy and restless. It might have been because all I could think about was going to war. Whatever the reason, I wouldn't be able to sleep. And it was the weekend, so my alarm wasn't going to go off at home and make me fall asleep here. It was going to be a long night.

I paced my room for a little while because sitting only made me feel more anxious. To distract myself, I pulled out my sword and started going through my offensive and defensive exercises. After beating Devin in a duel, I felt a lot more confident in my swordplay. As I smoothly moved through the drills, I continued to feel even more confident. Maybe I wasn't very much of a match for Juliet, but soon I would be.

I froze on the spot when I heard a faint noise coming from outside of my room. There was a *click*, and then what sounded like footsteps and a few quiet grunts. As I listen to the strange sounds it brought back memories of a vision I had when I first came to the Dream World. As I recalled the vision, I realized I had already seen this exact moment.

This was what happened right before I died.

Chapter 30

The Sleepless Night

Full of panic, I began to search my room, unsure of what I was actually looking for. I had to get out before they reached my door and trapped me inside. I glanced at my sword and took a couple of deep breaths. I just had to wake Autumn and Juliet, the three of us should be able to take them. I crept to my door and put my ear against it to listen. I heard footsteps and grunting and then there was a pause. *Click.* The footsteps and grunting increased as I assumed that they rushed into a room.

I quickly opened my door and hurried into the semi-lit hall toward Autumn's room. I looked back and saw another open door just two away from my own. I banged on Autumn's door then rushed over to bang on Juliet's.

"Juliet! Autumn!" I screamed. "Come out here quick! We're in danger!"

If they had already fallen asleep, then I was dead. My heart began to race as a black figure and three round creatures came out of the room. The part of the hall they were in was dark because the candles were out, but I didn't need light to know that I was staring at a Mors Somnia and three Nightmares.

As the creatures paused in front of me, Autumn came racing out of her room with an arrow nocked in her bow. Just as quickly, Juliet raced out of her room with her sword in hand. They both moved next to me and stood ready to fight.

"Why are you here?" Juliet asked.

"Isn't it obvious?" the Mors hissed in a high, squeaky voice. "To end you and take Chaz prisoner."

"I dare you to try it."

I think the Mors laughed. It sounded very wet, almost like he was choking. "You stand no chance."

"You underestimate us," Juliet replied.

Autumn quickly let loose an arrow, hitting one of the Nightmares. It began to disappear as the Mors made a screeching noise and rushed towards us. Two blades seeped from both of his arms as Juliet and I raised our swords to meet him in battle. He only took a few seconds to reach us, but once he did, Autumn had already gotten rid of the other two Nightmares.

The Mors attacked me and Juliet at the same time with each sword. Only because of my ability to see things before they happened was I able to block his attacks. He swung its sword so fast that I could barely keep up.

I searched the future for any possible way to land a blow, but all I saw was myself getting diced to ribbons. I decided I would focus on defense instead and let Juliet take care of the offensive part. I didn't know if she would be able to pull it off though, it was awkward fighting an opponent with someone else so close. I had to make sure I avoided getting in her way, while at the same time avoid hitting her with my sword. So far, it was a real struggle for me.

Suddenly, the Mors jumped at the wall and kicked off of it, sending himself into a spin with his blades outstretched. He looked like a tornado of death as he spun toward us. Juliet and I barely dove out of the way in time to avoid getting sliced. We had both dove in opposite directions. I landed on one side of the Mors and Juliet landed on the other. Autumn was on the same side as Juliet. She began firing arrows at him as it raced toward them. he swung its sword at each arrow, swatting them out of the air like annoying bugs.

I rushed at him from behind, expecting to surprise him as Juliet struggled to block both swords. Once I reached him, I was the one who was surprised as he quickly turned around and kicked me, sending me sprawling. In the instant that he kicked me, Juliet showed no hesitation by cutting his head clean off. The creature fell to the ground and disappeared.

I got kicked so hard that I wasn't able to breathe for a few seconds, I just lay on the ground in pain. Autumn and Juliet raced over to help me up.

"You okay?" Autumn asked. "Is anything broken?"

"No," I wheezed. "Just got the wind knocked out of me."

"If it wasn't for you distracting him, I wouldn't have been able to kill him," Juliet said. "I thought I was going to die."

"Next time, you be the distraction." My ribs were a little achy, but I didn't think they were broken. At least I hoped they weren't.

"How did they get in?" Autumn asked, sounding a little panicked. "Do you think there's more?"

"I don't know, Autumn," Juliet replied. "We need to let everyone know what happened."

"Do we even know where everyone lives?" I questioned. "Like Master Grayson or the Archduke?"

"I know they all live close to the rest of the nobles, near Fynn's family."

"I guess it would be a good idea to inform the captain of the army too," I added.

We left the hall and entered the dark waiting room, the only light coming from the bright moon, which spilled through the windows. We exited through the front doors and found four knights laying on the ground with their swords in their hands or at their sides. The sight made me feel sick to my stomach.

"This is awful," Autumn said with a whimper.

I would've responded, but I froze as I heard the sound of a struggle in the distance. I heard metal clinking against metal, and men shouting. I searched the dark courtyard but didn't see anything.

"It sounds like there's more," Juliet said. "Let's go."

We raced down the cobblestone path, and just past the

drawbridge was a knight locked in combat with a hooded attacker. Another knight lay a few feet away, probably dead. When the hooded attacker noticed us, he quickly finished off the other knight, as if it was nothing. As the knight fell to the ground, he turned to us.

"Well, well, well," the attacker said in a raspy voice that obviously belonged to a man and not a Mors Somnia. "I'm surprised you're all still alive. You must be tougher than you look."

"Who are you and what are you doing here?" Juliet demanded. I was impressed by her composure.

"Isn't it obvious?" the hooded man replied. "I'm with the Quin Anulus and we're here to knock this city to the ground."

"Just you and a few Nightmares?" I asked.

"The army will be here by morning. Too bad you three won't."

After he spoke, he made a clicking sound and something slammed into me from behind, knocking me flat on my face. I saw stars and my nose exploded with pain as it started to bleed. Something heavy moved onto my back, pinning me down. I craned my head to see a fat Nightmare perched on top of me, staring at me with its monstrous black eyes.

I turned my attention to the others to find Juliet locked in combat with the hooded man while Autumn was being assailed by one Nightmare after another. She would shoot one and then it would quickly be replaced by another, they seemed to just appear out of the night. I knew if I didn't help Autumn, she would quickly be swarmed by them. I tried to wiggle out, but the Nightmare was so heavy that I could barely move or breathe.

I looked to Juliet's duel again and noticed that they would pause and circle each other after a series of attacks. He must have been able to daydream too, that was why Juliet was still struggling to gain the upper hand. She was barely able to keep up with his attacks. I had to do something, or both my friends would die.

I looked down at my right hand and saw my sword laying right next to it. I grabbed it, but as soon as I did, the Nightmares tongue shot out and wrapped around my arm. I struggled against its tongue as it tried to pull my arm towards its mouth. I knew that the tongue was too strong, so I twisted my wrist so that my sword was pointing towards the Nightmare. I let it pull my arm, which sent my sword right into one of its eyes.

After the creature disappeared, I got up and raced towards Autumn. The Nightmares were no longer appearing, but two raced toward her at the same time. As she fired an arrow at the one in front of her, another came from the side and leapt at her, knocking her over.

As I neared, it turned to me and lashed out its tongue, once again wrapping around my sword arm. It jumped at me while its tongue was still fastened around my arm, so I punched it in the face with my free hand when it came close. It let go as it rolled away towards Autumn. She pulled out her dagger and finished it off with a quick stab.

I turned back toward Juliet and saw her sword locked

in place with the hooded figure's as they pushed against each other. The man no longer had his hood up, but it was still a little too dark to get a good look at him. All I knew was that he had a manbun and a square chin. They stared fiercely into each other's eyes for a minute when suddenly, he threw his head forward, smacking Juliet's forehead with his own. She staggered backwards and fell onto her rear.

"Stop!" I heard Autumn scream when the man was about to bring his sword down and finish her off. I was surprised when he actually did stop and glare at her. I turned to find her aiming her bow at him with an arrow ready to fire.

"Step away," Autumn said, her voice unsteady. "I will shoot you."

The man stepped away from Juliet and lowered his sword. "You would if I tried to harm your friend." he said. "But now you won't. You don't have it in you to shoot me unless you or your little friends are in danger." He started slowly backing away. "See, it's such an easy shot. Too bad you don't have the guts to do it. You're just an annoying kid." He smiled at her before he turned around and ran.

I ran to Juliet and helped her to her feet. She held onto my arm for a minute, trying to steady herself.

"You okay?" I asked. She had a small gash on her forehead, and she looked a little dizzy.

"Other than my killer headache, I'm okay."

"Nice job, Autumn," I said, turning around to look at her.

She stood in the same spot, staring at the ground, trembling as tears began to fall from her eyes. Juliet and I both moved to her side.

"What's wrong?" Juliet asked, wrapping an arm around her.

"This is too much," she said quietly. "All of this crazy stuff we have to do is too much. I was fine with killing those monsters, but people? I'm just a teenager, I can't kill a person. I shouldn't be expected to do this." She began to sob.

"You're right, Autumn," Juliet said. "We shouldn't be expected to do these things, but unless we fight, innocent people are going to get hurt. That's the thought that keeps me going. There are thousands of people who look to us for hope. I don't want to kill any people either, and I don't plan on it."

"That's the difference between us and them," I said, staring sadly at the dead knight on the ground. "The Quin Anulus will kill human beings, but we don't have to. We won't." I felt anger flare up inside of me as I thought about what the Quin Anulus had done so far, and what they were going to continue to do. I wouldn't let them win, I had to stop them.

Autumn started wiping her eyes. "I'm sorry. Let's keep going."

"We still need to warn everyone," I said, taking the lead.

We continued on our way past the drawbridge into the fountain area. I quickly scanned the area for movement before we made our way through. Just as we were about to continue, a few Nightmares seemed to just appear out of thin air right in front of us. I quickly counted four of them.

"Let's take 'em out quick," I said, charging toward the nearest one. It leapt at me and I sidestepped out of the way, while at the same time thrusting my sword into its direct path. The nightmare sailed right into my sword, slicing itself in two. I turned to find only one nightmare remaining. It leaped at Autumn and she shot it out of the air as it sailed toward her.

"Nice," I said, turning my attention to Juliet who looked like she was struggling to stand up. Her eyelids started opening and closing very slowly. "Autumn, I think she's falling asleep!" I ran over and steadied her as her head began to slowly bob up and down.

"Juliet, you have to stay awake," Autumn said, shaking her shoulder.

"So . . . so tired." She said, her eyes continuing to open and close. "I just . . . need to rest for . . . a minute."

"You can't!" I said. "We need you! Stay awake!" That was the last thing we needed, Juliet to fall asleep and leave us. I couldn't help but freak out inside as her head continued to bob sleepily. Someone was probably trying to wake her up on the other side.

"Please . . . for a minute," she slurred.

Supporting most of her weight, I half dragged, half helped her walk over to the fountain.

"What are you doing?" Autumn asked from behind

me.

"Waking her up," I said.

Once we were at the edge of the fountain, I scooped some of the cold water into my hand and flung it at her face. She jumped back and began spitting like something nasty got in her mouth.

"What did you do that for?" she asked, obviously a lot more awake than before.

"Chaz," Autumn said. "There's someone coming."

I turned to find a hooded figure approaching. He was at least twenty feet away. He pulled out a sword as he approached.

I looked at Juliet and found her sleepily blinking her eyes and dipping her head again.

"Autumn, keeping splashing Juliet with water." I said, handing the sleepy girl off to her. I turned to the approaching figure and pulled out my sword.

"Please be careful, Chaz," Autumn said desperately.

I approached the person I assumed was a member of the Quin Anulus and stopped about ten feet away. "Leave us alone," I said, sounding a little pathetic.

The person didn't stop or slow. "You're coming with me," he said.

He quickly closed the distance between us, and before I could even try to see the future, he started attacking. I blocked two of his attacks before my sword was knocked out of my hands and his was near my throat.

"Really?" he scoffed. "That's it? You're so helpless, it makes me want to laugh."

I felt embarrassed and ashamed by how easily he beat me. As I tried to come up with a plan, the hooded man turned his head to the left like he noticed something down the street. I turned my head as well and saw a robed figure walking down the street towards us. The hooded guy lowered his sword and turned to face the approaching stranger, taking two steps towards him. Once he was close enough, I realized it was Seer Farnsworth. He came to my side and pulled a saber similar to my own out of his robe.

"Don't try it, Keaton," Farnsworth warned the hooded man. "I have already seen at least twenty different versions of this fight, and let me assure you, you don't win a single one."

Keaton made a 'hmph' noise and then said, "Whatever you say, old man." He turned around and jogged away, quickly disappearing into the night.

"Thanks, Seer Farnsworth," I said, turning around to see if Juliet was still awake.

She sat on the edge of the fountain looking more alert than ever as Autumn stood by her side, gazing at the seer in awe. We walked over to them and Juliet stood up.

"I feel like I just woke up," she said.

"You're not sleepy anymore?" I asked.

"Nope."

"Do you think someone was trying to wake you up?" Autumn asked.

"No, it was my alarm."

"Who sets an early alarm on the weekend?" I asked, dumbfounded.

"I have a big dance recital to get ready for." She said defensively. She stood up. "I'm ready to go."

"Alright." I turned to the Seer. "What are you doing here, by the way?"

"Like I said earlier, I have seen this night many different times, and I knew where I was needed at the exact moment."

"That's amazing!" Autumn said. "What should we do next?"

"What you were already planning on doing," he said. "We need to first inform Captain Fynn and his family, and then wake up the rest of the city. The war has started."

I shivered at his last sentence. Just like that, it was time for battle.

"When did you realize it had started?" Juliet asked.

"The moment I found two Mors Somnia in my bedchamber." He started walking away. "Let's go."

Two Mors Somnia had managed to sneak into his room and try to assassinate him and he was still alive? That meant he had to be the greatest swordsman in the Kellamare. No one could take on two at once. As I followed him down the street, I silently wished that before the night was over, I would get to see him fight multiple Mors at a time.

On our way to Fynn's house, we finally ran into some good guys. They were two knights just making their usual rounds through the city. When the Seer questioned them, they told us they hadn't seen any unusual activity.

"Wake the city, war is upon us." The Seer said before

we continued on our way. We reached the home of Fynn's family without a sign of anyone else. A couple of windows in the house still had candles burning near them, so I assumed they were still awake. Farnsworth marched up to the front door and banged loudly.

"Albor! Fynn!" he yelled. "The city is under attack! War is here!"

I heard scuffling in the house, and after a few seconds, Fynn's father, Albor came rushing out holding his sword. "What is this you speak of?" he demanded.

Right then, Fynn came rushing out as well, chain mail spilling out of the bottom of his vest.

"A small group of Quin Anulus members have invaded the city," Farnsworth explained. "We have already run into a few of them. The majority of their force have not yet arrived. They will be at our walls before dawn."

"Why would they send a small group inside of our walls?" Albor asked.

"To assassinate as many key players as they can before the war begins."

Just as he finished speaking, a loud bell sounded in the distance. It clanged over and over again. It was sure to wake up most of the city.

"I will prepare my men," Fynn said, racing back into the house.

"And I will round up as many able-bodied men as I can," Albor said before he raced down the street.

Seer Farnsworth turned his attention to us. "You three will come with me. There is much to do if we want this night to play out in our favor."

As we followed Farnsworth, the city really came to life. Candles began to light up in windows of dark houses, knights ran around gathering gear and shouting orders, families were being directed to safe houses and bunkers throughout the city. The air was filled with worry and fear as wives begged their husbands not to go and children cried at their feet.

I was surprised when I realized we were heading to the entrance of the city. "Where are we going?" I asked.

"To check on our men patrolling the walls," The Seer answered, glancing toward the wall to the right of the city entrance.

I followed his gaze and noticed at least five silhouettes on the top of the wall. Steel clanged against steel as they danced back and forth. We reached the stairs of the guard tower that was connected to the wall. Farnsworth looked back and paused for a few seconds before he began to ascend the steps. We followed right behind him as he climbed up the dark tower.

"There's something you must know," he said as we climbed. "Even though I have seen this night many times over, there are still events that I cannot prevent from happening. There will be many deaths tonight. I wish it wasn't true, but it is. Of course, as I said before, the future is unwritten, and it is still possible to change it. Let's do our best tonight to protect those we love."

Though the stairs continued to go up, there was an opening that led onto the wall. We exited and made our way to the figures who were once fighting. All was silent and there wasn't much movement either. On the ground closer to us was someone sitting. There was a Mors approaching the person on the ground while two other Mors stood still a few yards back. All around us on the ground were lifeless bodies. I noticed only one or two breathing.

We approached the person sitting on the ground, and once we were close enough, I realized it was Raiden. He was holding a nasty cut underneath his right arm. I noticed that Jo was lying on the ground next to him. His eyes were closed, and he looked a lot more beat up than Raiden. As we approached, Jo's body began to slowly turn into dust and float away. It was the strangest sight and I hoped it only meant he had fallen asleep. The Seer stepped in front of Raiden to face the Mors. The Mors stopped in its tracks and became still.

"Is he alive?" Farnsworth asked Raiden.

Raiden nodded as he wiped a dirty hand over his forehead. "Barely. He must have fallen unconscious and returned to the Waking World."

Seer Farnsworth pulled out his sword and started toward the closest Mors.

"Don't," Raiden said, standing up. "There were a lot of us, and we still couldn't stop them."

"I know exactly how this will play out," Farnsworth said, raising his sword as he continued. "Don't interfere and this should be over quickly."

"Let us help you" Juliet said, stepping forward.

"Trust me, Juliet. Stay where you are."

I couldn't believe what I was about to witness. Seer Farnsworth against three Mors Somnia? There was no way he could win. But if he did win, and I got to witness it, then my life would be complete. I had never wished so hard that I had a camera with me.

As he approached the closest Mors, it raised its sword while the two behind remained in place. As quick as a blur, the Mors dashed at Farnsworth and slashed its sword horizontally. Just as quickly, Farnsworth sidestepped and ducked, easily dodging the slash. And in one swift movement, he pivoted on his left foot and stabbed the sword through the creatures back. Just like that, it dissolved and disappeared.

The other two Mors must have realized they underestimated him because they both began to advance at the same time, their blades held ready. The Seer's body followed the Mors that began circling him until he stood facing it with the other one straight behind. The one behind rushed forward soundlessly while the one to the front advanced as well.

Without looking, Farnsworth brought his sword over his head and behind his back, blocking the first attack from the Mors to his rear. As the one to the front slashed at him, he ducked the attack, which ended up cutting off the head to the Mors to his rear. As Farnsworth rose up, he brought his sword up with him, cutting the last creature in half vertically.

After they both dissolved, he sheathed his sword and made his way back towards us. I couldn't believe what I had just witnessed. Seer Farnsworth was a living legend. He was better than Yoda. I was a little disappointed that the fight didn't last longer, but I still I shouted in triumph and pumped my first in the air.

"That was amazing!" I exclaimed.

"Can you walk?" Farnsworth asked Raiden. "We need to get you medical attention."

"I think so," Raiden answered. As he slowly rose to his feet, pain flashed across his face.

Suddenly a strong wave a drowsiness hit me. I felt so tired that I knew I could fall asleep standing up. It became hard to think. Getting rest was all that mattered at the moment.

"I need . . . sleep." I said, looking for a spot to lay down.

"Oh no!" someone said. Was that Autumn?

"No, you don't, Chaz," Juliet said, suddenly beside me. I felt a smack to my face, and I was shocked out of my stupor for a second. I wasn't supposed to go to sleep. My friends needed my help. But maybe I would be more helpful if I took a nap first. I had just started to close my eyes when I received another slap to my face.

"You helped me stay awake, so I'm going to help you this time," Juliet said, pinching my cheeks. I was starting to get annoyed. I was so tired. Why wouldn't she just let me sleep? I tried to fall to the ground, but she wouldn't let me.

"Stop," I said, starting to feel more alert. Slowly the drowsiness faded, and I no longer felt tired. "Oh great, I didn't set an alarm, so that means someone was trying to wake me up."

"Are you normally a heavy sleeper?" Juliet asked.

"Not at all. They might think I'm dead or something."

"And they will probably keep trying to wake you up."

"Not again," Autumn complained. "What do we do?"

"We have to keep Chaz awake," The Seer said. "We need all three of you tonight."

Chapter 31

I Crush a Monster's Heart with My Hand

This was definitely the scariest and most intense moment of my entire life. I knew nothing in my life could prepare me for this. I stood in a dark field outside the walls of Kellamare with my sword in hand. The moon was full, but it was still too dark to see the large number of knights on horseback that were gathered a few hundred yards in front of us. I didn't need to see them to know that there were tens of thousands of them ready to defend the city. I also knew that Archduke Bradford, Captain Fynn, Master Grayson, and other friends were at the head of that army.

I looked around and took in the significantly smaller horseless army that I stood at the head of. We consisted of a few thousand untrained men with simple weapons and a determination to protect their families. Thankfully, this little army was only supposed to be a second wave, or a backup. We probably wouldn't see too much action. At least that was my hope. I glanced to my right and saw Autumn, Juliet and Seer Farnsworth. I turned to my left and saw Devin, Charley, and Garriton. I really hoped that I wouldn't have to see any of them get hurt.

We had only been out here ready for war for about twenty minutes. After we rushed Raiden to the infirmary, we helped wherever we could to prepare for the coming battle. At first, we were preparing to defend the city from inside the walls, but the Seer insisted that in order to win the war we had to meet them outside. He had seen various possibilities of the war, and he said the only way to come out on top was to meet them head on with two waves.

Everyone thought the idea was insane until Archduke Bradford agreed to it. Of course, Juliet had volunteered to stand at the head of the second army, so naturally Autumn and I came with her. It took a couple of hours of preparation until we made our way out here. The Seer even knew exactly which direction they would come from.

While all that preparation was going on, I had a few more sleep attacks. Autumn and Juliet did well at keeping me awake, but there were some close calls. There was one point when the drowsiness didn't wear off for almost ten minutes. And that was when Juliet decided to keep dunking my head straight into a barrel of water. I wasn't happy about her trying to drown me in that moment, but I was grateful when I finally did come back to my senses. Even hours later without another incident, I was still a little worried about it happening in the middle of the battle.

I turned my attention back to my friends, wondering

how they were doing. I looked at Juliet and saw the usual determined look on her face. I shifted my gaze to Autumn and caught her already staring at me.

"You okay?" I asked.

"I'm scared." she said. "But I'm sure most of us are."

"Yeah. I'm scared, and I don't think I'm ready for this. But I'm not going to let any of that stop me from keeping you safe. Stay close to me."

She smiled for the first time since all this crazy stuff had started. "Chaz . . ." She paused. "I like you a lot. I just wanted you to know that."

I was very surprised by her confession and I didn't know how to respond. I knew she had liked me for a while, but this was the first time she had the courage to actually tell me. I definitely liked her too, but her friendship was too important to me to risk it by starting a relationship. I felt very conflicted.

Before I decided how to respond, a deep horn sounded in the distance. It was the signal. The war had officially begun.

The thunder of hooves striking the ground filled the air as the first wave charged forward.

"For Kellamare!" Garriton shouted, raising his sword in the air.

"For Kellamare!" the rest of us roared as we raced through the grassy field. We jogged towards the battle for a few minutes before the actual sounds of war even reached our ears. The quiet night quickly turned into a symphony of metal scraping metal, men screaming, horses whinnying and the sound of grunting Nightmares. As we came closer to the other group, I realized that some of the Nightmares were already breaking through their ranks and heading straight toward us. Thanks to the full moon, we were able to see the swarm of what looked like giant frogs heading our way, their grunting growing even louder.

"Hold your ground!" Garriton commanded. "Let none pass!"

It only took another minute until they were upon us. The night was a blur of swords flashing and tongues flailing. There was so much going on that I didn't have much time to think. I opened my mind to the future and went to town on those monsters. A Nightmare leapt at me and I ran my sword through its throat. I sidestepped another one and cut it in half. I grabbed a tongue wrapped around my arm, pulling the Nightmare towards me before I jabbed my sword in its face. I kicked one like a soccer ball sending it right to Juliet who chopped it in half as it sailed through the air.

Things weren't going quite so well for everyone. I saw a Nightmare leap onto a man's back, sending him sprawling into a group of other Nightmares that immediately began to trample him. A man got his sword ripped out of his hands by a long black tongue before it tossed it back at him, piercing him in the ribs. Someone else got lifted up and then smashed hard into the ground by the tongue of a massive Nightmare.

The seemingly endless battle against the creatures went on for who knows how long, then everything quickly began to change when a Mors Somnia and a hooded guy of the Quin Anulus joined the fray. The Mors immediately began mowing down men with its black blade. The hooded figure with his strange weapon went straight for Devin.

The weapon he held was unlike anything I had seen before, it looked like a pole with a short sword on each end. The hooded man quickly spun it around over his head and behind his back like he was showing off before he engaged Devin in a fight. Once Garriton noticed, he began plowing his way through Nightmares, trying to reach Devin. He was eventually able to join the fight as well, and together, he and Devin took on the hooded figure.

I turned my attention back to the Mors. The men were doing everything they could to move out of his path as he made his way towards Autumn and Juliet. Autumn was easily picking off Nightmares with her bow as Juliet covered her back. I turned to search for the Seer and found him already dueling the huge Mors with the deep voice I had seen in Beckstead. Where did that one come from?

I ran to Juliet and Autumn, reaching them before the Mors did.

"We've got company," I said, gesturing to the monster that was only a few yards away.

"He's not the only one," Juliet said. I turned around to find another Mors heading toward us. "There's no one else who can help us right now. You take one, I'll take the other. Autumn, you watch our backs. You can do this, Chaz." She charged towards her foe, leaving me all alone with mine.

My hands began to sweat like crazy as I tightened my grip on my sword. I knew I wouldn't be able to win in a sword fight against the Mors, but maybe I could stall it until Juliet was finished with hers.

"Stand down." The Mors commanded in a slithery voice. He stopped just a few feet away. "You are not the one I was sent to destroy."

"Never." I said, searching the future for a way to hurt him.

Without another word, he attacked. I blocked and dodged as I searched for an opening. The Mors wasn't the fastest one I had seen, but he was definitely strong. Every blow jolted my arm and I knew I wouldn't be able to take it for very long. He must have also known I would tire quickly, because he didn't try anything tricky or really try to slip past my defense.

My arms quickly grew weak and I hadn't been able to find any openings. As I blocked another swing of his sword, I kicked at his legs, hoping to trip or make him stumble, but he didn't move an inch. I skipped backwards as my toes flared up in pain. It felt like I kicked an iron block.

The Mors pressed towards me and started attacking again. I became desperate and tried to sneak in an attack, but I quickly realized that it was a mistake when he knocked the sword out of my hand and hit me on my left shoulder with the flat of its blade. Pain exploded from my shoulder as I fell to my knees. The smallest amount of movement made it hurt even more; it had to be broken or dislocated.

I tried to stand back up, but he put a hand on my hurt shoulder and shoved me to the ground. My vision went mostly black as the pain threatened to knock me unconscious. I looked around for help, but no one seemed to notice me. Most of the men had given us a wide berth, and who could blame them? They weren't knights, they were just men trying to protect their families.

I looked up at the Mors to find him smiling down at me, relishing in my helplessness. "You're all alone," he gloated, picking up my sword. "You can't stop me from slaying your friends." He tilted his head to the right and an arrow sailed harmlessly past, missing by inches.

"I'm still here," said Autumn's voice. I turned around to find her a few feet away, nocking her last arrow. This whole scene was too familiar.

"Autumn, he's not going to kill me," I said. "Get out of here."

She pulled the arrow back. "You told me to stay close to you."

The Mors moved past me and began walking toward Autumn. Still aiming at him, she began backing away.

"Autumn, run!" I shouted. I got up and looked for anything I could use for a weapon, but there was nothing. I felt angry, scared, and sick with worry as I tried to figure out what to do. Autumn let go of her last arrow, but the Mors easily blocked it with a flick of his sword. I had to do something.

A random knight noticed what was going on and

charged in our direction. He quickly closed in on the Mors and attacked without hesitation. He put up a good fight for maybe ten seconds before the Mors cut him down and continued towards Autumn. Sickened by the sight of more death, I quickly started towards the Mors. Every step sent waves of pain into my shoulder. Autumn pulled out a knife and held it up like she was going to stand her ground and fight. As I quickened my pace, I noticed another one off in the distance appear out of thin air and attack the Seer, who was making his way towards us.

As I began to wonder how they just appeared out of thin air, I remembered Devin saying that they were pretty much just big masses of nothing. But if they were nothing, how could they also be tangible at the same time? Maybe they were only tangible when they wanted to be? It didn't really make any sense to me, but it gave me a crazy idea.

I didn't know what else to do, so I punched my hand forward into his back, willing my hand to go through it. I was surprised when my hand did go right through it, sinking inside his chest. The Mors let out a high-pitched squeal that hurt my ears as I felt around inside. It felt really weird, like there was something there, but at the same time, it felt like there wasn't. It would've been impossible to describe.

The creature continued to squeal as I moved my hand around, searching for some way to harm him. There had to be something in him. I pushed my hand forward a little bit more and finally felt something solid, it was the size of a marble and it was near the front of the chest. The little marble was cold and weighed nothing. It felt like a squishy bubble. When I grabbed it, I suddenly got hit with a big wave of emotions, and they were all negative.

I felt sadness, regret, fear, depression, doubt, hurt, frustration, and more. I felt so ashamed of myself and what my life had become, I felt like I was suffocating. I wanted to escape all of the negative emotions, but I didn't know how. In my panic, I clenched my hands and squeezed the bubble like a stress ball. There was a loud pop and then the Mors Somnia was gone.

I stared at my hand, expecting it to be covered in monster blood or bubble juice, but it was clean. I looked up to find Autumn staring at me in confusion.

"Um . . . what just happened?" she asked.

"I totally just reached inside him and crushed his heart or something," I replied, excited.

"That sounds gross, but nice job."

She quickly closed the distance between us and gave me a hug, squeezing me tightly before letting go. "Thanks for saving me."

"Don't thank me yet," I said, picking up my sword with my left hand. My right shoulder still hurt too much to move.

I began to survey the battlefield, looking for more hearts to crush. I finally felt like the superhero I was supposed to be. I looked around and noticed the Nightmares had slowed quite a bit. We weren't swarmed by them like we were before. But even then, there were still a few Mors Somnia cutting people down with ease. I suddenly remembered Juliet and began searching for her. I found her walking towards us with the Seer's arm around her neck as he limped beside her. When we started towards them, I was quickly reminded about my shoulder again as it flared up in pain.

"Seer Farnsworth, are you okay?" Autumn asked once we reached them.

"I wouldn't be if Juliet hadn't come to my rescue," he answered, sounding old and tired. A strip of his robe was cut off and wrapped around his calf. "I wasn't able to predict everything that would happen."

"We saw you do something to that Mors, Chaz," Juliet said. "What happened?"

"I killed it from the inside somehow," I said, grimacing at my shoulder pain. "I think I might have dislocated my arm."

"We'll have to find someone who can fix that," the Seer said. "For now, maybe you should help me walk so Juliet and Autumn can continue to fight off the rest of the Nightmares."

I felt slightly annoyed and ashamed as I put the Seer's arm around my neck and watched Autumn and Juliet head off to fight more monsters. Before I even hurt my arm, I wasn't much help, and now I just had to sit on the sidelines and let the girls do the dirty work.

"What do we do now?" I asked, glancing around. Men and monsters were becoming scarce on the battlefield. There were a lot less people standing than when we had started. I caught sight of Devin still struggling against the hooded guy, but I didn't see Garriton anywhere. I searched until I saw him on the ground, struggling to stand up. "We have to help them."

"I don't think there's much we can do," Farnsworth said, sadly. "We will only get in the way."

I continued to watch as the hooded guy and Devin fought back and forth, Devin was mainly on the offensive, trying hard to land a hit. It was no use though. The hooded guy's weapon was impossible to get passed because he used both ends so skillfully. Once Garriton finally got to his feet, the hooded guy cut Devin's arm and smashed him in the face with the handle of his weapon. Devin fell to the ground and didn't get up.

The man was about to finish him off, but Garriton quickly closed the distance between them and grabbed the hooded guys weapon with both hands. Garriton tried to wrestle it from his grasp for a minute, until he got kicked in the gut and fell onto his back. Hooded guy didn't hesitate to stab Garriton in the chest with his weapon.

"No!" I screamed as Garriton fell to the ground.

He turned to face me before he vanished in a blur of darkness.

Chapter 32

Ultimate Chaz Mode

I quickly helped Seer Farnsworth over to where Garriton lay and we both fell down at his side. I gazed from his pale face to his fatal wound. After seeing all the blood he'd lost, I knew there was no saving him.

"Garriton?" I said, hoping he wasn't gone yet.

He opened his eyes slightly and gazed at us a moment before closing them.

"Brother!"

I turned to find Charley racing over. As he crashed to the ground next to us, I was able to fully see the awful condition he was in. His face looked like it had taken a brutal beating; one of his eyes was swollen shut and he was covered in cuts and scrapes.

"Brother, please, no!" Charley cried. "Don't leave me."

"I'm sorry . . ." Garriton began weakly, choking as he spoke. "I'm sorry, Charles."

Tears began to fall from Charley's eyes. "You have

nothing to be sorry about. You have been the best big brother I could've asked for."

"I love you, Charley." Garriton closed his eyes. "I'm glad . . . that even after death, we still got to . . . grow up together. Tell Fynn . . . thanks for all the . . . adventures." Garriton's body relaxed as his chest rose then fell one last time.

My eyes brimmed with tears as Charley let out a pained yell before he leaned down and sobbed on his brother's chest. Why did he have to die? Why did anyone have to die? I wanted to feel angry, but I couldn't. There was nothing there. I felt empty inside.

The Seer put a hand on my shoulder as Devin walked over and plopped down next to us. He was holding his arm as it bled.

"Let's get that wrapped up," Farnsworth said, tearing a strip off of his robe.

As I stared at Garriton's lifeless body, I began to wonder where he was now and what he was doing. "What happens after death?" I asked, not really expecting an answer. "Is it just like a never-ending sleep? Or is there something else?"

The Seer finished tying the strip around Devin's arm before he spoke. "It's certainly not a never-ending sleep. You could say it's finally waking up."

We sat there for a few minutes as the sun finally began to rise over the horizon, lighting up the day and warming my skin.

"Remember when I told you about the insignia of the

country?" Devin asked.

"It's a symbol for hope," I answered.

"No matter how dark the night or stormy the day, the sun will always return again with light and warmth."

I felt a little ray of hope from his words as I watched the sunrise. Maybe things would be okay.

Chaaaaazzzz.

The familiar multi-toned, icy voice seemed to penetrate my mind. I rose to my feet and searched the grounds. It couldn't be him. Not now. As I searched the field, I didn't see anything out of the ordinary. Most of the fighting was over. Those who weren't fighting were tending to the wounded and checking for signs of life in those who lay on the ground. I spotted Juliet racing in my direction with a look of worry on her face. Wondering what was going on, I turned around, and that's when I spotted him.

Maybe twenty yards away was a Mors Somnia with the lower half of one leg missing. It was my dad's Mors Somnia. He was balancing on his one good leg and one hand was wrapped around Autumn's waist while the other hand was holding her head. Her eyes were closed, and she looked unconscious. There were three Nightmares there as well. They were snapping at Autumn like they were trying to get a taste of her, but he kept pushing them away.

I felt a burning anger course through me as I sprinted towards the Mors. If it had harmed Autumn in any way, I was going to make it pay. Actually, I was going to make it pay no matter what. I didn't need my sword to do it either. I was going to reach inside it and destroy it like I did to that other Mors earlier.

Running hurt my shoulder like crazy, but I didn't care, I had to save Autumn. Juliet was right behind me with her sword drawn. Right before we reached them, the Mors let go of Autumn and she flopped to the ground. He got down on his hands and one foot and quickly raced away while the Nightmares trampled Autumn and licked the air in a crazed frenzy. It only took us a few seconds to take out the three of them. When they were gone, I knelt down next to her just as her body started to turn to dust and float away.

"No, no, no!" I cried as tears threatened to spill from my eyes. "What's happening? She can't be . . ."

"She probably just fell asleep," Juliet said, sounding unsure. "I bet someone back home was trying to wake her up."

I desperately hoped that was all it was. But what if those monsters did something to her? What if they hurt her? Why did she only start fading away after they trampled her? What if she was gone and I never got to tell her how I felt? It was all my fault for not staying close to her, I should've kept an eye on her. The rage continued to boil inside of me until I felt like I couldn't take it anymore.

I stood up and pulled out my sword. I looked off into the distance and found my dad's Mors Somnia standing there staring at me, like he was daring me to do something.

"What are you doing, Chaz?" Juliet asked, wiping a tear from her face.

"I'm going after it," I said, stepping forward.

"You'll get yourself hurt. Besides, I just remembered

that–"

I didn't let her finish, I raced away as fast as I could. This time I was going to make sure that one of us didn't leave alive. As I raced towards him, a few Nightmares began making their way into my path, cutting me off. I felt annoyed that they were going to slow me down. I wanted so badly to destroy the Mors, and the Nightmares were just a waste of my time. I began to search the future for the fastest way to get rid of the ones in my path. After I saw it, I tried to push the future to hurry up, I willed myself to already be there running my sword through the first one.

I was so angry, and yet so in sync with the future, I didn't really know what was happening. Suddenly I *was* there, shoving my sword into the first Nightmare. Then, I willed myself to be at the next one, and there I was, bringing my sword down onto its head.

I must have been so numb with anger and so full of adrenaline that I didn't even notice myself running to each Nightmare, I was always already there, cutting each one down as I went. After there were no more Nightmares in my path. I looked ahead and saw him a good distance off. I began to search the future until I found the moment when I was already fighting it. Once I found it, I willed myself to be there.

Just like that, I appeared right in front of the Mors Somnia. He seemed surprised that I got there so quickly as he sprang away and crouched low. Maybe I was really speeding up time? Whatever I was doing, it felt natural. I felt like I had control of the future like I never had before.

I watched as large black claws morphed out of the Mors' fingertips and he let out a growl. I raised my sword and got ready to strike.

"Why hasn't your leg grown back?" I taunted, also a bit curious.

"Because Robert no longer feeds." The Mors hissed. "He no longer suffers. And it's all your fault."

I wasn't exactly sure what it meant, but I didn't really care. "How bout I take off another limb?"

He growled again and sprang at me quicker than any creature I had encountered before. I didn't want to waste any more time with this piece of garbage, so I urged myself to be behind him, and that's where I appeared, slashing my sword down at his back. The Mors twisted around just in time to block my sword with his claws before he sprang away again.

"I see you've learned some new tricks," he hissed, an annoyed look on its face.

No more talking. It was time to finally end him. I appeared right in front of him, thrusting my sword at his chest, but once again, he knocked my sword out of the way with his claws before I did any damage. He swiped his other claw at me, and I was barely able to spin out of the way, getting a small scratch on my back. I appeared at his side, swinging my sword towards his neck. As he ducked, I suddenly appeared above. I landed on him and pushed my sword into his chest as he fell to the ground. My dad's Mors Somnia let out a final screech and then dissolved.

I knelt on the ground as the adrenaline started to fade.

That's when the pain in my shoulder and the exhaustion finally started to catch up with me. I actually did it. He was finally dead. Dad would finally go back to normal. I dropped my sword and sat down on my rear. I just wanted to go to sleep. The drowsiness was starting to hit me again. After a minute or two of sitting on the ground, Juliet stopped next to me and rested her hands on her knees, breathing hard.

"Chaz, you . . ." she said between breaths. "You . . . how did you do that?"

"Do what?" I asked, staring numbly off into the distance.

She took a minute to catch her breath. "You kept disappearing and appearing somewhere else. You know, like you were teleporting! It was the craziest thing I have ever seen."

"Really?" I kind of suspected I was doing something like that, but I wouldn't have believed it unless someone else saw it. Plus, how was that even possible?

"Really! You ran after the Mors and all of a sudden you appeared next to the first Nightmare. After you killed it you appeared at the next one. You killed all of them within seconds before you teleported to the Mors." She paused. "Chaz, whatever you did was crazy insane. I've never heard of anyone doing anything like that."

Laughter boomed from somewhere off in the distance, startling us both. It sounded like it was so far away, but it was still pretty loud.

"No one has done *this* before either." A voice boomed

out in the distance.

I felt a tight grip around my neck, making it impossible to breathe. I grasped at the invisible clamp around my neck and felt nothing there. Suddenly, I was lifted off the ground by my neck and pulled away from Juliet. I zoomed through the air like a dog dangling on a leash. The ground was a blur as I raced across the battlefield. My vision started to go black from the lack of air. Before it completely left me, I found myself literally in the hand of Victor, being choked to death. After I recognized him, he dropped me, and I fell to the ground gasping for air.

"I told you the Quin Anulus has powers beyond your imagination," Victor said, grinning from ear to ear like a kid opening presents on Christmas. "I can bend reality to my will in ways you couldn't comprehend."

I slowly stood up and took in my surroundings. The area was a lot more dry and yellow compared to what I had seen so far of Elegit Terram. The mountains towered above us; they couldn't have been even a mile away. The road led to a small pass that went right in between the mountains. I hadn't studied the map enough to know where I was.

Standing behind Victor was four hooded figures. One was a lot smaller than the rest and I was pretty sure it was Ben. I glanced around before I turned my attention to Victor. "What do you want from me?" I croaked. I was surprised my voice actually worked after getting my throat crushed.

"I already told you what I want" he replied casually.

"I want you to join me. Especially after what I saw you just do. It's pretty amazing that you were able to figure out how to do something like that without the assistance of the Mors Somnia. You're the first one who has learned to do that on his own. Of course, I learned how to do that and more a lot faster. What I just did to you was only a small glimpse of my power."

"I already told you that I won't join you."

Victor shrugged. "It doesn't matter if you say you won't, I have ways to make you do what I want. Some of it involves corrupting the dreams of those you love, like you've already seen me do. But of course, it would be so much better if you came willingly."

"Why?"

"Your willingness is the key. Let me show you something." He made a gesturing motion with his hand, as if revealing a piece of art.

At his signal, the other members of the Quin Anulus removed their hoods. I recognized three of them. To his right was Ben and the woman named Victoria who was at the conference in Calverstone. To his left was a man I didn't know, but he had a familiar man-bun and a square chin. To my surprise, next to him stood Ken, the Asian guy who told me about the butterfly swords.

After they revealed themselves, I noticed everyone's shadow, besides Ben's, started lifting up from the ground and taking shape in the air. Slowly, faces appeared on each one as they solidified. It was their own faces. They each had their own Mors Somnia standing next to them. I stepped back in horror as all of the creepy Mors smiled at me. Victor's was especially disturbing because it looked so much like me.

"W-what is this?" I stuttered.

"This is how we are so powerful." Victor replied. "We bind ourselves to our own Mors Somnia's, becoming one with them and ridding ourselves of all fear."

I glanced at Ben curiously, wondering why he didn't have one. He looked a little uncomfortable.

"Some are still in training." Victor said, noticing my gaze. "This is why we need you to join us willingly. It will not work otherwise."

"Why me, of all people?" I asked. "You didn't know I would be as powerful as I am when I first talked to you."

"There are a few reasons. One is because you remind me so much of myself." He smiled. "The other reasons I will keep to myself for now. It's time for us to go. Congratulate the Seer for making your victory today possible. When you're ready to join the Quin Anulus, you will find us in Dolorem Terra. Or as I like to call it, *Imperious*."

He gave me one last smile before they all disappeared.

Scared, confused, and in pain, I finally laid down on the ground and let sleep overtake me.

Chapter 33

Everything Just Might Be Okay

I woke up to the sound of an unfamiliar beep. It was slow and steady, and I knew it wasn't my alarm. My bed was a whole lot more comfortable than I was used to. Something even better was the fact that I was no longer in pain. It was completely gone. My shoulder felt fine.

I opened my eyes and found myself in what looked like a hospital room. Everything was white, there were lots of machines around me, and my finger had a clip on it that was hooked up to a beeping heart rate monitor. The sun shone directly outside my window, blinding me whenever I moved my head just an inch to the right. I glanced around the room and saw Dad sitting in the corner on a chair. He was typing away on a laptop.

"Dad?" I said, my voice really dry.

He looked up from the laptop in surprise. "Chaz!" He set the laptop on the table next to him and came over and gave me an awkward, tight hug. "You're finally awake. You really freaked out your mom, you know."

"What happened?"

"You've been in a coma all day. We tried to wake you up this morning, but you wouldn't even move. After trying for almost an hour, your mom got scared and called for an ambulance. They brought you here, and after they couldn't wake you up either, they decided you were in a coma. They've been running tests all day and they still haven't been able to figure it out." He put a hand on my shoulder. "I'm glad you're okay."

"Where's mom?" I asked.

"She went to pick up Garrett from Grandma's. She'll be back soon."

I lay back onto my pillows as all the memories of the past day in the Dream World came rushing back. So much had happened. The Quin Anulus were a bunch of psychos, we had won the war, Dad's Mors Somnia was gone for good. Autumn was . . . What exactly happened to Autumn? Not until now did I remember that even if she did die in the Dream World, she would still be alive here. How did I forget that? I was so angry that I could have gotten myself killed. I had better call her. But not while Dad was around, he would be too curious.

"What have you been doing?" I asked. "Just surfing the web?"

"Not quite," he said, gazing at me thoughtfully. "I don't know exactly what it was, but something happened while I was sitting here waiting for you to wake up. Out of nowhere, I got these strong feelings of . . . hope. And not just hope, but a motivation and a desire to be better, to finally do something with my life." He paused and stared at the wall. "I don't know how to explain it, but it's like I finally woke up. I decided to start looking for a better job. And I've also been thinking about going back to school and chasing my dream of starting a restaurant. I know it won't be easy, but I at least want to try."

"That's amazing, Dad! I'm so happy you want to try it again. I'll do everything I can to help you get there."

"You've already been a big help," Dad said, squeezing my arm. "Thanks for always believing in me."

It was about twenty minutes later when Mom and Garrett got back. When they found me awake, they both cried. They hugged me for a long time and wouldn't let go until I told Mom she should tell the nurse I was awake. Before the doctor let me go, he asked me a lot of questions, like what I did the day before, what I ate, and other random things. With all the questions he asked, I might as well have told him my social security number and blood type. After we finally got home, I headed straight to my room and grabbed my cell phone.

I had three missed calls from Autumn, but nothing from Juliet. I immediately called her back and impatiently waited for her to pick up.

"Chaz!" Autumn screamed into the phone. "Are you okay? I've been so scared. I've been trying to get a hold of you and Juliet for a while! Is everything okay?"

"I'm okay, Autumn," I said, so happy to hear her voice. "I've been worried about *you*." I started feeling a little choked up. "I saw my dad's Mors Somnia holding you, and you weren't moving, and by the time we reached you, you started to disappear."

"It's okay, Chaz. I'm perfectly fine. I was already about to fall asleep when he snuck up on me from behind and grabbed me. I was too tired to fight back and the next thing I knew I was in my bed at home."

"I'm so glad you're safe."

"Same for you. What happened after I left? Is Juliet okay?"

"Juliet is fine," I said. "A lot happened. I don't know where to start. But there's something more important that I need to tell you first." I paused, not sure exactly what I wanted to say. "You know what, I'll tell you everything in person when I come visit you in Colorado tomorrow."

"Chaz . . . what?" Excitement spilled from her voice. "What do you mean?"

"I'm going to come see you tomorrow. It's not a very long drive, and my friend Jake has cousins out there. I'm sure I can convince him to drive me. I'll tell my parents we're going to hang out with them for a couple of days."

"Chaz!" she screamed into the phone, hurting my ear. "I would love that so much! I've never seen you in real life before! We should invite Juliet too."

"Good idea. I'll tell her as soon as I can. We can all hang out for real."

"Without having to worry about getting attacked by monsters," she added.

I laughed. "True. I can't wait. I'll see you soon, Autumn."

"See you soon, Chaz."

Later that evening, I talked to Jake about taking me to Colorado so he could hang out with his cousins and I could meet up with some friends. When he asked me what friends, I told him I met them online. He thought it was a little sketchy, but he was too nice to say no. After I talked him into it, I tried to convince Mom to let me go, but she said I would have to wait until next week so that we could make sure my health was okay.

An hour after that, I finally got a hold of Juliet. She had woken up not too long after I had, and her family was convinced she was in a coma as well. But she ended up waking up before they took her to the hospital. I told her about my plan to visit Autumn in Colorado and she said she would for sure come too. For some reason, the idea of meeting them both of them in real life was kind of scary, yet exciting at the same time.

Chapter 34

There's Always a Prophecy

The bright sun burned hot on my neck as Juliet, Autumn and I followed Archduke Bradford up the steps to one of the smaller houses in the nice part of Kellamare. Seer Farnsworth's house wasn't too far from Fynn's parent's houses. The nice little cottage home almost sat on a hill, so we had to climb many steps to reach the door.

When we first came back to the Dream World after the war was over, Bradford had us fill him in on every single thing that happened that night and the morning after. Fynn was there as well, the news of Garriton's death was very hard on him, he had to leave the room. I told the Archduke everything about my exchange with Victor and the Quin Anulus. He was greatly disturbed from hearing about the things Victor could do. He was also very impressed with the things I told him I could do. He had me try to demonstrate for him my teleporting abilities, but I couldn't figure out how to do it again. Thanks to Juliet's witness, he still believed the whole story.

For the next few days after, we had many meetings discussing what other things we might be able to accomplish with our reality bending powers. We also discussed the Quin Anulus and the Archduke's upcoming challenge for his office. Life became nothing but meetings and I was quickly getting tired of it. The only thing I liked was getting to make fun of Kaden for not being there during the war. He had gone to bed early that night, so he wasn't there for any of it. I joked about it every chance I got.

This morning, during one of our meetings, we were informed that the Seer's health had been getting worse ever since the war. He no longer had the strength to get out of bed or do much for himself. Apparently, he had something very important he needed to tell us before he passed on. I really hoped that he was just exaggerating, and he wasn't really about to die. I really liked the old man. He had saved my life multiple times.

When we reached the front door, Bradford knocked. After a few seconds Constable Darven opened it from the inside.

"Thank you for coming so quickly," Darven said with his usual friendly smile.

"Come on in."

The inside of the Seers house was very simple and fancy at the same time. It had a white marble floor, white walls, and small chandeliers hanging from the ceiling. There was a fireplace in one corner with an ugly floral couch facing it.

We followed Darven through the house to a door off to the side. He knocked before opening it. We walked into the small room to find Seer Farnsworth lying on a bed. He looked older and frailer than I had ever seen him. His prominent wrinkles and droopy eyes made him look like he had aged at least ten years since I last saw him.

Darven pushed some cushioned chairs near the side of the bed for us to sit in. We all sat down, and I suddenly felt very eager to hear what he was going to say.

"There are a couple of reasons why I invited you all," Farnsworth wheezed. "First, I wanted to let you know that I am certain my time is coming to an end. I believe the mantle of seership has chosen another." He turned to look at the Archduke. "I believe Darven has been chosen. I now ask you; will you accept Henry Darven as the new High Seer of Elegit Terram."

"I accept him," The Archduke said.

"Wonderful." Farnsworth smiled. "The second reason I brought you here is because I have received a prophecy."

"A prophecy?" I questioned.

"There's always a prophecy," Bradford commented, more to himself than anyone else.

"This particular prophecy was certainly a surprise," The Seer said. "Normally they come to me in visions. This one came to me in words as I slept last night. When I woke, I quickly wrote it down so I wouldn't forget. I have a copy of it for you three."

"Why us?" Juliet asked.

"I have a feeling it concerns you most." He handed

me a sheet of paper with elegant cursive handwriting on it. I knew I wouldn't be able to read it, so I handed it to Juliet.

"Too fancy for you?" Juliet asked, smirking.

"Just a little," I admitted.

"I'll read it, but don't expect me to read your birthday cards from your grandma for you as well."

Everyone shared a laugh.

"Go on and read it aloud," The Seer said.

Juliet cleared her throat and started reading.

"Three Waker's shall come to the world of dream,
all but unlearned and untested children they will seem,
three will not be essential, but three will be needed,
without the three, the one will be defeated,
it begins with the return of the blessed wayward son,
then the three gifts of prevention shall join as one,
the gift of visions will do more than improve the eyes,
the gift of premonitions will feel more than truth from lies,
the gift of protection will save more than those who call,
join them together and the Quin Anulus will fall."

After she finished reading, there was a short pause.

"I wish the whole prophecy was as specific as that last part," I complained. "And why are they always a complicated poem like that?"

"At least there's no question as to what will happen when the prophecy is fulfilled." Darven replied with an amused smile.

"Right now, it's hard to know for certain," the Seer began. "But I think we might already know who the three Wakers are."

"Well, Chaz definitely has the Gift of Visions," Juliet said. "And I think Autumn has the Gift of Premonitions. I have no idea what the Gift of Protection is though."

"Well, I think you're pretty good at protecting me and Chaz," Autumn pointed out.

"I bet the Wayward Son is Kaden," I said. "That guy thinks the whole world revolves around him. His brain has got to be very *wayward*."

Once again, everyone laughed.

"Well, it's all just speculation," the Seer said, sounding tired. "I'm sure all will be revealed in time."

"And what about the mystery of Chaz and Victor?" Bradford asked. He looked at me. "I know we haven't yet brought up the fact that you two look so much alike, but it must be addressed. Especially after discovering that you both have a gift with visions *and* you both can bend reality in ways that haven't been seen before."

"I honestly don't know anything about that," I replied. "I was freaked out when I realized how much we looked like each other. And I have no idea how I did what I did with the teleporting. I was just really angry, and I wanted time to speed up."

"Interesting," Bradford commented. "Farnsworth, do you have any insight on the matter?"

"Like with the prophecy," he began, "I can only speculate. But I am convinced that Chaz and Victor are connected in a way they just don't know about. I think Chaz might be an essential key to stopping Victor."

I felt a little embarrassed as everyone turned to look

at me.

"Well, I think that's enough speculation for one day," Bradford said, standing up. "We will let you rest now. Thank you, my friend."

We all said our goodbyes and headed out the door. For some reason, I felt like I might not get to talk to him again.

• • •

"I can't wait for tomorrow." Autumn said, her blue eyes beaming. The three of us stood in front of her bedroom door.

"It'll be an interesting next few days." Juliet said.

"Why do you say that?" I asked.

"Because we'll get to hang out like normal kids. *And* meet Autumn's parents."

"Yeah, what did you tell them about us?" I asked.

"I just told them you were both friends I used to hang out with in elementary school." Autumn replied. "Then you guys moved away, and we've kept in touch ever since. I feel awful about lying, but I don't want them to think I'm crazy."

"I'm just glad you didn't tell them we met online," Juliet replied, glancing at me.

"Hey, it's all I could come up with on the spot." I said defensively.

"Well, it's bedtime. See you two tomorrow."

"See you tomorrow," Autumn and I said at the same

time.

Juliet walked away and Autumn surprised me by giving me a quick hug.

"Goodnight, Chaz. See you tomorrow."

"See you tomorrow, Autumn."

Chapter 35

A Pretty Good Ending

I stepped out of Jake's car in Grand Junction, Colorado and shut the door behind me. The day was warm enough that I finally decided to brave wearing shorts and a t-shirt. I breathed in the smell of fresh-cut grass and stretched my cramped legs.

"See you tonight," I said through the window to Jake.

"Should I wait to make sure they're not creepers?" he asked, seriously.

"Naw, I'll be fine. If I need you to come and pick me up, I'll call you."

"Alright, be careful, Chaz." I turned around as his Jeep pulled away.

I stared at the brown brick house that was supposedly Autumn's and wondered what she and Juliet had been up to. Juliet's plane had landed only two hours ago so they probably hadn't done much yet. I walked on the perfectly green lawn over to the driveway and made my way up to the front door. I felt awkward as I passed the big windows that decorated the house. Autumn and her family were probably watching me right now.

Before I even had a chance to knock on the door, it flew open and suddenly Autumn had her arms wrapped around me

"I can't believe you're really here." She said.

Juliet stepped out of the house and smiled at me. "You look even lankier wearing shorts," she teased.

Autumn finally pulled away and looked me up and down. "Don't let her tease you. You look fine."

It was so weird finally seeing them in normal clothes again. Autumn wore denim shorts a striped shirt and a maroon baseball cap. Juliet was wearing white shorts and a yellow shirt that said 'Cali'.

"This is crazy." I said. "I've been seeing you two for months in my dreams and now here you are in front of me. What do we do now?"

"Whatever you want to do," Autumn answered. "I can show you my favorite places in town, we can go eat, or we can just hang out here."

"I don't know about you two," Juliet said. "But I'm actually pretty hungry."

"I'm down to get something to eat," I replied. "But first I need to talk to Autumn."

"Oh yeah," Autumn said." I forgot you said you had something important to tell me."

I glanced at Juliet and she gave me a knowing smile. "I'm guessing you want to talk to her alone. I'll wait inside." She headed inside, but before she shut the door she winked and made a kissy face.

"What is it, Chaz?" Autumn asked, eagerly.

"I don't really know where to start. I guess… well…" I paused. "You remember right before the battle started when you told me you liked me?"

"Yeah," she said, shyly.

"I wanted to respond, but I didn't. It's just that, things were really crazy, and I had no idea what was going to happen, I didn't have much time to think about it either. All I knew was that I love having you as a friend, and it would be awful to lose you. And I couldn't decide in the moment if I wanted a relationship with you because I thought . . ." I realized I was rambling on and it wasn't making much sense.

"What I'm trying to say is, I do like you Autumn. I just didn't want to say it because if I did end up losing you that day, it would've made it so much harder. Then there's Victor to worry about. I don't want him using you as leverage against me."

"Chaz, he would use me as leverage against you no matter what. He's already my enemy and I'm one of your best friends. I don't think being in a relationship would change that much. Besides, he can't mess with my dreams if I'm always in the Dream World."

"Yeah, that's true. But there's always the chance of us breaking up, and if we break up then we could never go back to being friends. At least not as good as friends as we were before. You know what I mean? I would hate for that to happen."

She didn't respond for a few seconds. She just smiled before throwing her arms around my neck. "Well, let's just never break up," She said into my ear.

Well, I guess if her mind was made up, then so was mine. When she pulled away and looked up at me, I leaned forward and kissed her on the lips.

Smooth Chaz did it again.

Acknowledgements

There were so many people who helped me start and finish this book, hopefully I don't leave out a single one. First of all, I would like to thank my good friend Ben Coles for motivating me to do something with my life and chase my dreams. If it wasn't for the great talks we had at work, I would have never picked this project back up. Another big thank you to my wife, Ashlyn Adams for believing in me and allowing me to spend so much time writing. I would also like to thank her for being a great editor and proof-reader.

I want to thank Jewel Adams for spending so much time editing and giving me some much-needed advice. Thank you, Seanté Nielsen for editing and proof-reading as well. Thank you, Cherie Fox for the amazing art-work on the front cover. Thank you, Sean Adams for all the book publishing advice and guidance.

And a special thanks to all of you who have constantly been telling me that you're excited to read my book and kept asking when it would be out. That alone helped me stay motivated to keep writing and get the book finished. Thank you to my friends who some of my characters were inspired by.

And last but not least, thank you reader for taking the time to finish this book. I hope you'll stick around for the next one!

About the Author

Daniel J. Adams lives in Utah with his wife Ashlyn and his dog Wednesday. He currently works as a dental assistant and loves almost anything to do with teeth. He also has his own DJ business that keeps him busy on the weekends. He has many hobbies and just a small few of them include playing musical instruments, reading books, dancing, yo-yoing, catching Pokemon, and playing Mario Kart. Daniel has always dreamed of being an author and eventually his friend convinced him to chase his dreams and do it, which is why he decided to write Dreamchasers, hoping to inspire others to do the same.

Find me online at:

Danielj-adams.com
Instagram - @danojadams
Facebook - authordanieljadams

www.ingramcontent.com/pod-product-compliance
Lightning Source LLC
Chambersburg PA
CBHW030828110726
47900CB00006B/1792